A FAMILY LIKENESS

by

Anna Gilbert

Dales Large Print Books
Long Preston, North Yorkshire,
BD23 4ND, England.

British Library Cataloguing in Publication Data.

Gilbert, Anna
A family likeness.

A catalogue record of this book is
available from the British Library

ISBN 978-1-84262-798-3 pbk

First published in Great Britain in 1977 by Hodder & Stoughton

Copyright © 1977 by Anna Gilbert

Cover illustration © Susan Fox by arrangement with
Arcangel Images

The moral right of the author has been asserted

Published in Large Print 2011 by arrangement with
Anna Gilbert, care of Watson, Little Ltd.

Dales Large Print is an imprint of Library Magna Books Ltd.

Printed and bound in Great Britain by
T.J. (International) Ltd., Cornwall, PL28 8RW

1

One day in June for a few hours I escaped. Until then I had not thought of myself as a prisoner.

My grandmother was in her room. I crossed the hall on tiptoe, drawing my skirt aside to evade the bared fangs of the tiger-skin. The front door, for once, stood open. Beyond the shadow of the house the field blazed with buttercups. One could wade in them knee-deep, I discovered, then scramble out into the bridle-path without being seen from the house; and so I, escaped, just as I was, in a muslin dress and heelless slippers, with only a garden hat; best of all, alone. It cannot have been the first time but I remember it with the freshness of novelty; and it had been so easy. The ecstasy of it wafted me up the hill to the carriage road.

There I would have turned back had it not been for Mrs. Masson. She changed the direction of my outing (as she was to change the direction of my life). Yet all she did was to come out of the Lodge, put up her honey-coloured parasol a shade lighter than her gown, and walk off across the park with the obvious intention of calling on my grandmother. There was nothing in her slender figure to account for my instinctive recoil. The waterfall flounces at the back of her trailing skirt, exquisite as they were, did not quite justify the feeling that I preferred to see her walking away; and I would be needed to help with the conversation.

Instead of going home I went quickly along a narrow path between dry-stone walls. At the end a gateless gap opened upon a hidden valley: a breathtaking view of hills; at my feet a grassy slope facing south; a few cottages; a derelict farm; between willows, a stream.

The day was sultry. A peculiar veiled brightness gave to the grass a lurid green, to the roof-tiles a hectic red. Perhaps I too was a little feverish. What else could account for my strange new mood of independence, or the touch of excitement with which I picked out and recognised – halfway down the slope and almost covered with elder-blossom – the well.

I had never seen it, only heard of it from Emma at an age when every well must be a wishing well.

'I don't know about wishing.' Emma had been cautious. 'Old? Old as the hills. They say the water has special powers in sickness but I don't know.'

She had always been too busy to take me. My French governess had a particular aversion to muddy walks. Besides, as she pointed out when the question of wishing arose: 'What could you possibly wish for? You have everything a young lady could want.'

Over the years I had forgotten the well but here at last it undoubtedly was.

I laid my arms on the coping of cool stone and saw where the limestone had been patched here and there with brick: beyond, nothing but darkness. Peering into the hollow gloom, I breathed an atmosphere as old as the earth itself. It filled my mind and heart with a sense of ancient sadness lingering from an age beyond memory. The silence rose like an invitation: a challenge.

To wish was ungodly. My grandmother had made this and every other moral issue absolutely clear. It showed an imperfect resignation to the will of Heaven. Besides, an existence as narrow as mine encouraged no vision of change so that I could scarcely have shaped a wish – on my own.

It shaped itself. It came up from the dark depths and flooded my consciousness without my help. I seemed to hear it without speaking: to feel it without willing.

'Let me be free of it all, of Barmote – of the family. Free, free. Help me.'

The sky had darkened. The upper air was still. Greatly venturing, I took a stone, dropped it in the well and listened. The pause lengthened, seemed endless, until at last from down came a faint responsive splash: a reply.

Instantly from the depths I looked up into the blue-black zenith and saw the sky scored by a fork of flame. A great roll of thunder shook the valley from Long How to Gib Rake and subsided, growling, down by the stream-bed. The clouds opened and bombarded me with rain.

I crouched there, looking at the point to the north where the jag of lightning had struck and persuaded myself (awed but curiously without remorse) that it could not have missed the tower of Barmote Hall just over the brow of hill.

In less than a minute the rain had reduced my dress to such limpness that I might have been naked. Soaked, shivering, shedding combs and pins from my tumbled hair and leaving one slipper in the wet grass, I ran for the nearest cottage.

In spite of the storm the door stood open. By the hearth a woman sat sewing, leaning close to the fire so that its light fell on her work. She jumped up, startled, then relieved.

'It's Miss Tessa. You frightened me for a minute.'

'You know me?'

'Know you?' The question evidently surprised her. 'I saw you at the well just now, like a spirit all in white.'

How could she not know me? Who else would roam the countryside in such a garb? I felt a sudden doubt as to the suitability of the unstiffened muslins my grandmother insisted on as the only proper wear for a young girl of gentle birth. Could she, in this one thing, be wrong?

'May I come in for a little while?'

'You're welcome as flowers in May.' She drew a chair to the fire. 'Come away from that draughty door.'

'Shall I close it?'

'It won't close easily. It's such a bad fit and the floor rises just there.'

It was of earth, covered with a clipping mat or two and so uneven that I stumbled on my way to the hearth.

'Reuben's going to put it right before the bad weather comes on.'

'Bad weather!'

I glanced at the window-panes awash with rain. We both laughed.

'It was sudden, the storm.' She wiped the poker and thrust it into the heart of the fire. 'The air felt heavy but I thought it would clear. That lightning made me jump. Like a judgment, you might think.'

She offered the chair but I took off my floppy straw and sat on the fender. She poured something from a pitcher into a mug and set it on the hob.

13

'I see you every Sunday in church but I've never seen you close to. No wonder they call you the Lily of Barmote.'

'Oh no, please. I don't like it. It makes me feel – unlike a real person.'

I slipped off my surviving slipper, its blue rosette now no more than pulp, and dabbed at the mud-stains on my white stocking in an attempt to seem prosaic and practical.

'I hope I haven't gone too far.' She looked anxious. 'Only I've heard so much about you from Reuben, my boy.'

'Reuben? Is he... Our Reuben?'

'Your groom.' She hesitated between pride in him and discretion. 'It's natural he should talk about you. You're the only young thing at the Hall besides himself.'

Drawing out the red-hot poker, she thrust it hissing into the ale, left it a minute, then handed me the mug.

'I've never drunk it before.'

I found it comforting, as satisfying as a meal and I watched as she took up her work again. She was a pleasant-looking woman, of middle-age, with a serenity of manner one could not help respecting. She was stitching gloves. A pile of cut-out skins lay on the table.

'You're clever at it.' She had been working a buttonhole and now went to the table and fitted the two sides of the glove to a metal vice on a little wooden stand. 'Does it take long?'

'I can make a dozen or more pairs in a week. The money keeps me in flour and soap and candles. Now that Reuben's so well placed at the Hall, I don't know how to be thankful enough. He's earning ten pounds a year and his keep, as you'll know.' I was silent, having had no idea of Reuben's wage. 'And being so near, he can come home regular. Those are his.' She nodded towards a row of books on a corner shelf. 'He likes to read. His father was the same.'

The family had evidently seen better days. The furniture was good, the dresser well supplied with blue and white tableware. The strangeness of my predicament, the warmth, the ale – loosened my tongue.

'You're happy then?'

At once I regretted the note of surprise in my voice. I felt too the awkwardness of not knowing their surname.

'Things could be worse. They have been. And they could be better.'

'You mean – your house?'

A stream of water had found its way through the sagging lintel and was creeping down the wall inside the door.

'I live in it but it isn't rightly speaking my house.'

Was it tact that prevented her from saying more? With surprise I realised that the house was mine, or would be some day. Like almost every other house in the district it belonged to the Jasmyns. The thought made we uneasy. I got up.

'You can't go in this weather with nothing on your feet.'

'I must.'

She came with me to the door. The rain had eased but what had been a path was now a stream. The cottages below clung mutely to the wet hillside, giving no sign of life. We stood isolated, the two of us, and in our solitude, equal as we might not otherwise have seemed.

'But there's no harm in dreaming,' she said. 'I come from Maresbarrow, you know, and what I would like, when Reuben's worked his way up to a good position, coachman, maybe...'

I heard no more of the dream. We had both caught sight of a figure hurrying along the path by the stream.

'There's Reuben now.'

At her call he waved, came quickly up the hill, stood flushed and pleased beside us.

'Come on in. You'll be wet.'

'No, mother. I was looking for Miss Tessa. Mr. Steadman saw her coming this way. "Our young lady's over the hill somewhere," he said when the storm came on. "You'd best fetch her, and there's nothing for it but the spring-cart in this weather."'

'Does my grandmother know?'

'She asked for you, miss, and she was

16

given to understand that you would be sheltering in the barn. But there's a real to-do up there. The flagstaff's been struck by lightning and the lane's flooded...'

'I must go at once.'

'It won't take more than ten minutes once we get to the cart. I've got it on the road by the bridge.'

His mother was rummaging in a cupboard.

'There's this.' It was a man's coat of some sort. She put it round my shoulders and handed me my ruined hat. 'She'll catch her death, Reuben, in her stocking feet.'

'There's no need.' Without hesitation, as though engaged in the swift dispatch of a mailbag he picked me up. 'See you Sunday, mother.'

'Thank you, thank you,' I called to her as Reuben squelched down the hill. She stood nodding, calm and unsurprised on the threshold, until we reached the path at the bottom.

Neither of us spoke a word. But as we slithered through the mud and up the incline to the bridge, when my hat fell of and Reuben contrived by going down on one knee to rescue it from a dripping clump of ragwort, all at once (I don't believe it was the ale) I began to laugh. Could this be how people felt on holiday, literally lifted above the earth with nothing expected of them?

My feet dangling, I felt as light as air. The air itself was full of the cool scent of elder flowers. The rain fell on my face. I tilted back my head and felt the cold drops on my throat.

Steadman was hovering at the open door when we drove up, and behind him Emma. From their quick glances into the depths of the hall I sensed that there was no time to be lost. Reuben was down in a second, was carrying me up the steps. It was nervousness this time that made me smile. Certainly I was smiling when Steadman stood aside and my grandmother appeared, her wide black skirts filling the doorway. Perhaps she mistook my nervousness for coquetry. My raffish, disordered appearance must have dismayed her. She was intensely angry but not with me: with me she was never angry. The full force of her fury fell upon Reuben.

'What are you thinking of? Put Miss Tessa down at once. How dare you presume...?'

Her cap-strings quivered. She was flushed, actually incoherent. Just for a moment I saw her for the first time as old and feared she would fall.

'Directly, ma'am, if you'll pardon me.'

Reuben stepped past her and set me down gently on the tiger-skin rug. Glancing up at him, I awoke. It was as though I looked at the spring-cart and saw it turn into a person; a human being on the brink of disaster. He was much taller even than my grandmother. He looked down at her as he said without resentment but with a formality unknown at Barmote especially in a groom, 'I had no thought of presuming, ma'am, beyond my duty.'

'You have gone too far. You can...'

But before she could finish, he interrupted swiftly: 'I give warning' – though his voice shook, his manner was magnificent – 'that I'll be leaving as soon as you can suit yourself with another groom.'

'You on go now, at once. Take your things and go. Once a servant over-reaches himself' – my grandmother spoke with her head high as though addressing the foxes' masks on the wall – 'he will do it again.'

Reuben's face puckered a little. He swallowed, hesitated, turned to me as if to say goodbye. But the look we exchanged was not of farewell but of greeting as though having seen each other daily for years, we had at last met; as though having ridden at a respectful distance behind me mile after mile, he had suddenly caught up, overtaken me and turned to smile; for in spite of everything he was smiling now.

But he went down the steps without another word. I heard his feet on the gravel tramping away. Only then did the others emerge from the transparency into which they had faded, and take on substance. A gentle swaying at the foot of the stairs made me think for a moment that the newel post itself had moved; but it was Mrs. Masson who stepped from the shadows in her honey-coloured gown, her hand extended in its unwrinkled glove. She had seen everything, I thought, hating her, mistrusting the upward curve of her lips as she said good-bye. The door closed.

The hem of my wet skirt brushed the bared fangs of the tiger. Shuddering, I drew it back. The servants had disappeared. I was alone again with my grandmother and her terrible, demanding love.

2

I had disappointed her again: had fallen behind once more in the endless struggle to become the person she wanted me to be: an embodiment of the virtues of all the Jasmyns: of all the Jasmyns the best, being – as I was, save for a distant cousin or two – the last.

'You have strength of character, Tessa, I know it. You must have: you're a Jasmyn. But there is a lightness in your nature. Unless you control it, it may lead you astray. Your behaviour this afternoon, for instance...'

Immaculate once more in a white dress. I sat bolt upright in the armless chair at her side where I had learned all I knew, above all how to keep still. It is not easy to sit upright with one's eyes downcast, but this art at least I had so thoroughly perfected that every fibre of the red plush border on my grandmother's footstool had for me a distinct identity.

'You have a responsibility to behave with seemliness and dignity...'

I listened as the homily took its course, each phrase as familiar and incontrovertible as the chime of the clock.

'Remember, you are the last of the Barmote Jasmyns. *There is no one else.*'

By saying it so many times my grandmother defeated her object. Her very insistence that there was no one else created for me the idea of a person who would have liked to be but was not a Jasmyn. Though she never mentioned him, I always supposed that she was thinking of the Indian gentleman. Long ago – I knew about him only from servants' gossip in which a wealth of drama compensated for a shortage of facts – he had unexpectedly appeared at Barmote, claiming to be a grandson of the Rodney Jasmyn who had begun the long family connection with. India. He had, I gathered, melted away as mysteriously as he had come: but on many a dark night, groping my way candleless to bed, I had almost met him on the stairs, a figure like Ali Baba brandishing a scimitar.

Grandmamma's feet moved as she took up the cup of soothing tisane Emma had brought her. My escapade had certainly upset her and, I remembered remorsefully, she had always disliked thunderstorms. For the most recent one – it was now evening – I felt responsible. The Hall had had a narrow escape. How oddly I had behaved at the well! Having been brought up to believe in Providence, I could not easily accept the idea of a coincidence and the response to my unfortunate wish had been unnervingly prompt.

Of course I hadn't wanted to be free. Who in her senses would want to leave Barmote Hall, the only house of any importance between Spandleby and Maresbarrow; and who – I patted her hand in compunction – would want to leave grandmamma? She was so loving, kind and good that even my stupidest mistakes were soon forgiven if not forgotten. 'I forgive you, Tessa.' The longed-for words had ended each troubled chapter of our existence together; only the oftener they came, the less their power to soothe. Soon inevitably, there would be something else to forgive. Even her occasional harshness – no, it was only firmness really – as she had explained time and again was for my own good: she was always thinking of me. Sometimes she seemed to know my very thoughts as now when she said: 'I have no one but you, dear. You are the only one spared to me.'

As a little girl I had liked to hear the story of how I had miraculously survived the Indian Mutiny. In those early days I had believed myself to be the only survivor. Both my parents and hundreds of solders, innocent women and children had perished; but Heaven, as my grandmother saw it, had preserved me from all evil. Neither sabre, knife nor gun, hunger, thirst nor fever had power to harm me. Sometimes, oppressed by the weight of my inadequacies, I drew comfort from the thought that there must after all be something special about me. I had been singled out – doomed, I almost felt when low-spirited – to survive.

My grandmother had never doubted it. She had been already widowed when my father, her only child, a Captain in Her Majesty's 32nd of Foot, had fallen in Sir Henry Lawrence's ill-fated sortie against the sepoys at Chinhat. The news had not reached Barmote until after Lucknow was relieved. Alice, my mother, had died, of a lingering fever, it was thought, in the last days of the siege. Almost all we knew of her personally had been contained in a handful of letters written before the fearful events that engulfed her. She had been allowed to fade into the obscurity from which her marriage had briefly rescued her, the sister of a clergyman's wife.

'But,' grandmamma said, 'anyone may carry a clergyman these days and especially in India.'

A marriage in India was to be disparaged as scarcely a marriage at all. That was another thing she stressed, though my parents' marriage had in fact been irreproachable; the Governor himself had attended the ceremony.

One positive fact about my mother I had soon learned. She alone could have bequeathed to me the lightness of my nature to which grandmamma was now referring. That could not have come from the Jasmyns. I was ashamed of it and of my mother. She was, as my grandmother gently implied, best forgotten.

The cup rattled in its saucer as she set it down between the little pile of devotional books and the ivory-handled reading-glass on her table. Looking up cautiously, I was surprised to see her hand tremble as she raised it uncertainly to her face. It was a strong, handsome face, still feminine – the eyes bright and dark; the complexion inclined to olive with a warm red on the high cheekbones; a face which, if one watched it anxiously all the days of one's childhood, became the face of an oracle. Isolated from the rest of her body, between the lace collar and dangling cap-strings, against the crimson velvet of her highbacked chair, it impressed itself upon my consciousness with a lasting intensity which has even now the power to restore her presence, as if she still sits high above me looking down. Perhaps she does.

But that evening, in the first flush of a new independence of vision, I recognised in her face the marks of suffering; an habitual melancholy. How she must have suffered, in the distant days of bereavement, shut up alone at Barmote!

Then, in August, 1858, had come a letter, written from an inn at Gravesend by an army surgeon who had come home by the Cape route with some of the survivors of the 32nd Foot. It conveyed little more than the bare fact of my existence: 'Captain Jasmyn's infant daughter'; a perfectly new, unknown Jasmyn. In my arrival in the care of a nurse were united the mysteries of birth and resurrection. Like Jairus' daughter, I seemed to have risen from the dead though at an earlier age. So far as could be calculated, for one of my peculiarities was that I had no known birthday, I was not two years old when my grandmother first laid eyes on me.

'I had travelled post most of the way to Gravesend. There was no railway at Spandleby in those days. You were quite alone in that dismal room. The nurse had gone into the bedroom and I was glad of it. There was nothing to come between us from the very first.'

Our meeting had combined with the magic of a fairy tale the grace of a revelation.

'The very sight of you restored my faith. It has never since flagged, I thank God. I thought, "In that little fair creature has been preserved the lifeblood of the Jasmyns. All the wrath of the enemy could not prevail against us.'"

Her clear-cut features would soften as she spoke, her eyes would fill with tears; and I would sit, lost in the wonder and romance of the story and when it ended, crushed with the burden of all that was expected of me.

'You were so beautiful, Tessa, sitting among the cushions. Like a little flower. You looked straight up at me and held out your arms. I was perfectly convinced that in some inexplicable way you recognised me. You don't remember of course…'

We would gaze at each other solemnly and I would concentrate all my mind, closing my eyes and clenching my fists in the effort to remember from those first moments the birth of our relationship. But it had long since been blotted out by the unceasing activity of the years between, for grand-mamma had lost no time in bringing me to Barmote to begin the arduous task of train-ing me in a manner befitting my prospects.

But first I learned that my nature was sinful. I must pray that God in his mercy would give me a new nature to enable me to do battle with the old. Whether this new nature was actually granted to me I was never sure; but the sense of being engaged in some worrying inner conflict rarely left me.

Reading, memorising, writing in my commonplace book, needlework – each hour had its allotted duty.

'You must take out all the stitches, Tessa,' when I proudly showed the first line of my sampler with its superfluity of mm's: 'Rememmber now thy Creator in the days of thy youth.'

'You must learn to discipline your thoughts...'

The taking out had proved more laborious even than the putting in. The tears, the pricked fingers, the tangle of wools and threads, these I was given to understand must be endured as necessary obstacles in the steep and thorny climb towards the moral heights we both sought, for it was a united struggle; we were engaged in it together.

'It grieves me as much as it does you, dear. More, in fact.' High above me in the throne-like chair she sat with her hands folded, occupied only in the grief of it, while far below, stitch by stitch, step by step, I made the slow ascent. She had tried so hard to implant in me the sturdy growth of seriousness and resolution, to root out my natural frivolity. I could see that now; but there had been moments of resentful despair as once when I had triumphantly produced a line of perfect stitching.

'Very good. Now to show that the effort is worth more than the achievement, I suggest that you take it all out and do it again.'

So sad and painful an experience must

have done me a great deal of good. It convinced me, for instance, that though God might punish me for my wrong-doing, he would not reward my virtue...

'I wanted to talk this over with you, Tessa.' Grandmamma glanced at the clock. It was a quarter to eight. 'I want you to examine your conscience and tell me quite frankly what you were *doing* this afternoon. A walk? On your own?'

I explained.

'But why, when you knew Mrs. Masson might call? I found myself actually apologising because you weren't here. She was surprised, naturally. I believe you know how anxious I am to make her feel at home here. It is so difficult to keep a tenant at the Lodge. The Warmans stayed barely a year. You behaved so – lightly. I hope you may be no worse for the wetting. But it has helped me to make up my mind. I want you to...'

I had been expecting it. She was going to make me promise never to go out alone without telling her first. Once I had promised, there would be no hope of escaping again. A promise was binding, a matter of conscience. 'You must give me your word, Tessa,' had too often sounded in my ears like the grating of key in lock, the slamming-to of iron gates. Knowing what was to come, I burst into speech. 'I believe, grandmamma, that you had quite the wrong impression of Reuben. He was perfectly respectful and his poor mother – they were truly kind. She was so very pleased to have him in good service; and Reuben was so helpful to me when...'

I stopped abruptly. She had never known how Reuben helped me through the great tragedy of my life, the death of Lance, my retriever. Only recently had I remembered it myself, having taken it for granted at the time that Reuben would dig the grave and lay poor Lance in it; but now I recollected that Reuben had done much more: he had grieved for Lance as I had done though naturally not with the same deep anguish. The funeral rites had been brief and stealthy for Lance had outlawed himself by worrying sheep and been shot for it. Grandmamma knew nothing of the grave inside the hedge bordering the bridle-path or of the commemorative cairn.

'Grandmamma would think a headstone wrong,' I said, 'for a dog, especially as things have turned out.'

'A cairn is different,' Reuben said, laying out the foundation with a deliberation that seemed touched with some other feeling than sorrow. Was it anger? 'If she finds out, you can say I did it. Heathen ways are only to be expected from the likes of me...'

To leave the sentence unfinished had been a mistake. Grandmamma looked at me sharply and I said hurriedly, 'Could we not perhaps keep him on after all?'

'It's quite out of the question. He shall have his wages to the end of the quarter but he must go. I know his sort. Besides, you're too old now for ... to be ... I can't tell you what a shock it was to see you in the arms of a rough country fellow. I can scarcely speak of it. With your hair hanging down and your feet without shoes, you looked – *wanton*. Had I not known it to be impossible, I would have thought... And Mrs. Masson...'

The pauses suggested unmentionable behaviour of such depravity as made me hot with shame. The clock struck eight. I rang the bell to summon the servants to prayers. Instead of Exodus IX, the usual reading after a thunder-storm, my grandmother read from Proverbs XI. 'A fair woman without discretion' could only refer to me. 'He that troubleth his own house shall inherit the wind...' Grandmamma did not turn to me when she read the words and I was grateful. Watched as usual by the elephants perched uneasily on their coronets in the Indian carpet, we knelt. Kneeling, I examined my conscience: I resumed the burden of my responsibility. But she had not after all insisted on the promise. Contrite and thankful, I rejoiced in my deliverance from the pitfall, knowing nothing of the precipice ahead.

31

The next morning, when I had helped my grandmother with her letters and was taking my bible to the window to study the day's portion of the Book of Joshua, she suddenly said, 'I feel, Tessa, that it would be a good thing for you to have some younger person as a companion.'

'I should like it.'

'Very much,' I was about to add, in my astonishment and delight but I restrained myself in time and said, 'If you would.'

Grandmamma was so very sensitive. It would hurt her to think that I might prefer someone else's company to her own. Nevertheless I glowed, in my ignorance, with enthusiasm, imagining some agreeable girl of my own age. We would talk, make toast... I had read a story in which girls were perpetually making toast. Or better still...

I wonder if Mam'selle would come back,' I suggested, remembering not to speak too eagerly. 'I've had no one to walk with since she left.'

She had come in October two years ago, in 1870 that must have been, and had left in the following March. We had been constant companions and parted in tears.

'It was strange, wasn't it, that she didn't stay? I thought she liked it here.'

Grandmamma did not reply. She had never insisted on my taking walks. It occurred to me that until we found a new groom, I wouldn't be able to ride either.

'I was really thinking of the future,' she said. The glow faded. I sat down at her side.

'The most suitable – the safest companion for you would be a husband.'

I had always known that I must marry. The matter had never been discussed but I had somehow become possessed of the idea that by marrying I would discharge an obligation to the dead Jasmyns. They would be gratified, perhaps finally appeased. On some distant day, by the sacrificial act of taking a husband, I would wipe the slate clean once and for all of my debt to the family. The notion had not been displeasing, but I was not prepared for an immediate sacrifice

'I shan't always be here. You'll never manage the estate on your own. The investments have done well. There will be a good deal of money.'

I tried to picture myself in black, wearing my grandmother's chatelaine, gravely turning over papers with Mr. Pawley the lawyer and pointing out with a gold pencil the things he had overlooked. Could I bring into my voice the touch of sharpness with which she sometimes spoke to Burnside the bailiff as they wrangled about rents and livestock?

'You'll need someone stronger than yourself who will help you to fight for your rights.'

'Fight?' The word surprised me. 'Who would there be to fight with?'

'There's always someone – or something – to fight. With your appearance and as an heiress, you would be absolutely at the mercy of fortune-hunters or some romantic whim of your own.'

'But, grandmamma,' I felt relieved; the oversight had been so obvious. 'There's no one to marry. I don't know one young man who would – want to.'

I quickly reviewed the local gentry, not for the first time. There were no young people at Spandleby Hall or even at the Rectory. A faint hope that grandmamma might be planning a season in London made me look up, and the hope died. Her expression troubled me. Her face was flushed. She stroked my hair but avoided my eyes.

'Your life has been sheltered. Too much so. I see that now; and for that very reason it's important that you should marry – suitably. Besides, there is the family. It must go on.'

Of course. Destiny had saved me for that very purpose; had snatched me from the jaws of death so that there might still be Jasmyns at Barmote.

We sat silent as we had done for many an hour on many an interminable day when afternoon was distinguishable from morning only by the slow movement of light from the lozenge-shaped window-panes across the panels of the chiffonier and over to the glass door of the china cabinet. I stared into the fire, so often my refuge and consolation and found in its warm heart, inspiration: something else my grandmother and even Providence had overlooked.

'But don't you see?' I shook her hand playfully, confidently. 'If I were married I wouldn't be a Jasmyn any longer. I should have to go away and my children wouldn't be Jasmyns.'

Oh, the blessing after all of being a woman! Had it not been for my deep attachment to Barmote – and to grand-mamma – the prospect of marriage might have become almost attractive, the very direction in which freedom might lie; and again I thought guiltily of that extraordinary combination of events at the well.

Then I saw that my brilliant discovery had not moved her, at least not in the way I had expected, though she was moved. She drew her hand away and sat twisting her rings as she sometimes did for minutes together.

'You hadn't thought of that,' I persisted, teasing.

'Oh yes, I had thought of it. You can't imagine how much or how long I've prayed for guidance.' She took a deep breath. 'You would still be a Jasmyn and your children would be Jasmyns if you married a Jasmyn.'

It was only a moment before I understood

and felt quite simply a withering of the heart as if something fresh and green had died of a blighting frost. Stretching out a cold hand, I found that the fire was giving out no heat.

'You mean Cousin Ashton? You want me to marry him.'

She nodded. In each of her dark eyes burned a small bright flame. I saw that with all the fanaticism of her nature she meant it to be so.

3

'But he's so old.'

It was a lament, not an argument. One doesn't argue when the sky suddenly darkens.

'Ashton is a little older...'

'Ten years at least.'

Our connection with the family at Stydding was distant, dependent on nothing closer than the same great-grandfather. Had it not been for the name, my grandmother might have deliberately lost touch: she was not sociable. But she herself had been one of the Stydding Jasmyns, a second cousin of my grandfather.

'Who could be more suitable, dear? Ashton has the maturity you lack – and may never have, I'm afraid.' She had found her confidence again now that the subject was broached. 'We need the kind of help he can give on the estate. You don't know, Tessa, what a burden it has been to bear so much responsibility alone.'

I had no experience of rebellion. The habit of obedience, imposed on me in infancy by a will far stronger than my own, had become almost an instinct; but now a purer instinct awoke and told me, speaking from the depths of my nature, that here was a thing I could perhaps refuse to do.

'You have it in your power to make me so much happier, dear.'

She took out her handkerchief almost surreptitiously, not wanting me to know that she was crying. It was unusual for her to cry. Even then I didn't actually see the tears but the drooping sadness in her whole demeanour made me ashamed. The agony of disappointing her had always been more than I could bear. A week of hurt silence when I had pleaded to be sent away to school after Mlle. Quéva left, had cast an almost ineffaceable gloom. Another such ordeal in the immediate future frightened me more, just then, than the prospect of a lifetime devoted to Ashton.

And as she explained, with a gentleness that seemed to me very touching, I was lucky: Ashton was no stranger but actually, though distantly, one of the family. I had said myself, only a moment ago that there was no one else; and there never would or could be a young man better suited to be master of Barmote.

'Since it can never be my own son,' she reminded me. 'I have lost so much – so much.'

When she let me go, suggesting that for once as the day was fine I might take my books into the garden, I was astonished to find that it was still early. It was not years since the blow had fallen: only an hour, in which grandmamma had explained to me the advantage, the wisdom, the necessity of marrying Ashton with such patience that in the end she was exhausted. I left her, lying back in her chair with her eyes closed and knew that she was hurt by my withdrawal into silence.

Even on a bright day it was hard to find a sunny spot in the garden. The house had been built in the early seventeenth century with its back to the south-west winds which in those days were thought to bear fever-laden miasmas. In 1805 Rodney Jasmyn had added a battlemented tower to house a library and those of his Indian treasures that could not be accommodated in the house. It also served to rob the garden of light from the east. Except in high summer, the steep rock-pierced slope behind the house cast its shadow for the whole afternoon. I knew exactly where sunlight would fall and at what hour; but on that morning no heat or light could reach me. On the terrace, in the arbour under the rock, I saw only Ashton, as vividly as if he had already moved in.

For that was just what he would do. Doubtful of everything else on earth, I knew that between them they had planned it. My grandmother could not have spoken so confidently of the marriage if she had not first discussed it with Ashton himself. In sudden enlightenment I understood his half-hearted interest in his father's cotton mill; his leisurely travels on the Continent; his occasional visits to Barmote. He had been filling in time until the place became his own. To become master of Barmote, its land, farms and cottages and all our great-grandfather's Indian treasures, he had only to marry me. I felt the painful difficulty, the impossibility of resisting when it had all been arranged years ago.

Emma was watching me from the kitchen. She must know of course. She and Steadman knew everything. I went round to the front of the house and leaned on the garden railings. After yesterday's rain the buttercups shone brighter than ever in a field of golden silk. I was lucky really...

With a tiny feeling of relief I recollected that Ashton as a small boy had known my father and admired him. I had been quite a little girl when, on visits to Stydding, it had been thought suitable for me to watch Ashton conduct the siege and defence of his toy fort. They were military operations, not games. Ashton, home from school for the holidays, was already too old to play. It was through the bloody sieges of the fort that I learned my family history. There was a cruel gusto in Ashton's treatment of the sepoys, made from black darning-wool and pipe-cleaners, that conveyed to me the horrors of the Mutiny more effectively than any history book could have done.

'Oh, please don't do it,' I cried more than once as he fired the wretched natives from his cannon or hanged them from gallows made of wire and pencils.

'Don't be silly. Nothing's too bad for the brutes. They killed your father, don't forget, and tortured innocent women and children. The things they did were too frightful to tell you.'

The elation in his light blue eyes conjured up for me an infinite frightfulness, shapeless, nameless, that woke me screaming in the night.

But he had not, in spite of these manoeuvres, gone into the Army: he had waited for me.

Even more than the hideous carnage on the cobbled causeway of the fort, I had feared Ashton's white mice. Enjoying my fear, he would open the cage and let them creep, smooth, pink-eyed and snuffling, round his bony wrists. Once as I retreated, he caught me at the door and laid one of the mice on my neck, lifting my hair to expose me more intimately to the brittle touch of the small feet. The warm smell, the tickling fur, the exploring nose, reduced me to such a state of demented hysteria that my frenzy

41

frightened even Ashton. But when he put the mice away and picked me up to hush me, not so much in penitence as in fear of the grown-ups, the sense of loathing persisted.

'You're like a little white mouse yourself, Tessa,' he said, diminishing my pride still further.

Not all his courteous treatment of me in later years could blot out the memory of that infamous nursery but as time went on, my grandmother gradually discontinued her visits to Stydding. The drive was too long; her friendship with Ashton's mother cooled; her attention became fixed, more unflaggingly than ever, on me.

Emma's skirt brushed the stone steps.

'Here's a cup of hot chocolate for you, miss. It'll do you good.'

She set the tray down on the garden table.

'Oh, Emma, do you know what is to happen to me? Whom I'm to marry?'

'I can guess, miss. I've seen it coming.'

With the buttercups behind us we faced the heavy rectangle of the house. The last of the morning sun had moved from between the tower and the east gable, leaving the garden in shade.

'If you ask me,' Emma said, 'one man's much the same as another when you're married to him.'

Through some trick of intermingling light

42

and shade I saw for the first time that the trees in their dense summer foliage were so disposed as to form dark lines stretching out from the darker central mass of the house like spokes of a wheel; but as I looked, the clouds changed, the trees lost their density and wavered gently, no longer spokes but groping tentacles...

'It isn't as if you'll have to go away,' Emma said. 'You'll go on living here always.'

In the time that followed I looked back on my childhood and early girlhood with affection. Narrow, disciplined, tedious as the days had been, they had passed smoothly, untouched by any deep unrest. It was easy now to overlook the small anxieties, the constant sense of my shortcomings and to remember only the security before the pattern of our lives altered. It frightened me to see the change in my grandmother. Sometimes I found her drooping listlessly in her chair as if too tired to do anything at all. Seeing me, she would give a guilty little start, take up her needlework and begin to talk brightly with a brave attempt at cheerfulness. I fancied that her face had altered; yet, studying her features anxiously, I could see no real change in them except perhaps a loss of firmness; but she certainly walked more slowly. Once she swayed and had to clutch at me for support.

'It's the pain again,' she said. 'Here in my chest. No matter. It will pass.'

Holding her with all my strength, I felt in my whole body how much she needed me.

'No, no, dear, I'm not unhappy,' she said once when one of her deep sighs had roused me to ask. 'Besides when one's heart has been broken, one doesn't look for happiness again.'

She opened her little brown copy of *Daily Light* and read with a sad serenity that made me sad too. But I was not serene. It was as clear to me as daylight that I was breaking her heart all over again.

'It seems so strange, doesn't it, dear, after all these years when my every thought has been for you – when we have lived together in such harmony...' her smile was so tender that I realised all over again how hard it must have been for her to be sometimes a little – harsh, 'that you can't give me the one thing I want most – for you.'

She would never, could never force me to marry Ashton.

'In a matter such as this you must make your choice with perfect freedom, Tessa darling. At your age naturally you can't be expected to see the advantages as others can, though I must in fairness to you say that I have never known you stubborn before. Not that I'm reproaching you, dear. Only I do worry about your future. What will become of you if I die and leave you unmarried? If you were married, I believe death would come as a blessing. I should welcome it after so much suffering.'

I had never thought of her dying. It had troubled me once when Emma said, 'She's been a fine-looking woman in her day,' as though her day had declined. To me, since there was no one to compare her with, she was not old: she had no distinct and separate qualities. How can one judge the height of a mountain when it fills the view? Grandmamma was absolute, immortal. But now I lay awake at night worrying about her health. Though she rarely complained, I guessed that the pain continued to trouble her.

'Don't look so anxious, dear. It may be only a nervous trouble. It will pass when... I don't really need a doctor.'

In my ignorance I had not thought of taking advice but now I reproached myself and with Emma's support called in the doctor who spoke of possible heart trouble, prescribed digitalin and forbade excitement.

'As if,' grandmamma said, shaking her head with a wry little smile, 'the trouble were only a physical one.'

It never occurred to me to question Ashton's suitability as a husband: the advantages of the match were too obvious even to me for argument. It was just that I could not for the life of me say, though I did try, 'I'll marry Ashton if he wishes.' My lips would not encompass the words.

'Let me write to Ashton.' Grandmamma made the suggestion quite suddenly one evening when I was setting out the board for backgammon. It was some time since we had played, though she loved the game. Fortunately the casting of lots was sanctioned by the bible. Since it was not chance but providence that influenced our throws, we played seriously. 'You've almost grown up since he was last here. At least you can have no objection to getting to know him again.'

'No.' I sprang up, upsetting the board, and rushed to the window. 'Not yet. I don't want to see him. I couldn't behave naturally after all this.'

'How can you speak to me like that, so roughly?'

I turned with an apology to find her groping helplessly for her drops.

'Are you in pain?'

She nodded with a look of suffering. I measured out the exact dose with the painstaking care the doctor had enjoined and held it to her lips. If she had died, it would be I who had killed her. When half an hour later she said feebly, 'I have so many worries at present. Ashton might have advised me. He has such a cool head.'

46

'Let him come.' It was a relief to give in and see her smile again. 'If you wish.'

She looked so much better that I set out the board once more, feeling happier.

A fortnight later Ashton came.

From behind my curtain I watched him as he stepped down from the carriage: a tall gentleman in an Inverness cape. It was the one moment of his visit that I could look down on him, secure from the influence of his personality. He paused on the gravel sweep and looked down the garden to the fields beyond; then turned to the house, appraising its heavy stone façade and twin gables with the deep porch between.

When I went downstairs, his manner to me was affable. There was a hint of old comradeship in his greeting.

'Little Tessa. After so long – and you are just as I remembered you only taller and more...' His smile and nod suggested that the unspoken comparison was a flattering one.

He was one of the fair Jasmyns like myself and unexpectedly handsome as he stood on the hearth-rug fingering the seal on his watch-guard. There was a touch of elegance in the low velvet collar of his morning coat of fine worsted. My grandmother, there was no doubt of it, was pleased with him. I forgot the bony-wristed owner of the white mice. In the atmosphere of light family talk the situation became manageable.

Ashton had broken his journey to visit a friend at Maresbarrow.

'Packby is a pretty keen man of business. We had an interesting talk. Do you know, Mrs. Jasmyn, that you have a gold-mine on your land?' He laughed at our surprise. There was a largeness in his manner that inspired confidence. 'A particularly useful kind of grey sandstone, nearly as coarse as Bramley Fall stone. There's a bed of it over the river from Betony at the north end of Gib Rake. Rodney Jasmyn took some of it for his tower, just a handful. Apparently there's a good demand for that weight and quality of stone in the engineering world. Would you like me to go into the possibilities of quarrying?'

They talked of it a good deal. I listened and found the subject tedious; but I liked to watch Ashton. It was a change to have someone other than grandmamma to watch.

On the drive from Spandleby railway station Ashton had looked about him.

'The road between the village and the Hall must be drained, Mrs. Jasmyn. I'm not surprised that you have difficulty in keeping a tenant at the Lodge. It would be worth your while to improve the approach, even make a new drive. The cost?'

They discussed the necessary alterations;

the advantage of putting in a new hot-water system at the Lodge, even a bathroom. My grandmother smiled; the sun came out; we all three walked for a while on the sheltered terrace at the back of the house.

But more often, Ashton and I took our walks alone. My natural inclination was to listen while he talked but the dread that he would talk of marriage drove me to chatter endlessly, foolishly, lest a pause in the conversation should give him his opportunity. Though I knew that if he chose, he would interrupt me, pleasantly enough, and have his say, still I struggled desperately to ward off the silence into which sooner or later the fateful words would fall; and all the time I was aware of having nothing to say to him, no experience to draw upon. In society ladies talked of books and music; of their stay in Baden-Baden or Pau. I felt unequal to any discourse based on the Book of Joshua. My knowledge of music took me no further than the careful execution of a Minuet with Variations after dinner.

I remember, however, that we did talk about the Jasmyns. Since the weather often kept us indoors and the house was full of their spoils, the topic was unavoidable. One dull morning I found Ashton in the gallery which ran round three sides of the hall.

'We need more light here, Tessa. There's nothing to distinguish this place from the family vault especially with all the dead Jasmyns hanging about.' He was looking at a portrait of the Rodney Jasmyn who had built the tower. 'Our mutual great-grandfather. You have him to thank for it all. The black sheep who founded the family fortune.'

The painted face, florid above the high, intricately swathed cravat, gave no clue to his history. Some scandal had driven him to India in the days of the third George. He had gone out in disgrace as a clerk to the East India Company and returned in triumph, a Nabob. As my grandmother said, no one ever came back from India poor. Rodney Jasmyn had come back very rich. The source of his wealth was never discussed. The lacquered cabinets, jade vases, ivory-carvings and silver ornaments had represented only the exposed tip of a supporting mass of gold and rupees. In three generations the fortune had dwindled but when my grandmother had come to the Hall as a bride, the family had lived in a style beyond the dreams of their simple country forebears.

'I wonder what he had done. The thing that drove him away, I mean.' Ashton glanced at me, measuring my innocence. 'But Rodney's life was one long scandal, I suspect, until he came home, acquired the manorial rights and learned to behave like a gentleman.'

Like Ashton himself, I thought, comparing the two confident, fair-complexioned faces, except that Ashton would find it easier even than Rodney had done to become lord of the manor.

A movement in the hall below made me look down over the balustrade. On the Jacobean table by the inner wall a red-shaded lamp burned low as it always did throughout the day. The only other light came from the one stained-glass window and from the wood fire. Against their dark back ground of English oak the Eastern trophies glowed, faintly luminous: a pair of huge china vases, a brass gong, a case of stuffed parakeets, a picture of dark-eyed girls dancing in a pale yellow garden. On a marquetry table on the half-landing a set of jade toilet bottles made their own faint moonlight. I waited, expecting to see Emma or Steadman cross the hall, but no one came.

'...a much more interesting question.' I had lost the thread of Ashton's remarks. 'Yes, indeed. We can guess why he went away. But why did he come back? They always do, don't they? But suppose he came back for the very same reason he went away; to escape from an entanglement. There must have been some foundation for the rumour.'

'Which rumour, Ashton?' I asked politely.

'You've never heard the story of the Indian gentleman? Oh, you have? You do have other topics of conversation then besides repentance and how to avoid the snares of the flesh. They still talk about him at the Duke's Head although it happened in your grandfather's younger days.'

'What exactly did happen?'

'A gentleman from Calcutta – with an Indian servant – put up at the inn and lost no time in calling here. That wasn't surprising. He claimed that the Hall was his; that his grandmother had been Rodney Jasmyn's wife.'

'Do you mean that our great-grandmother was his second wife?'

'Something of the sort.' Ashton looked thoughtfully at the portrait. 'Mrs. Jasmyn has never told you, of course.'

'She dislikes talking about India.'

There had been another reason then, besides her reluctance to revive memories of the Mutiny. When she insisted that Barmote was to be mine, perhaps she was thinking of the Indian gentleman. Poor grandmamma! She had so many worries and her passionate concern for the family possessions was her one weakness; unless – I floundered – it was her strength. In no respect, surely, could grandmamma be thought of as weak.

'Some things may be best kept dark. In any case there's no hope – or danger – of uncovering old Rodney's secrets now.'

It was chiefly because he came close to me

and took my hand that I said quickly, 'What happened to the Indian gentleman? Do tell me.'

'Your grandfather was a regular sport. He invited him to stay for the grouse and took him out for long days on the moors. It happened to be a particularly wet August. The weather and food together were too much for the poor fellow. He left at the end of a week and was never heard of again.'

'Then our great-grandmother had everything and the other wife had nothing?'

'Who knows' – Ashton hesitated – 'what she had.' He put his hand under my chin so that I had to look up at him. 'And now we'll forget her, shall we? She has no part in the family history, if she ever existed.'

'But the Indian gentleman,' I said, with an obscure feeling that he had been unfairly treated, 'he existed. You said he was still talked of in the village.'

'It was probably some old fellow at the Duke's Head who spun the yarn in the first place. Oh, there may have been an Oriental pedlar selling scarves who called at the Hall one day. A foreigner of any sort would be a rare bird in these parts. You won't find a cottage in Barmote where they haven't heard of him and they'll all have heard different things.'

A sudden sense of darkness and mystery, a shrinking from the past and especially from the strange land of my birth made me burst out, 'It was Rodney Jasmyn who started it all, the uncles going to India, then my father. I wish it hadn't been so.'

'You would have been poorer, my dear.'

'There's too much of everything. They oppress me, all these things. They darken my life.'

He must have heard the change in my voice. I heard it myself like a cry for help.

'That's because you are too much alone here, Tessa.'

I had given him his opportunity. He followed me as I moved away. In a panic I went quickly to the top of the stairs, pretending to see Emma. But it was not Emma who came out from the deep shadow under the gallery. Firelight reddened her trailing grey dress with its over-skirt of russet velvet as she stepped past the hearth and into the shadow again. She must have come out of the sitting room. I went down, wondering why Steadman was not there to show her out and half hoping that she would leave without seeing me; but she tilted her head in its flower-laden little hat and looked up smiling. There was nothing for it but to introduce Ashton.

She chatted pleasantly but not a minute longer than politeness required.

'The weather hasn't kept you indoors, Mrs. Masson?' Ashton opened the door.

'Unless it actually rains I pay no attention to the weather. Besides, it's no more than a short stroll to the Lodge.'

She drew up her skirt with a pretty little gold claw. We watched her walk round the house to the path that led across the park. I noticed it then, an incongruity; or rather I felt it without knowing what it was, like some flavour in an elegant confection that didn't quite belong; an element which – whatever it was – may have accounted for the reserve I had felt in her company from the beginning.

'Who is she?' Ashton asked abruptly. 'I know she's the tenant at the Lodge but who actually is she?'

'I don't know. How can one know who a person is?' I put the question with no thought of being profound, yet half aware that it raised other questions whose widening ripples extended beyond my range of conjecture.

Mrs. Masson was an excellent tenant, Burnside said. It was foolish, more than that, utterly unreasonable to feel sorry that the strolling distance from the Lodge to the Hall was so very short.

4

Miraculously Ashton's visit came to an end without a formal declaration. Some business or social engagement recalled him unexpectedly to London. I drove with him to the railway station at Spandleby for the pleasure of the drive back and felt so light-hearted at having escaped that I could behave more naturally than at any time since his arrival. Indefinitely postponed, marriage seemed not quite intolerable. Besides, as grandmamma delicately pointed out, the fact of being married to Ashton would solve all my problems. The reluctance to have him near me, the fastidious dislike of certain things about him – these would be forgotten the instant I became his wife.

'Marriage will make all the difference,' she said, and the bliss of returning to a life without Ashton made it possible, however irrationally, to believe her.

She had spoken with the old tender smile I loved; and I loved it more now that it was touched with the sadness of a future parting. Yet surely my marriage would not part us. It would simply mean that there would be three of us here at Barmote instead of two.

'We've been alone, dear, so long.' As so often happened, grandmamma's thoughts coincided with my own. 'It won't be easy for me.'

I felt remorseful. Intent upon my own interests, I had forgotten hers. She too would find it difficult to admit a third person to our partnership. If Ashton's visit had placed a strain on me, it must have exhausted her. She may have resented his proprietory manner. She could hardly have approved of his habit of sauntering about the rooms and picking up a piece of jade or an onyx paperweight as if assessing its value.

'It will be very suitable. But there's no need for haste.' She lay back in her chair with a luxurious air of having all her time to herself. 'So long as I am here, an engagement will suffice. My mind would be at rest.'

'Let's stay as we are.' I set up the board for backgammon, hoping even more fervently than usual that grandmamma would win. She so disliked losing and I was invariably lucky in my throws. 'We're quite comfortable, just the two of us. Besides, Ashton may not want it now that he has seen me again.'

'I'm sure he wants it very much. But young men are in no hurry to settle down. You need not marry before you are twenty at least, unless I die before then. But you must promise, Tessa, that you'll accept Ashton's offer. There must be a formal engagement. As it is, while you are under age, Pawley says there will be complications. I want everything settled. Then if anything should happen to me, you could marry at once.'

Even the fearful word 'promise' had less than its usual power to daunt me.

'You won't die, grandmamma, not for ages.' And I began then and there, in defiance of her religious teaching, to pray that she would live forever, on earth and in the flesh. We played backgammon in the firelight until it was time for prayers.

All the same, though Ashton was handsome, suitable in every way and much kinder than I had dared to hope, I still could not bring myself to give the promise she wanted. It would be as binding in conscience as the settlements, once signed, would be in law. Common sense told me that if she died I must turn to Ashton because there would be no one else; but to give so fixed a shape to the vague bright future was more than I could force myself to do.

How long the respite lasted I cannot now recall. I know that the brief happiness was delicately poised. It was as though I had never been happy before, now that the small familiar problems had been eclipsed by the one overwhelming anxiety which had itself drifted away like a cloud to give a spell of heaven-sent sunshine. Thanks to what grandmamma called the lightness of my nature, I was able to enjoy a precarious contentment without giving much thought to the day when the wind would change.

The letter seemed innocent enough. I had no suspicion that it would work against me: the only letter on the afternoon post one day in late autumn. My grandmother looked at the unfamiliar writing before handing me the envelope to slit open with the ivory paper-knife.

'It's from Alistair Darlington.' She read the letter carefully. 'He's a Colonel now, home from India for good after twenty-seven years' service. He's living at Cheltenham.'

'Father's friend? He must be the Captain Darlington who took out the ruby to my mother...'

I should have learned by this time to avoid any mention of my mother. Grandmamma's face hardened. The ruby too had always been a sore point.

'I've always regretted letting it go but your father was so insistent that she must have it. He had no moderation where she was concerned. Darlington was in every way reliable, naturally, but if I had followed my own inner prompting, the ruby would never have left Barmote and you would have had it. You will be the first bride for four generations not to wear it. As it is...'

It had been swallowed up in the confused events at Lucknow. I cared nothing for the ruby. It was no more than just that it should have returned to India whence it had been looted in the first place from the palace of one of the Mahratta princes, to fall into the rapacious hands of my great-grandfather. But grandmamma saw its loss as one more example of my mother's fecklessness. Had she been a lady of family, she would have taken more care of so valuable an heirloom. She had written about it as if it were no more than a pretty trinket.

I knew better than to defend my mother, judging her to have been a poor, ineffectual creature. Even her letters had not been worth keeping. Once in a sentimental mood I had asked if I might see them. The silence that followed was impressive. Its implications as the speechless seconds passed made me hot with embarrassment.

'I destroyed them,' grandmamma said at last. Her eyes, uplifted to the blue lozenges of sky beyond the window-panes, were shining darkly. From that heavenly upward look I knew that it had been a good thing to destroy the letters.

Once raised, the subject of the ruby was difficult to dismiss. It was well known, grandmamma declared, that many ladies had kept their treasures safe throughout the entire one hundred and fifty days of the siege and had brought them out sewn into their petticoats. When I ventured to mention (for it seemed an argument in her favour) that my mother had in fact died during the siege, it was brushed aside as a trivial circumstance.

'She could have made some arrangement. The truth is – it grieves me to say it – Charles's marriage was a mistake from the outset. Nothing is more disastrous than an unsuitable marriage. Fortunately no such thing can happen in your case. Yours will be a perfect match. Between you, you will have considerable property. No one can dispute that.'

Clouds had gathered again. The letter had revived memories and anxieties though there had evidently been nothing disturbing in its contents.

'Colonel Darlington writes very civilly. He would like to come here but his health is uncertain. He has suffered a good deal from the climate and an old wound.'

She might almost have added 'fortunately' so little did she seem inclined to receive him. No plans were made for his visit. Meanwhile other things combined to upset her. Ashton's friend Packby had written asking for an appointment to discuss the possibility of quarrying at Gib Rake. She had also to make up her mind about the draining of the carriage road, whether to put the work in hand at once, or wait until the spring. I had never seen her so fretful and undecided.

One November afternoon I found her as usual by the fire, huddled in an assortment of the Rampu Chudder shawls she loved. It had been a dreary day. The Hall was situated in such a way that on all but the stillest days we were troubled by the sound of the wind. My grandmother's sitting room at the very centre of the house was more sheltered than the hall and upper rooms: its heavy furniture, thick carpets and curtains muffled every sound; but on that particular day a ceaseless rustling had penetrated even there.

At the sight of me she began at once in a nervous, wailing voice quite unlike her usual low-pitched tones: 'It's no use putting it off any longer. We must make definite arrangements for your engagement at once, while I'm still able to see to it.'

The abrupt end to my long suspense, the sad sighing of the wind, the hopelessness of any dream I might have dreamed for my own future made use reckless.

'No. Please. Not yet. I can't promise. If you love me, don't make me.'

I almost shouted, shaking hysterically and stamping my foot.

'It's because I love you...'

'No, no. Don't ask me again.'

My own intense excitement made me blind to hers but presently I saw with horror that she was changing before my eyes – had actually changed into a hideous stranger. Her face was strangely twisted; her beautiful deep-set eyes glared: an ugly spluttering sound in her throat gradually took the form of words.

'I can't bear it. You're killing me...'

She slid down in her chair, her head lolling sideways. I sprang to the bell-pull and tugged it again and again. Faint above the wind, the bell clanged in the depths of the house. Emma came running, then Steadman.

'Oh Emma, is it my fault?'

They pushed me aside and exchanged looks.

'It's the real thing this time,' Emma said, undoing grandmamma's collar. 'We must have the doctor.'

Somehow they got grandmamma to her bedroom and Steadman rode off at a gallop.

'There'll be plenty for you to do by and by,' Emma said when hours later I was still hovering miserably on the landing, hardly daring to look in again at the bloated, lamp-lit face on the pillows. I went down and straightened the disordered sitting room. Beyond the window, above the black rock, clouds were tearing across a yellow sky. The sudden glimpse of movement and light were like a last reminder of freedom; or was it not, in my case the first, since at that time everything was new to me, above all the stifling fear of an imprisonment that would last all the days of my life?

I drew the curtains and went into the hall, where firelight fell on the tall, painted vases and picked out here and there in their contorted designs an impassive, oriental face. I knew their way of catching each random flicker of light and holding it for a moment before letting it go, those bland, pale faces with their upslanting, thin-lined eyes. The masks of foxes – the antlers of deer – made aquiline profiles in shadow on the wall as I side-stepped the tiger and went upstairs. At the end of the gallery a curtain lifted in the draught. The flame of the lamp sank and rose again to show Rodney Jasmyn hanging above his spoils. What would become of me if she died? How could I live here alone, wavering for ever between my fear of the place and the close attachment I took to be love.

Her door opened. The doctor came out.

'Is grandmamma... She's not...?'

'Mrs. Jasmyn is not fully conscious. She may recover. But she seems distressed. Something has been troubling her. Do you know what it is?' I could not answer. 'A second attack could be fatal. I'm sorry.'

I stayed there when he had gone, weighing one disaster against another, pretending that I could choose. If I promised, she might recover. If only she lived, she might live for years. In all that time I would be no more than engaged to Ashton. It was like the hope of eternity. If she died now, I had not promised; I would be free. But what in the world would become of me, alone here at Barmote?

It was not the power of reason that made me push open her door at last; nor even the desperate impulse of a gambler, risking for a few years of freedom a lifetime of captivity. Only the familiar longing to please her, to be at peace with her, drew me to her bedside. I bent over her poor twisted face, looked into her prominent, expressionless eyes. It was love for her that made me say, 'I'll do whatever you want, grandmamma. I'll marry Ashton if he wants it. I promise.'

5

The whispered promise stole to whatever core of consciousness remained and lured her back to life. At first there was no sign that she had heard but by the next morning she had rallied. I flattered myself that I had saved her, thinking more of my power than of her victory, and wore myself out in waiting on her.

'She can't bear you out of her sight,' the nurse said, planning no doubt a half hour of leisure for herself.

In a few weeks grandmamma was strong enough to sit in a chair. So far as I recall – for long confinement to the house had made one day very like another – it was mid-December when she came downstairs and we were able to resume our old ways. I remember feeling grateful that she was so little changed. The dreadful staring look had gone. The nobility (I thought) of her features was unaltered.

In my reduced state tears came easily. They were tears of relief that made me bow my head over my work to hide them. We had sat for a while in quiet companionship when, looking up, I found her eyes fixed on me with an expression that startled me: a feverish concentration which, though it was certainly directed towards me, expressed no closeness of interest but rather a feeling of separateness as if she were looking out from some urgent inward crisis and seeing me as an external object to be dealt with in some way.

A creeping wind pushed open the door. I got up to shut it. She caught my hand as I went back to my chair.

'I feel much better,' she said. 'You have looked after me so well, darling. I'm quite strong enough to talk. We must talk about your engagement to Ashton.'

Weary from lack of fresh air and sleep, I stood by her chair, my hand helpless in hers, wondering how it was that the engagement, once only a possibility, had become a certainty.

'You must promise...'

'I have promised, grandmamma.'

I tried to draw away my hand but she held it firmly, placing her own on top of mine to press it down.

'Say it again.' An unfamiliar dark wilfulness suffused her lace. 'I want it, want it.'

Confronted with so nakedly hungry a purpose, I felt the strength ebb from my finger-tips.

'Ashton hasn't asked me to marry him.' A faint hankering after dignity made my voice shake. 'But if he does, I shall accept. I can see that it would be – sensible.'

'And when I die, you'll marry him at once. Say it.'

She pressed down my hand so fiercely that it seemed crushed against something flat that lay in her lap.

'If you die, I'll marry him at once.'

'There.' She let me go, sank back with a sudden change of manner and glanced at the object in her lap with a laugh that was gentle again. 'There now, look. I just happened to be holding it but I do feel, don't you, Tessa darling, that it has sanctified your promise?'

I looked down at the bible, its black leather covers worn with use.

'Put it on the table, dear.'

She raised a hand to rearrange her lace, then sat twisting her rings and smiling in her own quiet way.

The bible felt limp. It had the shabby look of a thing that had served its purpose. Some of the limp shabbiness had even passed into me as if I too had been used. I said nothing but for a little while after, a kind of nausea troubled me such as one might feel on seeing some loathsome, unsightly creature scuttle from a shadowy corner, pounce on its prey and scurry back. The sensation passed. Both Emma and the nurse said in their different ways that there was no accounting for the tantrums of invalids, especially the elderly ones. Odd quirks of behaviour, Dr Almore said, were to be expected after a slight stroke. We were lucky that things had been no worse; but there must be no repetition of the strain and excitement that had brought on the attack. As grandmamma's strength returned, so did her sweetness of manner.

I learned to keep my eyes away from the round table at her side where the bible lay because the sight of it never failed to remind me that I was bound for the rest of my days. Every promise must be binding in conscience; but the conscience (especially mine) may falter. The bible had given to my promise the unalterable mystery of a sacrament. I had made it, however unsuspectingly, under the scrutiny of a higher authority. The whole affair had passed into a loftier sphere.

In a way it was a relief to know that nothing on earth or in heaven could change it. The very enormity of it brought a kind of release. I could concentrate all my resources on the straightforward task of keeping grandmamma alive. When I had bathed her hands and face, rubbed her palms and temples with cologne, gently brushed her hair and held the cup of warm milk or arrowroot to her lips, I sat with her hour after hour, willing her not to die. I sometimes wonder if she knew that our relationship had changed. Did she pass from satisfaction to guilt, like an over-zealous gardener who cultivates a cherished plant to death?

As we grew a little further apart, I felt myself becoming more like her. Certainly in this one respect of caring for her health I achieved a singleness of purpose even she could not have surpassed. Sometimes too thoughts came to me in the very words she would have used: 'I have given you every hour of my life. Was that not enough? You shouldn't have asked for more.'

Yet surely it was grandmamma who had devoted her life to me. From the confusion of such thoughts I turned to more manageable things: footstools and screens, shawls and slippers, fans and cooling drinks.

In February Mr. Pawley came – and Ashton, who stayed a fortnight, insisted that I must have fresh air and exercise, engaged a new groom and behaved with such consideration that in any other circumstances I would have enjoyed his company. Afterwards I realised that from the day of our formal engagement, my grandmother made him a regular allowance. Certainly he appeared well satisfied. The household basked in his good humour. I remember the first brief thrill of pleasure when he put the half-hoop of pearls on my finger and how pretty (he said) it looked. He kissed me as he put it on and I felt older.

The one aspect of my engagement to be

70

positively enjoyed was the change it wrought in my appearance.

'It's time,' Ashton said, 'to rescue Tessa from those deplorable muslins.'

My grandmother was roused to send for Mme. Ballard who came down from London with two assistants and took me in hand. I rose to the occasion and discovered, Mme. Ballard was pleased to say, a natural elegance and taste. Not all the flounces and gauging in the world could alter my situation (and those were the days when forty yards of trimming on a dress would have seemed cheese-paring) but they did make it more bearable. It was understood that Mme. Ballard would make my wedding dress when the time came.

Ashton's visit interrupted our routine and when he had gone I continued to enjoy a little freedom of movement. Provided the nurse was with my grandmother, I came and went as I chose, savouring every second of my solitude. Even to walk to church became a joy because I was not yet walking there as Ashton's wife. Sometimes I stayed out of doors until it was dark, each phase of the moon reminding me how quickly a month can pass, how few months make up a year. I learned, too early in life, to measure time.

It was as though, closing my eyes to the distant view and concentrating my zest for life upon the present, I saw the world for the first time. Most of all I took to my heart the hamlet of Betony. It lay just the right distance away for a walk. Time after time I came to the gateless gap at the end of the narrow walled path with the same rapturous sense of freedom as the valley opened between the brown slope of Gib Rake and the greener flank of Long How to reveal the shining stream; and closer, at my very feet, the well, the red-tiled roofs and the empty farmhouse lying at peace with its fields.

The aspect was sheltered, the air mild. In the cluster of cottages, more than one front gate level with its neighbour's chimney, in the stunted fruit trees and low-leaning willows, I found a homeliness, a curious and quite illusory sense of returning to a way of life once familiar.

Afterwards I had only to step into our own hall to feel the used air brush my cheeks like a curtain to be stepped through; and sometimes it was quite an effort to go on past the tiger and the silent girls in the yellow garden to the sitting room in the very centre of the house, where my grandmother sat waiting.

6

One afternoon I came to the gap above Betony and saw a man at the well. He had evidently just wound up a bucket and secured the rope to the hook.

At first I could not place him. He was strongly built and plainly but respectably dressed in dark clothes. He took off his billycock hat, laid it on the grass and leaned right over the well, looking down as I had once done myself. Then exactly as I had done, he found a pebble and dropped it in. It was too late to warn him, in the light of my own experience, not to make a wish.

He heard me as I went down the path and his face lit up, with such a genuine pleasure in seeing me that I felt a rush of gratitude. It was some measure of the guilt and concern I had suffered.

'Miss Jasmyn.'

He thought me altered then. I felt a little sad at the departure of Miss Tessa.

'It's my clothes,' I said.

Yet I had changed in more than my appearance; had grown so much older in recent months that I could say to him without hesitation, 'I've been anxious about you, Reuben.

It was my fault that you were dismissed. If it were to happen again, perhaps I could...' But even if I had been half as callow and ignorant, what could I have done? 'How are you? Do you like your work?'

Emma had told me that he was working as assistant to an apothecary and druggist in Maresbarrow.

'Yes, I like it.' He had straightened up and seemed even taller than I remembered; but he was paler too.

'It's more confined. You can't be out of doors so much.'

'That's right. I felt shut in at first and the pay isn't much. But the work's worth doing.'

'More worthwhile than the work you left.'

It was impossible to keep from my voice a bitterness I would not have been capable of feeling a few months ago. Yet the bitterness should have been Reuben's. To have been at the beck and call of a useless girl for ten pounds a year and then to be dismissed for doing a little more than his duty! He was looking at me thoughtfully, observantly, and he did not contradict. He had always had – though not until now had I recognised it – a quality of independence; and all at once I saw how little scope there would have been for the exercise of such a quality on a coachman's box.

'You're having a holiday?'

'Just a day.'

'Mrs. Bateman will be pleased. She must miss you.'

I had found out their surname and that, to my shame, was all I had done. He nodded. His manner was entirely free from any sign of resentment. I should have known it would be so. But he seemed so altogether untouched by the disaster of his dismissal that after a rapid review of the situation, I said, 'Would you have – had you made up your mind to leave in any case?'

'That's it. I wasn't exactly dismissed, you know.' He smiled as if enjoying the memory of that dramatic moment in the hall. 'I didn't want to leave all this. No, indeed.' Already the hills were darkening but the spring air was moist and sweet. No one would leave Betony lightly. 'But the work was only a stop gap until something better turned up.'

'Then you didn't mind?' I was more than relieved, delighted.

He hesitated.

'There were some things I missed. But I was pleased enough to give warning before the old lady turned me out.' His words were disrespectful but he spoke so humorously that I couldn't take offence. 'I was cutting a dash, you might say. Thought myself a bit of a hero.'

'It was splendid.' I threw in my lot with his, feeling as reckless as a mutineer.

'With all due respect to you, miss, it goes

against the grain to work for the Jasmyns.' He picked up the bucket. It was empty. 'I reckon they've just about squeezed this bit of country dry.'

'Do you mean the well is dry?'

'I mean more than that. But the well is dry. Listen.'

He dropped in another pebble. We listened, looking into each other's eyes, sharing the experience of waiting, until at last instead of the expected subterranean splash there came the tiny thud of stone on stone.

'How can that be?'

'You see those trenches.' Strips of upturned earth scarred the hillside where workmen were draining the carriage road. 'They must have altered the flow of water in some way.'

'I didn't know it could happen like that.'

'It's not unusual. There used to be chalybeate in this water. That's why the local folk thought it was a healing well. Then after they started quarrying stone to build yon tower, there was no more chalybeate they say. But at least there was still plenty of water.'

'How do you know all this?' It seemed odd that he should know so much more about the land than I who would some day own it. I wondered if my grandmother knew about the chalybeate.

'I remember what my father used to say and I've read books. I know that people

76

can't do one thing without affecting something else. That's why we should all be pulling together, instead of drawing apart. It's the same with horses.'

I was impressed, knowing that what he said so simply must be true. It confirmed a vague disquiet I had already begun to feel.

'You blame us. It's our fault. You think we don't care.'

'It would be hard to blame you, miss. You're so young and you wouldn't hurt a fly. Only winding up the empty bucket made me feel right here in my heart what I've thought for a long time. Betony's finished. It's been dying for years and soon it'll be dead. Shall I tell you what it used to be like? Over there downstream on the other side of the bridge my great-grandfather Bateman had his manufactory. Just a little place. He made snuff-boxes. He built some of these cottages for his work-people. The Wagstaffs – they live down there at the bottom – were tinsmiths and coopers. They made well buckets among other things. Then there were the Cades farming over here at Betony Hay.' He nodded towards the long low roof of the farmhouse below on our left.

'What happened to them all?'

'The Wagstaffs are still here, labouring for the Jasmyns although John Wagstaff's a clever craftsman, brought up in the family trade. The French wars finished off the snuffboxes.

The Cades hadn't enough land to make farming pay. Some of us went down and the others went up, like buckets in a well.'

He had not said so but I assumed that the Jasmyns had been the only ones to go up. At the same time I realized that my grandmother was always afraid of our going down again.

'It happened bit by bit. My great-grandfather mortgaged the factory to yours. When the Cades had to sell a parcel of land here and there to make ends meet, it was the Jasmyns that bought it, and there was some argument about a boundary that the Jasmyns won. Those that hadn't money borrowed from those that had and then they couldn't pay it back.'

'There's talk of quarrying again,' I said timidly, 'over there at Gib Rake. Perhaps that will make work for the men here.'

'How are they going to get the stone away?'

So far as I was concerned the project had been mere theory. I had given no thought to its practical effects.

'It would mean either bringing a new road down here or laying a railway line up the valley, probably both. Ten years of quarrying,' Reuben said, 'and the whole place would be devastated.'

The thought was disturbing. I stooped and looked out from under the canopy of the well. With its two upright supports and the rounded tree-bole forming the winder, it made a frame enclosing a living water-colour of green slopes, brown willow boughs and silver-mottled stream.

'Do you know what happened that day,' I burst out, 'the day of the thunderstorm? I made a wish here at the well. It was childish and silly, I know; and one isn't supposed to tell a wish but it doesn't matter; mine won't come true: it never can now and in a way I didn't want it to. I wished to be free – oh, I don't know how – to go away, I suppose, to be a different person altogether, not a Jasmyn at all.'

I fumbled for a handkerchief, miserable and at the same time amazed at the disloyalty I had never acknowledged before; ashamed too, at least I would have been ashamed to cry before anyone but Reuben.

'It doesn't surprise me,' he said, 'that you want to be rid of all that. But I shouldn't have said what I said. The last thing I wanted was to upset you.' Then, for there was no stopping once I had started, as the tears ran down my face and soaked my good lace ruffles, he said, 'I haven't seen you cry like that since the day we buried poor old Lance.'

'Oh, Reuben.' I was in no state to resist the added misery and knelt down with my head on the coping and literally wept into the well. 'He wasn't old. And wasn't he beautiful

– and good until he did – what he did?'

'It was a shame.' He sounded angry still as he had been then. Yes, it was anger that made him slam down the stones to make the cairn. I remembered his flushed face and the wind blowing his hair over his eyes as it had blown the tall, trembling grasses by the hedge where I had knelt, waiting for the shot.

'I would never have believed it of Lance.' I looked down into the dark well and could see nothing but the coolness was restful to my inflamed eyes.

'He'd been where there were sheep a hundred times. I wouldn't have believed it if it hadn't been grandmamma herself who saw him.'

'Ay,' Reuben said, 'she was the one that saw him. The only one.'

'That was what was so unlucky. If it had been anyone else they mightn't have told and Lance might never have done it again.'

'That's true,' Reuben said grimly. 'He'd never done it before.' He had said almost the same words as we had stood, wretched and incredulous on either side of Lance's golden corpse. I had looked up into a sky of summer blue with great towering white clouds and said in stark misery: 'It's a lovely day for his funeral.'

What a baby I had been! And yet the agony had been as sharp as any I would ever know.

'I was so fond of him,' I said apologetically.

'Too fond,' Reuben said

'You mean, it's wrong to love an animal so much?' I said. As he made no reply, I was conscious of having indulged my feelings too freely and changed the subject.

'What are you going to do about the water for Mrs. Bateman?'

'I'll fill the bucket at the spring. It's better water but more difficult to get at. The one thing the Betony folk must not do is drink water from the stream. And that's what they will do. It's so much nearer.'

In the depths of my ignorance concerning the countryside that sustained me, my ignorance of the existence of the spring goes without saying; but a kind of earnest sense of duty made me plod silently behind him as he set off obliquely up the hillside. It was a few minutes before we heard the gurgle of water and saw it spouting from under the slab of stone that served as a spring-head, overflowing a shallow basin of natural rock and losing itself in a hidden runnel through the grass to the river below.

'We need a jug or a pitcher.' I stood by the spring as Reuben tilted the bucket first one way and then another without finding an angle at which the water could flow in freely. It would do nothing that was not free, I thought, watching its effortless flow from under the stone.

'I'll have to come back.'

'But how will Mrs. Bateman manage? It's so steep and even in fine weather it won't be easy to carry the bucket so far.'

'I'll get Tim Wagstaff to do it; but you know, I can't help saying it though I'd rather cut my right hand off than hurt you, Mr. Burnside could have had water piped to every one of these cottages for no more than it's costing to drain the carriage road, if he'd been instructed. He told me so himself.'

He explained where conduits could carry the water from the spring and how a system of tanks could regulate the pressure. The hamlet lay below us, giving as usual little sign of life except for a line or two of clothes dangling like people who had given up hope.

'You think we're letting it die.' And yet the breeze that moved the pinafores and night-shirts was rich with the scent of fertile earth. In the bare willow a thrush was singing. 'Somehow it doesn't feel dead. I love it, love it.'

At Reuben's feet the water sprang sparkling from the hill and fell in smooth folds into the basin, always the same yet endlessly renewed. He was watching it too. I forgot his criticism of my family and felt only the sympathy between us. With Reuben I had no need to talk unless I wanted to. Finding in his face the protective understanding I had always taken for granted, I said, 'I've known you since I was a little girl, Reuben...' then stopped. It was surely more than sympathy that made the familiar face unfamiliar. I had thought of him as a firm-looking young man but it was not firmness that I noticed in him now.

'Leaving you was the worst of it,' he said slowly. Without 'Miss Jasmyn' or any form of address, his words went straight to my heart. 'Wherever I look, it's you I see.'

There were pale mauve milkmaids growing by the spring. I gathered a few.

'I used to make you carry the flowers I picked. How you must have hated it!'

But I knew that he had not hated it. A sort of joyful confidence, a gush of happiness, a feeling of absolute trust in him, made me tuck the posy in his buttonhole. 'There. Isn't that pretty?'

Standing close to him, I remembered how he had lifted me from the earth into a new kind of freedom under the wet, flower-scented trees. Perhaps he was remembering too. The strange thought came to me that if only life could be restricted to a green hillside, an arch of sky and a thrush singing, then Reuben and I might be – friends. The thought faded in recollections so painful that without intending to, I said, and my voice as I remembered it afterwards had a high-pitched desperation in it, 'I didn't tell you what happened after I made that wish.'

'I don't see much sense in wishing.' He spoke with the same slow gravity. 'Especially to be someone different from the person you are.'

'That's just it. It's not only senseless but wrong. They punish you for it.'

'They?'

'Yes.' I waved my arm to include the attentive pagan gods of earth and sky as though all my grandmother's careful exposition of the Testaments Old and New had been lavished on someone else. 'Instead of being free, I'm to be doubly a Jasmyn.'

His face changed. He became quite still and attentive. Perhaps it was simply because he was there, the only person whom I could tell, that I told him, but it seemed at the time that I must.

'I'm to be married to my cousin, Ashton Jasmyn.' Dragging off my glove, not so much to show him as to convince myself, I looked at Ashton's ring. 'It's all been arranged.'

'It's all been arranged,' I went on saying to myself as I walked away across the grass to the gap between the stone walls. 'It's all settled and there's no sense in wishing, especially to be someone different from the person you are.'

For a moment I caught a glimpse of the sad mystery of things. Fluttering innocently in the wide air, the spirit could be caught, fixed, imprisoned in a particular self, whether one liked it or not.

Reuben was still standing by the spring as I turned into the darkly shaded narrow way. When I came out on the carriage road, the square tower reared its head over the crest of the hill. Rooks wheeled above the Barmote elms. I stood watching them soar and sink with the cold sky behind them. It was impossible just then, I found, to go home, when every impulse drew me back to Betony.

Some inkling of the feeling I should have had for Ashton made me lean my head against the wall, filled from head to foot with regret.

7

It had become a habit to use the bridlepath for fear of meeting Mrs. Masson; but I was lucky: there was no sign of her as I ran across the park though I could not be sure that she was not watching from the Lodge window.

It was quite a shock, when I had taken off my outdoor things, to find her in the sitting room pouring out tea.

'I have taken your place,' she said with her charming smile. She leaned forward to adjust my grandmother's shawl which had slipped from her shoulders, then handed me a cup and filled the pot from the spirit kettle. 'You're glowing after your walk. Did you enjoy it?'

'Very much, thank you.'

I swallowed my surprise as I sipped my tea. Yet after all it was not unusual for her to call. On reflection I discovered that she called quite often, indeed almost every day. If my grandmother was unwell, she made do with my company. If I was not at home, she simply left a card and called again the next day, setting convention aside on the grounds of grandmamma's ill-health and presumably my youth. She was always pleasant. Whether we drained the carriage road or not, here was a tenant who made no complaints, had no intention of leaving.

'I've been telling Mrs. Masson how well satisfied we have been with Mme. Ballard.'

'You have reason to be.' Mrs. Masson cast an experienced eye over the black velveteen facings of my green walking dress. 'She has managed the inner sleeves very well. I should be glad to have her address.'

On the subject of clothes Mrs. Masson and I found common ground. I felt her eying my merino as keenly as I was eying her winter beige. But gradually it dawned on me that there was a difference in the way we looked at each other. There was no doubt about it. Whereas I had been absorbed in the pleated edging of her draped overskirt, she had been absorbed in me, my whole person; more than that, my whole being. The startled sense of being entirely exposed made me – unobtrusively, I hoped – draw back my chair.

'No more, thank you.'

She had glanced at my cup with the most delightful blend of humour and kindness as though apologising for the hospitality she was dispensing on my behalf. The conversation lapsed. I found some difficulty in coming to its rescue, wrestling as I was with the uncomfortable sensation of still being too close to Mrs. Masson. It was surely that absorbed and unaccountably warm interest that had put me on the defensive from the first. Had I not suffered long enough from the suffocating attentions of my grand-mother?

Possibly Mrs. Masson had the same effect on others. My grandmother had sunk down in her chair and closed her eyes. With a revival of the old affection I pitied her. It was a protective pity. For some reason I saw the two of us, not as Mrs. Jasmyn of Barmote Hall and her grand-daughter in all the glory of a fashionable chignon but as an infirm and aging woman and an ignorant girl confronting some wholly indefinable danger. The fleeting notion escaped. Could anything be less dangerous than our secluded life at the Hall?

Besides, Mrs. Masson was not looking at me at all or at my grandmother: she was looking at the clock with the same unfailing interest. It was of walnut, mounted in silver gilt, a handsome piece, I realised, feeling an absurd impulse to pop it somewhere out of sight. Mrs. Masson compared it with her watch and felt for her gloves. My grand-mother roused herself guiltily.

'Mrs. Masson was saying, Tessa, before you came in, how much she would like to see round the Hall.'

'But Tessa is tired.' Mrs. Masson's voice was concerned, familiar, almost loving. It conveyed so much more than the situation warranted as to irritate me.

'Not at all. Would you like to see the gallery?'

The gallery, she said, was impressive. From the table laden with terra-cotta figures and bronzes she could scarcely tear herself away. The portraits – she looked at every one with close attention – were fascinating. The upstairs drawing room with its cloudy looking-glasses and shrouded chairs, its uninterrupted view of the louring crag, occupied her for quite ten minutes.

'This is thought to be rather unusual.'

It was a chair from the palace of Ranjit Singh, made of wood and lacquer overlaid with gold and festooned with red cord from which dangled gilt cones and bunches of gilt fringe like fairy brooms. The feet were in the shape of hooves. Nothing seemed more likely – the thought had often occurred to me – than their stirring into motion and trotting away.

'It really is unusual,' Mrs. Masson. said.

'I'm afraid you'll find the library very cold. It's in the tower.'

Not in the least. She had on her mantle, hat and gloves. But I must find a shawl. Waiting at my bedroom door while I put it on, she noted each item of furniture and nodded approval. She was remarkably easy to entertain. To take so obvious, so sincere a pleasure in other people's possessions was disarming.

I set off rather quickly along the unlit passage, unbolted the red-baize-covered door and ushered her into the lobby with its empty wrought-iron cressets, then through the oak door into the library, a square room lit on three sides by narrow lancet windows.

'No one ever comes here. It's a dreadfully cold room,' I said, my teeth already chattering. There was no refuge here from the wind. It enjoyed the uninterrupted possession of the place. In contrast to its feline mewing our remarks seemed more than ever stilted; but Mrs. Masson, undaunted, toured the shelves, pulled out a book or two and admired the cabinet of carved ivory with brass mounts.

'My great-grandfather added the tower in 1805.'

'That would be when he came home from India.'

It was not a question. She seemed familiar with the family history. I waited while she peeped out from each of the windows in turn, feeling it my duty to be proud of the library but unable to repress a tiny doubt as to its value; a sham tower of faked antiquity and full of unread books.

It would have been tasteless to express such an opinion when Mrs. Masson appeared so well pleased with all she saw.

'The Jasmyns were quite simple people,' I felt compelled to tell her, without at all understanding why, 'until my great-grandfather made his fortune. They were yeomen farmers, very comfortable.'

If there was a note of regret in my voice, she overlooked it. Turning, I found her toying with the handle of one of the drawers of the writing-desk.

'But now,' she said quickly, moving away, 'the position is very different. It is a splendid inheritance – not only the house but the land.'

I was surprised at the confidence with which she named the farms. She had certainly wasted no time in getting to know the district. Her eyes moved to my left hand.

'You must be very happy in your engagement. So very suitable. Mrs. Jasmyn has told me...'

'The name will go on,' I explained.

'Ah yes. You'll always be a Jasmyn. You have no other close relatives, I understand.'

It was like her, I suppose, to assume the forlorn expression she expected to see in me.

'You're so very young. It will be a long engagement?'

'Yes, quite long.'

'Mrs. Jasmyn is far from well. You must be anxious about her.'

'Grandmamma is much better.' I bolted

the baize door and we stepped into the comparative warmth of the house. 'She is really very strong; only excitement is bad for her.'

'She will live for years and years,' I added mentally. 'She must.'

'Excitement. Yes, indeed. That could be dangerous. Any sudden shock, for instance.' She paused at the head of the stairs. 'And her death – one must be prepared for such things – would leave you quite alone, except for your fiancé.'

She motioned me to go first while she gathered up her skirt.

'Nothing is likely to upset her. We live very quietly and see no one.'

There was no reply. I looked back. She had not after all followed me but remained in the gallery under Rodney Jasmyn's portrait. The setting of dark panelling and heavy gilt frames became her. She had – there was no denying it – an air of distinction; and why on earth should I want to deny it? I raised my voice.

'Barmote is not an exciting place.'

'Perhaps not.' She laid her gloved hand on the balustrade and came down a step or two. 'And yet,' she spoke with a casualness that afterwards seemed inappropriate to so interesting a remark – 'my Kate would very much like to come.'

'Have you a daughter, Mrs. Masson?'

I was astonished. She seemed an essentially solitary person.

'Yes. I have a beautiful daughter.'

She just inclined her head with a little secret look of real tenderness.

'I shall look forward to meeting her.'

The unexpected existence of a Miss Masson was as startling as an apparition.

'I've told Kate about you. You are of about the same age–'

Mrs. Masson broke off and seemed to hesitate. She was going to ask me how old I was. To avoid the uncomfortable necessity of telling her that I didn't know, I ran down the remaining stairs and so caught nothing of her next remark save the one word, 'Switzerland'.

'It is too secluded for her at the Lodge. She must have more society. You have been unusually fortunate in finding a husband on your very door step. So fortunate...'

She took her leave gracefully. On the whole my impression of her had improved but she was not an easy person to understand; so very well-mannered, gracious and self-confident and yet – it had puzzled me all the time and it still puzzled me as I closed the door – her hand as she gave me my cup of tea had been trembling and cold. She had been nervous.

She came again – and again. Nothing, it seemed, could keep her away. My grandmother enjoyed her visits and I grew used to them. Besides, we had a duty towards her as tenant and neighbour. The Hall provided her only outlet

'Run along, dear,' she would say, her voice full of affection. 'You look pale. A little fresh air will do you good.'

The opportunity to escape on my own was always irresistible. Yet often as she came, I never saw her coming across the park without some misgiving. Diminished by distance, between the tall trees, she appeared at first as a small figure, growing steadily taller as she approached until one saw the charming details of her dress; the carefully arranged pale brown hair under one or other of her expensive hats; the delicate pallor of the complexion she was always so careful to protect. She had only to set foot in the hall to impress upon it the warmth of her personality, to such an extent that all the ornaments, rugs, pictures, guns, daggers and gongs seemed to droop and wilt, so little did one notice them. One of the unusual aspects of my attitude towards Mrs. Masson was that the figure crossing the park seemed always distinct from the lady who, with increasing familiarity, moved about the Hall. For some reason the two never quite fused into one. But we did grow closer. It was impossible to resist her friendly overtures, her constant interest in our affairs.

'I like to know where I stand, miss.' Emma was in fact standing in the hall holding a tray and on it a glass and claret-jug. I had just come in from the garden. 'It's you I've been used to take orders from, or the mistress, and *requests* from the nurse. But if I'm to give heed to Mrs. Masson as well...'

'Mrs. Masson would only ask on my grandmother's behalf, Emma.'

'That may be. But this is the first I've heard of claret. Gruel, the doctor said, and milk-and-water, and the drops in an emergency.' She hesitated. 'It's good for you, miss, to have time to yourself and especially in the fresh air. Mr. Steadman says the same. But when you're not in, well, a gap can be filled.'

She followed me into the sitting room and said, pointedly addressing my grandmother, 'Will *you* be needing anything more, ma'am?'

I doubt whether Mrs. Masson noticed, all her interest being immediately fixed on me. As usual it embarrassed and repelled me. I moved away awkwardly and sat down in my own chair. It occurred to me that the furniture had undergone a slight rearrangement. My low chair had been moved away from my grandmother's. I now faced her across the hearth-rug. Mrs. Masson sat between us.

I had interrupted one of their long spells of gossip, about the family, no doubt. My grandmother, having few topics of conversation, had initiated Mrs. Masson into the Jasmyn cult of which, I realised long afterwards, she was herself both founder and high priestess. There was something irksome in the relish with which the two of them explored the family history and reviewed the family possessions while I, doomed to carry the burden of them to my grave, sat silently listening.

'Mrs. Masson thinks that I would be the better for an occasional glass of claret, Tessa.'

My grandmother looked at me anxiously as she often did now.

'We must ask Dr. Almore,' I said abruptly, 'before making any change.'

Mrs. Masson achieved something between a smile and a frown of surprise at my unusual firmness; but then she could not know my fierce determination to keep my grandmother alive, or how far beyond compassion it went.

'I don't doubt that the doctor will think it, as I do, a real life-preserver for an invalid such as Mrs. Jasmyn.'

At her choice of words, I wavered, knowing my ignorance.

'I'm so tired of gruel.'

My grandmother spoke fretfully. Her face looked pinched.

'A mere spoonful.' Mrs. Masson went to the table.

I made no protest. A wave of indecision, of despair at having constantly to weigh one problem against another, made me indifferent. Although Mrs. Masson presumed a little, her manner was reassuring: she knew what she was doing. I watched her hands moving competently over the bottles and phials as she tidied the medicine table. And after all the claret did grandmamma no harm. She sat up looking less frail and miserable. Mrs. Masson was so invariably kind, so much more experienced than I, that it was ungracious to repel her offers of help and friendship. Penitent, I looked up at her, feeling my face relax into a smile, to find her gazing at my grandmother with an expression that sobered me at once. But then, an elderly invalid with dull eyes and trembling lips and – I saw to my dismay – traces of spilt milk on her black dress, is not a pleasant sight.

I turned to the one topic certain to protect me from Mrs. Masson's too penetrating concentration on myself, the increasingly interesting subject of Kate. Since we were much of an age, comparisons were inevitable. Mrs. Masson was inclined to dwell on them.

'You are so very fortunate in your expectations,' she said in her gushing way, 'but Kate...' The pause made me more keenly aware than ever of my own shortcomings,

'...has so many accomplishments.'

She had had the best of masters for music and drawing, had travelled in France, Germany and Italy; was even now in Switzerland. At her expensive boarding school she had made suitable friends whose homes she visited: a Margaret Sutherland for instance, who was at present staying at her aunt's country home near Maresbarrow. It was a relief to learn that there was no prospect of Kate's coming to the Lodge, at least for some time. She both fascinated and frightened me.

'You have given a great deal of thought to her education,' grandmamma remarked. 'I hope when she is settled that her position in life will justify it. No doubt you have plans for her.'

Mrs. Masson made no reply. None was needed. It was evident that she had plans and not only for Kate, whose training had been as thorough in its different way as my own. I don't remember when or why the conviction seized me that every move Mrs. Masson made was planned. I had not yet reached the point of seeing an intention in everything she did; only that there was nothing haphazard about her from the tiny pearl buttons of her chemisette down to the black braid frogging on her yellow silk boots; no little touch of rashness.

When my grandmother sent me to fetch

some eighteenth-century maps of Barmote and Betony, Mrs. Masson's interest was not merely polite. She produced from her reticule a gold handled glass on a velvet ribbon and examined the maps in a keen, intelligent way though I personally found them dull. It was not surprising then that she took an interest in some of the family jewellery when my grandmother, flattered by her enthusiasm for the maps, took a fancy to show her some of the less valuable pieces.

I took them one by one from their lacquered boxes and spread them on the table: a necklace of gold filigree and turquoise; a white jade comb set with red and green stones in a design of birds and flowers.

'This is my favourite.'

Mrs. Masson looked critically at the gold half-moon set with jargoons, to be worn as a necklace, and shook her head.

'Too heavy for you, my dear. But there are several pieces here that would be suitable for a young girl. The seed pearls. Try them on. Undo your collar.'

We stood by the chimney-glass. The unfamiliar sight and feel of the pearls on my bare neck was intriguing. Grandmamma nodded. She liked to have the Jasmyn treasures displayed. Once she might have reproved me for vanity but she was changed. Was she so very much aged, so very much nearer the end? I glanced at her anxiously, then back into the glass to find Mrs. Masson's eyes fixed so intently on my reflection – or on the pearls – that I took them off quickly and put them away.

It amused her to put on one side the necklaces and eardrops particularly suitable for a young girl.

'And of course the heavier things could be re-set.' We laid them back in their cases. 'A fine dowry for any young woman, Mrs. Jasmyn. More appealing in their way, as jewellery, than more precious stones might have been.'

She was too polite to be derogatory but my grandmother flushed.

'The more valuable stones are in safe-keeping. There is a limit to what can be kept in a country house. I confess it has always grieved me that the ruby should have been lost. It was a pretty thing, a pendant in a gold and pearl setting. It disappeared – in India. I know who was responsible. It was no better than deliberate theft. But I dislike talking about it.'

Since her illness grandmamma had become less restrained in her manner. Her venomous resentment in speaking of the ruby – and my mother – suggested a wildness of judgment that alarmed me.

'The ruby was sent out to my mother,' I told Mrs. Masson when, having put away the maps and jewel cases, I walked out with her on to the gravel sweep.

'You don't remember her?'

'Oh no. I don't remember anything about India. I was only a baby. That's why I envy you and Kate, Mrs. Masson. You have each other.'

Any reference to Kate went straight to her heart. Her smile was almost tearful.

'But you and Mrs. Jasmyn have been all in all to each other.'

'There is a difference.' I heard myself with astonishment and felt guiltily conscious of disloyalty to grandmamma; but there was surely no harm in expressing a generalisation. 'A mother and daughter must always be closer than a grandmother and granddaughter.'

'Yes. It is the closest of all ties. The strongest and most lasting bond.'

We stood in the shadow of the house. Her eyes travelled over its façade. When she spoke again, her voice was low without its usual pleasant lightness.

'It should be so. There is nothing one would not do for a daughter: no pain, no risk one would not endure if it would make life better for her.'

A pang of loneliness, of envy of Kate made me say, 'I wonder if my mother felt in that way about me. You see, she scarcely knew me.'

'She must have felt about her daughter as

101

I feel about mine.'

'I should have liked some memento of her.'

Until that moment I had not once been aware of such a feeling. It deepened as I spoke into regret, in spite of all her faults, that my mother's form and features would never be known to me. Time like a great wave had carried her away into oblivion, leaving no trace of her – but me. I emerged from my reverie to find that the impossible had happened. Mrs. Masson had behaved rudely. With unbelievable rudeness she had walked away without saying goodbye, dragging her long skirt over the gravel and then the grass without the usual precaution of hooking it up with the gold claw that hung from her waist.

For a few minutes I had been drawn to her as never before; but I realised now that her gushing manner was affected, her interest superficial. She thought of nothing, cared for no one but the insufferable Kate. I began to detest the girl and all her accomplishments.

By the laurels where the path across the park began, Mrs. Masson had stopped and stood with her head bowed. I wondered if she was feeling unwell.

'I don't care,' I thought spitefully. 'We don't ask her to come here. If she wants help, she can ask for it.'

All the same I couldn't help watching her from behind the laurels as she walked slowly away between the trees. She disturbed me. Instinct warned me against her. On the whole it would be better if she stayed away.

8

As I said, Mrs. Masson changed the course of my life. It was to be a long time before I understood the nature and extent of her influence but she had already been the means of turning my thoughts in a new direction. Had it not been for her, I might never have felt any curiosity about my mother; but once Mrs. Masson had established herself in her new role as mother of a daughter with whom I could compare myself, by a natural transition, the process of comparison extended to include my own mother; and almost at once my regret that she had been so feckless and commonplace gave way to regret that grandmamma had not kept her letters. At times the feeling was almost indistinguishable from resentment; unless of course there had been something shameful in the letters. I imagined grandmamma casting them into the fire and looking up through the lozenge panes at the sky as if to purge herself of their impure influence. Such thoughts, alas, served only to increase my interest in the whole dubious history of my mother.

It was of no use to probe my grandmother for information. I must look elsewhere. By this time I had learned to be devious.

'Grandmamma,' I said as I sat with her one evening, 'did you reply to Colonel Darlington's letter?'

She looked up with pathetic eagerness from the page of her testament, which had occupied her unturned for an hour or more. I believe she was always hoping for some advance on my part that might lead to a renewal of our old intimacy. She had forgotten the letter. I found it in her letter case.

'He asks if he may come. How rude he must think me! But I would rather not revive the connections with India. Its associations are still so very painful.'

Between fear of exciting her and the longing to know more, I hesitated.

'I could write to him, explaining that you've been ill.'

'You could say that we shall look forward to seeing him when I'm stronger, in the summer perhaps, the late summer, or even in the autumn. The countryside looks very fine in autumn.'

I showed her my letter but not the postscript.

'Please, Colonel Darlington, tell me all you know about my poor mother. I should so like to hear it.'

Amazed equally by my boldness and deceit, I dispatched the letter and only then found time to wonder by what process of change she had become my 'poor' mother. Was it because she too had married a Jasmyn?

It may have been this strangely worded appeal that hastened Colonel Darlington's reply, addressed to me. It came almost at once. I took the letter to my room without mentioning it to my grandmother and read it with the trembling alertness of a traveller setting foot in an unknown land, a land, as it turned out, of unexpected features.

...So you are Tessa. I thought you might have been named after your mother... Your parents were more than kind to a lonely bachelor as I was then and still remain. I was their guest at Simla and I later met your mother very briefly at Lucknow. I wonder if you are like her. Alice was a radiant creature whom it is impossible to think of as dead... I have heard her spoken of as an example of gaiety and courage when both were needed. There is much that I cannot write but that I shall look forward to telling you when it is convenient for Mrs. Jasmyn to receive me.

Naturally the Colonel, or Captain as be then was, would see his hostess in a more favourable light than could be expected to illumine my grandmother's view of her unknown daughter-in-law. He was loyal to his old friends and I liked him for it; a little deluded too and for that I liked him none the less. He had failed to see the shallowness and social inadequacies that made my poor mother so very unsuitable a wife for a well-bred young man who would one day be rich; who was indeed rich then if he had come home to take up his inheritance.

Was I like her? Grandmamma had worked hard with my earnest though sometimes feeble cooperation to see to it that I was not. Radiance and gaiety were not qualities that flourished at Barmote. All the same I could scarcely wait for the polite interval of two weeks to elapse before writing to the Colonel again; and he with equal promptness replied. Our correspondence flourished to the extent of half a dozen letters. It provided a touch of mystery to be enjoyed to the full in an existence as uneventful as mine was at that time. We wrote only of my parents and their life in India. My letters were short, consisting necessarily of questions whose form I had difficulty in varying. Since my attention had recently been drawn to my own lack of accomplishments and elegance of manner, I developed a quite penetrating interest in my mother's.

I wonder if my mother was tall. I am myself five feet and three inches in height... Was my mother musical? Did she draw and paint well? I dare say she was well taught – I have not myself had the advantage of drawing lessons...

This combination of fact and surmise elicited the information that the Colonel was not sure of my mother's height, that she sang, played and sketched very well but that he chiefly remembered the charm of her conversation.

I believe he enjoyed the correspondence as much as I did. He lived a restricted life, in failing health and much confined to his over-large house in Cheltenham. He wrote of his early days with the Regiment and created for me a living India such as all the profusion of relics surrounding me at the Hall had failed to convey. It was an unusual relationship. More than once he hinted at some special reason for wanting to see me.

It is natural that you should be interested to hear details of the tragic end of both your parents. Your father's death was heroic. He should certainly have had one of the new Victoria Crosses. [There followed an account of his part in the fighting at Chinhat.] *As for your mother, unfortunately I can tell you little about the circumstances of her death. Indeed her presence at Lucknow came as a surprise to me. It was after Havelock's arrival and before Sir Colin Campbell's final relief of the Residency that we met by chance as I was leaving for a spell of duty with the guns at our outpost at the Farhat Baksh palace. The enemy had exploded a mine there and breached the wall. When we*

108

were relieved on 17th October (I have just refreshed my memory by consulting the journal I kept at the time) I returned to the Residency and was distressed to learn from Mrs. Inglis herself that your mother had died and been buried – as was necessary in those conditions – on the same day. There were so many hastily prepared and unmarked graves that I could not even pay my last respects to hers...

I read intently with a sense of distant sadness and half aware of some discrepancy in his story.

Though I could not know it at the time, our last farewells had been exchanged in that brief meeting on 10th October. I had found her in low spirits. You must remember the effect on her of your father's death. She was convinced that she too would die. She thought only of her baby. Until then I had no idea that Charles had left a daughter. Your mother was insistent that if she herself did not survive, you must be taken home to Barmote. 'Barmote will be hers,' she said again and again. I have cherished all these years a sentimental wish to see you and fulfil in person a certain obligation she laid upon me. Indeed I have been remiss in not doing so long ago but my health... [Before the evacuation of Lucknow he had been suffering from wounds and fever.]
I could not give the help and advice I would

otherwise have given to your nurse, a faithful soul, Susan or Sarah; I have forgotten her name. She had lost her own husband, poor woman, and at least one child, but she must have been a woman of spirit. She chose to come home by sea for the sake of your health instead of by the overland route though that would have been quicker. I dragged myself up to watch the women setting off in their dhoolies *on the four-day journey to Calcutta with so many delicate infants and invalids. All I could do was to write to Mrs. Jasmyn, telling her what I knew…*

So far as I knew that letter had never arrived. I tied up the Colonel's letters and put them away, then sat for a while at my window considering the few items of information that remained from my past like hazy landmarks in mist. All my early history was contained in the satinwood box where the letters lay; yet they told so little. I felt just then no more than a mild curiosity, a faint impulse to tidy up the facts. It had been a surprise to learn that my mother's death was sudden: I had formed the impression that she had lain ill for weeks. My chief feeling however was one of disappointment. My mother had only anticipated the doctrine my grandmother had been drumming into my ears since infancy: Barmote was mine.

My window overlooked the park, by nature an acre of rough grass pierced here and there by slabs of outcrop rock; but Rodney Jasmyn, having turned himself into a gentleman, turned the unpromising pasture, as best he could, into a park. Neither transformation, I dare say, had been entirely successful.

The trees, touched with the gold of a summer evening, stood so still that it seemed no wind could ever change them. But all at once there was movement. Jackdaws and rooks rose from the grass in a ragged black cloud. Mrs. Masson was coming. The birds scattered and cawed as if they found her as disturbing as I did; but she took no notice and watching her draw steadily nearer, I almost reached the point of recognising what it was about her that puzzled me. Then as she came closer and I saw her face, the discovery eluded me.

To sit with her and grandmamma for half an hour was more than I could bear. As Steadman let her in at the front door, I escaped along the terrace. There would just be time for a quick walk as far as the church.

Twilight gave a grey uniformity to the graves. On the plain headstones the same names appeared again and again. I could just make them out: Wagstaffs, Cades, Batemans, all of Betony; and next to them in neighbourly closeness, the earlier Jasmyns: Aaron who had died in 1750 and his wife Patience: quiet folk, I fancied, who had worked their own land. In those days it had been Barmote

Farm. The simple epitaphs made no mention of a Hall. With the natural rock behind them, Aaron and Patience had felt no need of a sham tower.

I pushed open the west door. It was too dark to read the inscriptions on the marble tablets dedicated to the later Jasmyns including my father and his father, both of them Charles, but their wording was familiar: I could read it any Sunday. Another memorial attracted my attention.

'Sacred to the memory of Rodney Jasmyn ... a wise Parent, an affectionate Husbande, a compassionate Magistrate, an Example of Christian Piety in his Life at Home and Abroad...'

All the same, on the quiet pages of the village history, my great-grandfather seemed to cast a shadow. It was in his time that the families drew apart, the Jasmyns going up and the Wagstaffs, Cades and Batemans going down. Without actually rejecting the description of his many virtues, I felt something inappropriate in the design of his commemorative window; the Good Shepherd surrounded by lambs with a border of inset scenes depicting sowers and reapers and sheaves of corn.

My reflections were pleasantly interrupted by the throb of music – and of the most secular kind: the music of Barmote Fair.

In the solitude of the porch I danced a few

surreptitious steps to the tune of 'Belle of the village' and came out into the warm dusk to see below on the green a yellow circle of naphtha lights. In years gone by the Wagstaffs and Cades, Jasmyns and Batemans must have gone to the fair together, some of them lovers perhaps... Here, generation after generation, their banns had been read, their children christened. My children would walk this path to church and my children, I realised incredulously, would be Ashton's.

The shock aroused me to a consciousness of my surroundings: the fading light: the silent graves: a voice calling me from the lych-gate.

9

'Reuben.'

'I wanted to see you.'

We met under the roof of the lych-gate; and even in the half light I saw and understood the change in his whole bearing.

'I was running away from Mrs. Masson.'

'They told me at the Hall that you'd gone out for a walk. I saw you go into the church just now and I waited.'

'Why did you want to see me?'

'Because I couldn't wait another day without seeing you.'

I believed him. It seemed perfectly natural, even inevitable. He spoke with such earnestness and agitation – his lips were pale – that I recognised in him the influence of the same transforming spirit that had, to my astonishment, changed me too.

'It seems years since I saw you,' he said, 'and I couldn't bear it any longer.'

It might indeed have been years since we had met, so radically had the lapse of time altered us. Whatever distance had separated us we had crossed at a single step; if such a distance had ever existed; I had forgotten it. Imperceptibly I had grown into the habit of referring every thought and feeling to his judgment, wondering at every turn what he would say and think when at some uncertain future time we met again. Now he stepped out of the dusk into the centre of my life, annihilating the rest of it. We were alone in a world extending no farther than the span of the tiny thatched roof above us.

The music had started up again though we could hear little more than its lumbering beat and now and then the fragments of a tune.

'Isn't it lovely?' I said, endowing it with my own rapture. 'Steadman said it was to be a steam organ this year. Did you know? I like that kind of music – as if it were hard work to be cheerful. Do you?'

He paid no attention; and the mood of pure happiness can have lasted no more than a minute before he said, 'I'm going away to London. I had to see you before I left.'

'To live?'

We were standing so close together that parting seemed no less remote than dying; but we gradually lowered our voices like conspirators meeting in a dangerous place.

'To work and study.' He spoke with a mixture of dejection and pride. 'Mr. Constantine, the gentleman I work for, has helped me. He's found an opening for me at the Royal Free Hospital. I want to be a doctor; a physician; and work here some day.

Others have done it, starting at the bottom. I've read about Dr. Snow and my father knew Dr. Marsden.'

He jerked out the statements without conviction as if speaking of events too far away to have significance and presently his voice faded into a gloomy silence. At the same time the organ laboured to the end of its tune. The warm evening took on a stillness so profound that I had the sensation of falling headlong into it. A bird flew into the black shadow under the yew. We both started.

'It'll take years,' Reuben said.

'Yes. Years. How many? I wonder.'

'I don't know. Seven at least. I'm so ignorant. It's the chance I've wanted all my life... Mother and I used to talk about it. And now that it's come, I'm as miserable as if I was lying in one of those graves.'

I stared into the dark shade where the Batemans and Jasmyns lay resting in a peace that seemed all at once complacent.

'You mightn't be so miserable there. Your troubles would be over.'

Beyond our small refuge the air was shedding its light so fast that the colourless earth seemed to spin. Dizzily I put out my hand to the iron latch.

'Don't go yet, please. I may never have another chance and I want to tell you. It's because of you that I want to better myself;

116

not that it can ever matter to you what I am, but by making the most of myself, I'll feel nearer to you.'

He could scarcely have been nearer. We were closer than we had ever been or could ever be again.

'When you come back I shall probably be married.'

I pulled open the gate and went out into the lane. The hedges were thick with dog-roses and honeysuckle. On the green below, the circle of light had brightened with the deepening darkness.

'They're enjoying themselves,' I said as the voices floated up to us. 'What is it like at a fair? There are gingerbread stalls, I know.'

'And hoop-la – coconut shies.'

He had joined me in the lane.

'A fat lady. A midget perhaps.'

'How small?' I asked, imagining a creature of exquisite daintiness.

'Somewhere about the size of Mrs. Cartwright's youngest next door to the Duke's Head.'

'Oh! Still I should like to go just once, and you could buy me a fairing, Reuben.'

My spirit soared above the conversation. I scarcely knew what I said or heard his answers as I fashioned in the incurable lightness of my nature a dream of Reuben and me, arm-in-arm between the gingerbread stall and the hoop-la, shouting above the music like real country people. But optimism could take me no further. Nothing could ease the anguish of knowing what I had missed.

We walked slowly along the lane, spinning out the distance and the time.

'You couldn't ... we couldn't somehow...? You remember what I said over there at the well about wishing?'

'That there was no sense in wishing to be different?'

'I thought myself so clever and now I do nothing else day and night but wish I was someone else.'

'It wouldn't make any difference. I'm promised to my Cousin Ashton. There's no changing it; and even if I hadn't promised, I don't see how...'

'Nor do I.'

Almost at once, it seemed, we came in sight of the Hall.

'I don't see how it could ever be.'

He opened the gate. Even then we lingered, I looking out at him, he looking in.

'Would you like me to visit your mother? Would she like it?'

'If you could see her once in a while until I can send for her, I'd be grateful.'

'You'll be going back to Maresbarrow now?'

'First thing in the morning. I could come round this way.'

'I wish you well, Reuben.'

'And you, Miss Tessa. I hope you'll be happy. I shouldn't have spoken as I did but I couldn't help it. You're the whole world to me.'

With every step, as I crossed the park, the sky shrank and the house grew until I could see neither stars nor trees, only the dark walls. This time, after the scent of roses and honeysuckle I noticed at once more vividly than ever the smell of stale old things and something more; neither the odour of musty cloth nor the perfumed oil from Indian marquetry, nor dust nor mice but a compound of them all that hung in the air to make it almost tangible.

On the table under the gallery the lamp burned as usual. In the firelight shadows moved. They had no power to frighten me. Nothing could frighten me now. What worse thing could happen to me than to see in Reuben's face the love I should have seen in Ashton's.

All the same I crept into my grandmother's room with a quickening agitation very like fear. She lay quite still in the candlelight, her eyes closed. I went closer. She was breathing. She was still alive.

Although we had said goodbye, I knew that he would be there in the morning at the gate or in the bridle-path.

Early as it was the air was warm. The tall grasses scarcely moved in the sheltered corner by the hedge where I had waited to hear the shot that killed Lance. I remembered how, when at last it came, so short and flat that I could hardly believe it was enough, the familiar landscape changed: the light grassheads close to my own withdrew as if they had separated themselves from the situation and looking up, I saw white-peaked clouds move calmly across the vast and comfortless blue.

The rectangle of stones marking the grave was overgrown now, half buried in grass; the cairn had fallen apart; the agony had abated a little; the memory not at all.

I had been grooming Lance outside one of the loose-boxes when grandmamma came out into the yard, dressed for her drive.

'I'm going, Tessa dear. You won't be lonely?'

'Look.' I passed the brush through Lance's pale silky coat. 'Isn't he beautiful? And he loves me, don't you? I can see it in his eyes. We'll have a walk presently, beloved.'

'It's a sin to talk in that way to a dog.'

I didn't look up but I could feel her between me and the sun and caught out of the corner of my eye the glitter of jet beads on her cape.

'Have you learned your verses? Then lock him up and go to your room, dear.'

I put away the brushes and waited for her

to get into the carriage so that I could arrange her skirt as usual but she made no move until I had shut Lance in – whining with disappointment – and fastened the door.

'Now go upstairs.'

She watched me go, not trusting me, I suppose, and it was quite a little while before I heard Steadman drive away. We were in Exodus at the time and by a hideous irony the passage was all to do with rams and bullocks and lambs. The verses flew into my mind: I learned them in a trice, ran downstairs, and saw at once that I had blundered again. The upper half of the loose-box door was open, the pin dangling free on the chain, and Lance was gone. It had happened twice before when I had not fastened the door securely. But there was no harm done. I would find him.

'Lance, come here, boy,' I heard my voice ring again in the free air, under the high-piled clouds. A dozen times I had seen his nose uplifted from the meadow grasses the moment I called: he was such an obedient dog. But before I could run to look for him, there had come the sound of wheels on the gravel and Steadman, stony-faced, brought back the carriage. They had been gone no more than twenty minutes.

Grandmamma never hurried but something in her way of getting down the very moment Reuben let down the step, impressed me with a feeling of urgency.

'Where's your dog, Tessa?'

Not 'Lance' but 'your dog', so that his escape became more than ever my responsibility.

'Lance has got out somehow, grandmamma. I did think I'd locked him up safely.'

'Then I was right.' She stood erect, her eyes uplifted to the distant sky. 'I was sure of it. I saw him just now' – the pause was terrifying – 'chasing sheep in the high field above Betony...' She came nearer and put her hand on my hair. 'There are lambs... He'll have to go, darling. I'm sorry.'

'Go where?' I asked, my heart pounding.

'He'll have to be destroyed. Once a dog takes to worrying sheep, there's no cure for it.'

'Oh, but he couldn't. Lance wouldn't do such a thing. I don't know how he got out but I expect he only wanted an outing on his own. It's quite natural. He only wanted to be free. It's such a lovely day...'

I made a frenzied tour of the garden, the buildings, the park, calling him, until he came out of the wood on the east side of the house, looking as innocent as could be. We had just time for a quick goodbye. He licked my hand as Steadman came out with the gun; and Steadman waited, giving me time to run away and hide.

It was Reuben who knew where to find me. He had come alone, bringing Lance covered with a sack on a handcart.

'We'll bury him here,' he said, and hacked down the bracken with a spade...

And he knew where to find me now. I heard him coming down the bridle-path. He stepped over the hedge and without – so far as I can recall – saying a word, began to gather up the stones of the tumbled cairn. I knelt down and we rebuilt it together, kneeling on either side, never touching except when his hand brushed mine as we lifted the stones. My eyes felt hot: I had scarcely slept; but a current of energy bore me up so that I felt weightless, charged with life: and below and beyond and around the exhilaration, making it all the keener-edged, was nothing but sadness.

'I'll think of you here,' he said. 'You'll come here sometimes.'

There would be blue sky again and high white clouds. It would be a lovely day – for a parting. My feeling of exhilaration gave way to misery as keen as that I had felt when we first made the cairn; but this would be more lasting. I could see no reason why it should ever end. Since the future was as empty of hope as it was long, we talked of the past; at least I talked. Long afterwards I realised how significant Reuben's silences had been.

'If only grandmamma hadn't been going to Spandleby that day, it wouldn't have happened. I mean, it might have happened but she wouldn't have seen.'

'It had to be, I suppose.'

I went over it all again as we fitted the stones into a broad pyramid, not only to recall Lance but because Reuben and I had shared the experience of losing him and in sharing had been united, no barrier between us any more than there was now as our alternate hands laid the stones; first his, then mine, time after time in a conscious rhythm. I knew that we were feeling alike just as we were remembering alike, so that in movement, heart and mind we were at one.

'The whole thing was my fault. I can't have fastened both halves of the door properly. You know, that was just like me; and yet I truly meant to. Over and over again I've tried to remember and each time I can almost hear the bolt going in, but I'm not sure about the pin...'

'It wasn't your fault. It's all wrong for you to feel guilty. I saw you shut him in.'

'Of course, you were there in the yard when they drove away.'

'Not just then. I was in the tack-room when she – Mrs. Jasmyn sent Steadman into the house for a bag she wanted.'

'I remember. They didn't go at once.'

Rattling through the verses in my room, I

had been aware of some delay.

'But you did see me bolt the door?'

'Yes.'

'Then that really is a relief. And the pin?'

He looked at me, as if hesitating. My heart sank. 'Then Lance must have undone the latch by jumping up. But you didn't see him get out or you would have stopped him.'

Reuben said nothing as he laid the last stone on the top of the cairn.

'Everyone goes away,' I said.

'There's no help for it. How could I stay, things being as they are.'

'We'll meet sometimes. You'll come to see your mother.'

'I've brought you something to remember me by.' He reached in his pocket. 'It isn't a liberty. Even Mrs. Jasmyn couldn't call it that. You asked for it.' He smiled and gave it to me: a fairing; a pottery group eight inches high; a dark-haired gentleman with a confident waxed moustache and a faint resemblance to the late Prince Consort, standing erect beside a seated figure not unlike the Queen. 'It doesn't quite come up to the sort of thing you have at the Hall.'

'Just look at them,' I said, stroking their smooth pink cheeks and glossy hair. 'They're so pleased with themselves and each other – in a world of their own.'

'You like it?'

I nodded, holding it carefully and feeling

that it was all I had; all I could have.

A bell rang in the house.

'I'd best be off now.' He had added two miles to his ten mile walk to Maresbarrow by coming round this way. I could tell that he had something more to say; but he hesitated, he who was usually so forthright. 'She hasn't–' He began again. 'Nothing has changed you yet. It's unbelievable, that you should be as you are living yonder.' He glanced over the meadow at the house and I realised, with distress, that he hated it. 'You'll have a lifetime of it. Wanting you to stay just as you are now is like asking for a miracle.'

His brow was anxious. Seeing the new shadow in his face, I knew myself to be the cause of it. It would settle and remain there throughout the endless years that would keep us apart. I held out my hand and felt his close round it with a longing like my own.

The sun was high enough to show the gleam of gossamer threads between the bracken fronds. Delicate as they were, they should have broken and disappeared as Reuben stepped out into the bridle-path; and yet, unable to raise my eyes to see the last of him, I saw them still, tenuous and clinging.

10

Next day the weather changed. Low cloud closed us in, leaving no more than a few wet laurels to mark the margin of an un-imaginable world into which Reuben had vanished for years; for ever. Imprisoned in the dim rooms, I had time to remember that when he had been part of my daily life I had ignored him. Only when it was too late had I begun to care whether he came or went. The hopelessness of our situation, the lack of any prospect for the future, fixed my mind wholly on the minute fragments of time we had spent together. So that it was in a bird-like state of spirits, alternately soaring and returning unwillingly to earth that I dreamily waited on my grandmother or drooped at the window, looking out on the glistening rock and drenched leaves. The weather kept even Mrs. Masson away.

The sudden return of summer at the end of the week brought release. It was mild enough to saunter down the bridle-path; mild enough for a young lady to have set up her easel in defiance of puddles where the hedge sank low to give a view across the meadow to the Hall.

I watched her through the hazy brightness of sunshine after rain with the same astonishment an apparition would have aroused; the same startled yet wholly pleasant awareness of the difference she made, whoever she was, by simply being there. From the first moment she charmed me. My instant conviction that she had every quality I admired – and lacked – was never shaken when I came to know her well. Her vivid colouring: blue eyes with dark brows and hair; the picturesque flow of her red dress; the rather rakish set of her gipsy hat; the quick resolution of her brush strokes – all established her as a creature of radiant life.

Catching sight of me, she smiled, brush suspended.

'I knew it. You were meant to be part of my picture. I saw you in the distance as you came out of the door and wished you would stand there for a while. You were exactly what was needed. I was feeling a lack of human interest. But this is much better.' She got up. 'I'm Kate Masson and you must be Miss Jasmyn.'

There was so much confidence in her way of holding out her hand that she might have been at home, I the stranger; but I liked it.

'I didn't know you were coming.'

'No one knew. I just took the law into my own hands and came.'

I looked at the sketch, interested to see

through the eyes of a stranger a place so familiar as to be in no way separate from myself. If she had included me, then I would have learned what I was really like.

'I could put you there.' She pointed to a space in the right forefront, 'and yet somehow,' she looked from me to the sketch, frowning, 'you don't fit or it doesn't fit you. The fact is I haven't caught it, I haven't caught it at all.'

'The house?' It seemed a faithful reproduction of the twin-gabled front, the rock, the tower. 'I dare say you thought at first it was just an ordinary farmhouse.'

I looked at her anxiously and was surprised to see her suppress a look of amusement.

'Oh no, not ordinary.' She began wiping her brushes. 'Why have I put in those long shadows reaching out like spokes – or tentacles? They must be there.'

'It's the trees.'

'Perhaps in another light... Oh, I'll tear it up and start again... The colours here are difficult. After Switzerland one feels the difference. This landscape is darker.'

'It changes all the time.' Would she understand if I told her how clouds and trees and hills were constantly at work to bring bewildering new relationships of light and shade so that a shadow might become a shape, a shape a substance? 'Sometimes I feel there is more here than I actually see.'

She had been looking round with the exploratory eye of a newcomer. Now she turned the same bright, intelligent – but slightly puzzled look on me. Had I not been fairly confident of my green delaine, I would have fancied some oddity in my appearance. She turned with dissatisfaction to the sketch.

'I haven't caught it. How could I?'

'Please don't tear it up. I think it's very good. If you don't want it, I should like to have it.'

'You would? Then it can't be so bad. I should like to give you something as a token of our meeting but something much better than this. I do hope we shall get to know each other.'

'I should like it.'

'When you opened the door and came out, a pale figure in your light green' – how glad I was that she had never seen me in my pallid muslins! – 'I could have fancied that you were escaping.'

'And so I was, after three days of rain.'

But she had seen in a flash what it had taken me years to discover. It pleased me to watch her putting away her brushes until, uneasily, I realised that we were not alone; for of course Mrs. Masson was there by the oak to the left of the path. She was dressed in the light brown tones like honey, that she often wore. They made her inconspicuous in the shade of the wide-spreading boughs. But as she smiled and nodded I noticed how remarkably pale she was, colourless as ivory but without its sheen. In contrast to her daughter, she seemed more lifeless than usual; and as we chatted, she glanced from Kate to me as if, having compared us in other ways, she could now compare us in the flesh. Presently, shivering a little, she excused herself and went home.

'Mother is not quite well,' Kate explained. 'It's a sort of ague she suffers from.'

We talked while the colours dried. Afterwards I walked with her to the Lodge. Here at last was the companion I had lacked all my life. My prejudices had been absurd. We might have known each other for years. From the beginning our relationship was one of effortless ease and – I thought – affection deep enough to give promise of a friendship secure and lasting; and in spite of the extraordinary strain put upon it, I was not much mistaken.

'Do stay for a while,' Kate urged one afternoon when I called to return a book, 'if it isn't too dull for you.' (She could have no conception of the sepulchral dullness of the Hall.) 'What shall we do?'

I hesitated.

'If only...'

'Yes?'

'How very pleasant it would be – more

than anything else I should like to make toast.'

She laughed so much that I was obliged to explain.

'I never met anyone like you, Tessa. You have the most exquisite sense of happiness as if all the world were fresh and new to you.'

I could not tell her of its bitter counterpoise. All I said was, 'It isn't the toast so much as having someone...'

'To make it with. I do agree. Do you know' – with another burst of laughter – 'I have a passion for making toast.'

And the toast itself on that holiday afternoon was delicious.

Kate knew that in coming to Barmote she had acted against her mother's wishes.

'Fortunately I had the excuse that Margaret Sutherland has invited me to Maresbarrow where she is staying with a relative for the summer. I shall go on to her from here. Mother had arranged a round of visits for me and wrote several times to tell me how dull I should find it at Barmote. She's been taken aback to see how happy I am, how entirely at home.'

'Does she find it dull?'

'No, indeed. One would think the place had some fascination for her. We heard that the Lodge was to let through a chance meeting with the Warmans at Lyme Regis just before I left for Switzerland. Mother wanted a change and thought it would suit her. She doesn't need society. She has lavished everything on me' – Kate became thoughtful – 'as though she stopped living on her own account years ago and formed the habit of living through me. I was a sickly child, given up for dead more than once. Having literally to watch over every breath I drew has made her over-anxious. Even now if I have a headache she sees me in a rapid decline.'

'Then that is one way in which were alike. Grandmamma has given her whole life to me.'

The similarity seemed to me quite striking. Waiting for Kate to confirm it, I was aware that the confirmation did not come.

'But then,' Kate said after a little hesitation, 'you'll be married soon, won't you? I'm sure Mr. Jasmyn will want it to be soon.'

'It won't be for some time, perhaps years. I may not marry until – while grandmamma is alive.'

I would have been happy to leave the subject, especially as Mrs. Masson had come into the room.

'But that's a shame.' Kate spoke warmly. 'Why ever not?'

The matter being so delicate, so hedged about with every kind of emotional complexity, I was lost for a suitable answer and resorted lamely to the very last thing I wanted to tell them: the truth, or part of it.

'Grandmamma thinks it best.'

But I told them no more; nothing of my own feelings – how could I? – and my reserve misled them as surely as if I had lied. I grew hot and uncomfortable as they looked at me, Kate pitying my condition as she supposed it to be, and Mrs. Masson? Her look was different but then she was always inscrutable.

That was not the only time the conversation turned upon my engagement.

'I have no inclination to marry,' Kate said once. 'Not for years. But I shouldn't say so to you, Tessa, for if ever a girl was in love! Come, you can't deny it. It's written all over you, the way you look and speak. Mother noticed it and said how blessed you are and how secure in your future. I hope you'll be very, very happy.'

Astute as she was, she misinterpreted my confusion. Of the circumstances of my engagement she saw no further than the pearls on my finger.

Shortly after Kate's arrival, Ashton paid us a visit. His mood this time was less affable. Besides, he must have found our Spartan way of life disagreeable.

'You and Mrs. Jasmyn live as if you were penniless,' he said as we walked in the garden one morning. 'This place is no more comfortable than a convent housed in a museum. You might as well be in that sister-hood – what's its name – on the river bank beyond Betony.'

'St. Agnes'.'

'You'd find the same atmosphere of repentance and reproach; the same boiled mutton and rice pudding.'

I thought him ungrateful. He did at least have hot water brought to him in the mornings. Gathering all my courage, I embarked on a little social life, persuading my grandmother that Ashton needed to be entertained in a quiet way. Since they were the nearest, the Massons were our most frequent visitors, especially Kate. Her mother came less regularly while Ashton was with us.

Kate was frankly interested in the Hall. She regarded it as a curiosity, the inside, as she put it, having so little relation to the outside. When I hinted once that the family trophies were not quite to my taste she said casually, 'When you inherit you can clear them all out and refurnish; or there must be attics where you can store the things.'

Perhaps in my zeal for company I invited Kate too often. At any rate Ashton developed a prejudice.

'Who are these Massons?' he demanded more than once and yet in fact he knew more about them than we did, having met the Warmans one evening when they had gone up to London from Dorset.

'They had been talked about a good deal in Lyme Regis; not in any scandalous way of course, but so little was known of their background that the ladies in particular were inclined to romanticise. When Mrs. Warman mentioned having spent a year at Barmote Lodge, Mrs. Masson said at once, "Do you mean the Jasmyns' place near Spandleby?" The very next day she asked for Pawley's address.'

'Imagine anyone knowing about Barmote. Was there anything else?'

'Only a general understanding that they had lived abroad, based on nothing more than a servant's mention of a tin-lined trunk, I fancy. Mrs. Masson didn't speak of it and Miss Masson was away a good deal, at school or on the continent with friends. Mrs. Masson is thought to be more than usually ambitious for her daughter. She has set her heart on her marrying well. If you're to spend much time with them, I shall want to be sure that they are suitable companions for you.'

'How could they be unsuitable?' I gazed at him in amazement. 'Kate is much better educated than I. You've heard her play and she has read a great deal. I feel her to be my superior in every way.'

'I should scarcely say that. Accomplishments can be picked up easily enough. Are they people of family? They live in comfort.

Do you know where their money comes from?'

'I have no idea,' I said, resenting his manner; and my resentment increased when one morning a small unpleasantness arose which kept the Massons away during the remainder of his visit. We were coming back from church, Kate and I ahead, Mrs. Masson and Ashton a few paces behind. A lull in our conversation made it possible to overhear theirs.

'I hope, Mrs. Masson, that you have not been persuaded to invest in the railways,' and when Mrs. Masson murmured what seemed to be a negative, 'You prefer minerals? Australian nickel is still doing well. However, if your means derive from land, you are wise to let well alone. Your late husband's family owns land in Dorset, I believe.'

Mrs. Masson, as a rule adept in controlling a conversation, seemed put out by Ashton's persistence and showed some reluctance to reply. Indeed she looked almost flustered and made a great show of stepping up on to the grass to avoid a deep rut, with her eyes lowered to the careful adjustment of her skirt, so that Ashton at least did not see her lips tremble. But Kate did and with a quick, puzzled glance at her mother, stepped back and took her arm.

'You're interested in investments, Mr. Jasmyn. Have you ever regretted not making a career in the City? But perhaps in your case no career was necessary. You are fortunate.'

Ashton looked vexed as Kate took charge of the conversation with a competence I envied. Mrs. Masson did not open her lips again. As we parted I noticed again how drawn she looked, while Kate, flushed with air and exercise, seemed to me quite brilliant.

'I tried to find out a few facts about the husband.' Ashton was unrepentant. 'When people cannot be frank about their affairs, one naturally feels there is something to conceal.'

'What sort of thing?' I asked.

'Nothing sensational I dare say. They could be small tradespeople who have done well and branched out. Successful milliners. But I don't think so. There's something I can't quite put my finger on. Has it ever struck you that Mrs. Masson might have foreign blood?'

It had not. My attention was invariably directed towards Mrs. Masson's clothes rather than to her physical characteristics. I noticed them later. Yet I had to admit to myself, though not to Ashton, that I had felt in her from the first some indefinable flaw.

'Her intonation is unusual. She has rather a clipped way of speaking,' Ashton said.

'If it were trade,' I broke in, 'Kate wouldn't hide it. She would think it trivial and affected to pretend.'

'Possibly. But does she herself know? And if it isn't trade, what is it? For there is concealment, I'm certain of it.'

The incident left me doubtful. It was impossible not to be influenced by Ashton, who knew the world and could have no interest in gossip for its own sake. I reached the conclusion with a sighing sense that his company would be more entertaining if he had. Since we saw no more of the Massons for a while, there was time for the small uncertainty to grow into mistrust, faint at first but increasingly difficult to dispel.

All the same I had only to see Kate again to know that she was incapable of deceit. The day after Ashton left I called at the Lodge and invited her out for a walk. If I was happy without Ashton, she too may have found relief in a change of company. I thought her quieter. Her mood was thoughtful but that may have been due to a chance encounter that depressed us both.

We were just turning into the bridle-path when a woman came trudging along the carriage road on our right; a poor woman with a bundle strapped to her back and a baby in her arms. Something about her – a dogged weariness – made us both stop and wait, disinclined – I'm sure Kate felt as I did – to turn our backs in case she needed help. As she came up, she raised her head. I think we both smiled and both saw a look of desperate appeal in her face though she had not intended to stop; nor did she speak until Kate said, 'You look very tired. Have you far to go?'

'Only to St. Agnes', miss.'

'Would you like to go into the house and rest?' Kate nodded towards the Lodge. 'They'll give you something to eat. Come, I'll take you.'

'No, thank you, miss. I can't wait. It's the baby. She's going fast.' She held the child close, rocking a little in the pain of her grief. 'I must get to the convent. The sisters have helped me before.'

We looked at the poor little grey-faced creature, her hands like tiny claws, as she breathed her last of the bright summer day. I could only cry in sympathy but Kate said, 'You mustn't give up hope. Look at me.' She stood, tall and beautiful in her blue zephyr dress, her eyes alight with a vitality of spirit that brought some faint change of expression even into the woman's face. 'I was like that when I was a baby. They gave me up for dead more than once; but I lived, didn't I? Didn't I?'

'Yes.' The woman gave a quivering smile. 'Only she don't take nothing, not so much as a sup of water.'

'I was just the same but I hung on. My mother told me. I wish you would talk to

140

her but you haven't time. And look at me now. Don't give up. You don't want to wait but I'll send the pony carriage after you to catch you up.'

'It would be quicker to go by Betony.'

I showed her the narrow way between the stone walls and told her to take the path by the river and round the wooded hill. 'Don't give up,' Kate called after her. 'Don't ever give her up. You needn't cry, Tessa. I don't believe the baby will die.'

'How can you know? So many babies die.'

'It's as though I remembered' – we walked into the shaded path between high hedges of elder and thorn – 'the one agonising need, to breathe and then to breathe again when all one knew of life was a tiny pulse beating in darkness; and then gradually the coming out into the light – and here we are.'

She laughed with sunlight on her face as we reached the spot where the hedge had been cut low, the place where we had first met. At this time of year the Hall looked least severe. Light for once bleached the rock behind. The heather rooted in its crevices blushed pink. Another summer was passing, I thought, subtracting it from the immeasurable but ever shrinking sum of the years before my marriage.

Kate looked at the house thoughtfully.

'You were right about the curious quality in the air; an atmosphere alive with possibilities. One never sees it all. There's always a cloud or a hump of hill or a clump of trees in the way.'

I missed the smile with which she usually mocked her own tendency to dramatise.

'I see questions everywhere. Do you know, Tessa, I sometimes wonder if I'm clairvoyant.'

'Oh, yes,' I said ardently, thinking it a compliment. 'I'm sure you could be. You're so good at everything.'

At that she did smile and hugged me. It was like having a sister.

'Have you ever...?'

'Do you know I...'

'Go on. What were you going to say?'

'I don't know.' The feeling had been fleeting, a memory of some sort. 'I've forgotten.'

'What's the very first thing you remember, Tessa?'

'I don't remember India at all.' By this time Kate was familiar with all that could be known of my history. She had even, having promised secrecy, seen Colonel Darlington's letters. 'Or even the inn at Gravesend. It's as if my life began here at Barmote.'

'I know what you mean. One can't remember life beginning but one might remember it beginning again because something marked a change, a difference important enough to linger in the memory.'

'I remember being here at the Hall in the

dining room on a Sunday. I used to have to stay there by myself between services while grandmamma rested.'

'But that must have been hours.'

'It seemed like years. No toys or books because of Sunday.'

For a moment I felt again the crushing tedium of those weekly ordeals: silent grey tracts of time when, stiff in my Sunday best, I formed my first notions of eternity.

'It was monstrous. Most children are allowed a Noah's ark on Sundays.'

Kate's expression of outraged candour amused me; but it occurred to me that there had perhaps been something unusual in my upbringing. Had those hours of solitary confinement really done me any good?

'You said you remembered the feeling of struggling to live.'

'I did say so; and yet it can't be possible, surely, to remember so far back. I must have imagined it. But it's true that the very first thing I remember is one or other of my illnesses; the feeling of anxiety brooding over me; and far, far away, I remember someone crying. I can still feel the pain of it. It seemed a sorrow nothing could ever heal.'

We moved on. Her mood changed.

'I met a gentleman in Switzerland who was interested in such things as mesmerism, animal magnetism and so on. He said that one could discipline one's thinking much more than most people do. The mind is an instrument. It's a question of concentration.' She treated me to a short lecture on the subject. 'It should be possible to recall past experiences. As to foretelling the future, that's another matter.'

The future did not interest me. I knew too well what it would bring.

'Emma knows an old woman on the Gibside road who tells fortunes with cards.'

It was all I could contribute to the learned discussion. I was humbly aware of its inadequacy even before Kate said, 'That's utter rubbish. Pieces of cardboard.'

We had reached the gates. I invited her in but she declined, hardly noticing when I left her standing stock-still, brows drawn down, staring fixedly at a clump of harebells with a concentration that filled me with admiration and envy.

In the hall I found a letter from Colonel Darlington. He was coming the next day.

11

The Colonel's visit, if, in view of its peculiar circumstances, it can be called a visit, was fraught with so much bother and vexation that for a long time I wanted only to forget it. In retrospect I see the incident as marking my first step towards the territory of gloom and shadow in which at the summer's end I found myself.

We had fallen, the Colonel and I, into the habit of ending our letters with polite hopes of an early meeting. On my part these were no more than a form of words; I had never envisaged an actual meeting at all.

'If Mrs. Jasmyn is able to receive me, I shall give myself the pleasure of calling at Barmote Hall on Wednesday.'

He was to visit a friend twenty miles away, would break his journey at Spandleby and drive out for luncheon, returning in time to catch the six o'clock train to Maresbarrow Junction.

I was thrown into a regular flutter, especially as he had also written to my grandmother. Had he alluded to my letters? Mercifully her letter was as brief as my own. It aroused in her, I sensed at once, a similar dismay.

'There isn't time for you to write to him, Tessa, to say whether it will be convenient or not.' She sat twisting her rings for quite a while before saying with an air of coming to a decision, 'Well then, he must come. But how tiresome it will be in the middle of the day! We shall have to entertain him during the whole afternoon.'

But how? Her dilemma was simpler than mine. My embarrassment if the Colonel should insist on talking about my mother in grandmamma's presence would be equalled only by my disappointment if we could find no opportunity of talking about her at all. I wondered if he would like to walk round the estate if the day were fine or the library – a bleaker expedition even at this time of the year – if it were wet. I rehearsed a few topics designed to bridge awkward gaps in the conversation or – to change the metaphor a little – to dam an unwanted flow. Kate would know how to entertain an elderly colonel. 'Old people like looking at curios,' she had once said. There were surely curios enough at the Hall to divert all the colonels in Her Majesty's Indian Army for the rest of their days. In any case, I had no time to consult Kate but had to be content with sending her a verbal message next morning, explaining that Colonel Darlington was coming and that I would be engaged until evening.

The day was warm. I wore my best striped grenadine. Grandmamma had evidently overcome her reluctance to receive the Colonel. She installed herself in the hall facing the door and manoeuvred me into the far corner, 'out of the draught' as she said with unusual solicitude; and how I longed for a draught of air as a stifling hour passed, bringing no sound of a carriage.

'I've done my best with the lamb.' Emma was red and cross. 'He's missed the train, Colonel or no Colonel. That's plain enough after all the fuss.'

We picked at our luncheon, making endless calculations. If the Colonel came on the next northbound train, he would arrive at Spandleby at ten to three. An hour's drive would bring him to the Hall in time to swallow a cup of tea and return at once to catch his connection for Maresbarrow Junction.

'It will be a short visit.' There was no denying my grandmother's satisfaction. 'And on such a hot day we can only be thankful.'

Renouncing her comfortable chair in the sitting room, she returned heroically to the hall and presently dozed off.

I felt quite put out, forgetting all my nervousness in the disappointment. There would barely be time to greet the Colonel, much less to hear from the lips of the only person who had known her, all the things I longed to hear about my mother. Emma and I discussed the preparations for tea which was to be brought forward to four o'clock sharp. Then I put on a hat, pinned up my skirt and set off for the carriage road, persuading myself that the Colonel might arrive by some other means; might even be already in sight.

At the point where the bridle-path joined the road, I waited. Minutes dragged by. A haze of heat hung about the trees and veiled the outline of the church a quarter of a mile away to the right. It would be cool in the church porch or under the lych-gate. I could sit there and listen for the horses pounding up from the village. But the effort of walking there was too great.

A flat-topped boulder offered a seat near at hand but I was unwilling to risk my grenadine and stood, ready to drop, as Emma would have said, gazing languidly at the church on the right and then at the Lodge with all its windows open, on the left. Yawning, longing to sit down, incapable of going home or settling to any occupation save that of waiting, I waited.

It was after I had stood there for perhaps half an hour that the afternoon began to take on the dream-like quality which has haunted my memory of it to this day; so that the warm air, the murmuring flies, the still trees, the mood of mild suspense are palpable again as they were then when I stood among the wayside sheep, turning my head this way and that like a drowsy clockwork toy; and gradually I became aware of movements in the nearest corner of the Lodge garden where rhododendrons grew close to the wall. Longing for company but loath to quit my post, I walked a few steps towards the Lodge. At the same time Mrs. Masson came through the gate.

'I was looking for Kate. Have you seen her? She went out before lunch without telling me. So unwise in this heat.'

So far as I was concerned, Kate had eclipsed her mother so effectually that I had scarcely noticed her for weeks. She had literally paled into insignificance. Now face to face, I saw with surprise that she was not as I had thought her to be. In a flash I perceived that the ravishing clothes and the woman inside them did not quite match. Had it always been so? Had I been so dazzled by the clothes as to overlook the woman altogether? Even now I could scarcely drag my eyes away from the frilled scarf drapery of her skirt with its tiny bows of heliotrope velvet. And yet, between the careful freshness of her muslin cuffs and the fidgety movements of the hands protruding from them, there seemed a disharmony. Her uncertainty of manner suggested some mental unrest such as might result from a calculation gone astray.

'Kate cannot have gone far, Mrs. Masson.'

'She said something about making a sketch of the church.'

'It will be cooler there. I thought of waiting in the porch for Colonel Darlington. He'll be driving by in a little while. Shall I walk along and tell Kate you want her?'

'Oh no, no.' She actually caught my arm to stop me. Through her creaseless glove of palest lavender I felt the firm grip of her hand. 'I'd rather you stayed with me.' Then, seeing my surprise perhaps, with an obvious effort she assumed a more normal manner. 'How is Mrs. Jasmyn? She will understand that I haven't been able...' She stopped. 'Did you hear something?'

I listened, sufficiently impressed by her unaccountable anxiety to feel almost nervous. From one of the Betony fields came the voices of reapers but close at hand there was no human sound except – again I felt a touch of alarm – the sound of her own quick breathing.

'I'll fetch her myself.'

With a snap, as if the trivial gesture were an act of recklessness, she put up her parasol. She had certainly taken every precaution against the sun. Her hat brim was six inches wide and draped with a gauze scarf so that the face under it had a remote look like one of the carved ivories I was so familiar with.

When she retreated under the parasol and drew down the scarf, the effect was to increase the feeling of distance like the placing of an awning over a sacred figure.

'I'll go. It's too hot and dusty for you, Mrs. Masson. It will give me something to do.'

'We'll wait a few more minutes. She may not be at the church after all.'

The clock struck three, marking that perfect hour of a summer afternoon when the stillness of trees and hills gives the illusion that it will last for ever. The influence of the scene should have been soothing. Mrs. Masson and I were equally unresponsive to it. We were both agitated, our remarks, as I recall them, jerky and ill-considered.

We shuffled, hesitated, until at last she said – and Ashton would have noticed the clipped precision with which she spoke, 'Would you come into the house and sit with me for a while until Kate comes back? If you would be so good as to fetch John, he can watch for the carriage while we are indoors.'

It would have been ungracious to refuse. Glad of any occupation, I fetched John. As soon as we returned, she took my arm and leaning upon me heavily, directed me towards the house again. Once indoors she seemed to recover; swiftly unpinned her hat; rang the bell; took cups from the china cupboard and made tea with surprising speed.

'Sit down, dear. You look tired.'

Unwillingly I sat down on the velvet sofa and instantly an extraordinary apprehension seized me. To the exclusion of all other sensations, I felt the absence of Kate. Infected by Mrs. Masson's fussiness, no doubt, I felt too a kind of anxious sadness as though Kate had really gone away; an unreasonable state of mind; she was probably sketching happily and would be back presently demanding tea; but it taught me how deeply I was attached to her, how grievous a real parting would be, though we had known each other for so short a time.

Mrs. Masson's dress rustled as she moved about the room then sat down at the teatable, half hidden from me by the high arm of the sofa. I felt trapped, stifled by the oversweet scent of roses and clove pinks from the open window. As I watched the agitated wagging of the pendulum of the French clock on the mantelpiece, all the small anxieties of the day quickened into a kind of fear. The very air vibrated with uncertainty. I could have believed that something was happening out there in the heat and dust of the road; some threat more potent than physical danger. Each facet of my small world flashed upon my excited fancy: my grandmother alone – asleep – at the Hall; Kate – where was she?; the Colonel, faceless, unimaginable...

'You're quite fagged out.' Mrs. Masson

leaned towards me, holding out a steaming cup. She may have seen the anxiety in my eyes. Her own were steadfast now and intent 'Drink your tea. You'll feel better.'

I drank thirstily. She must have taken the cup from me; I don't remember; but I do remember how Mrs. Masson seemed to fade from the room; the wagging of the pendulum became less agitated, then ceased; the room itself faded; until, much later, from a subterranean darkness I looked up into distant daylight and knew that someone was looking down at me: my mother: or Kate? The dream dissolved, leaving a loneliness and longing, as if a bond had broken. With a confused impression that it had been the well-rope that broke, I awoke and saw Mrs. Masson bending over me.

'You fell asleep.'

'Where is Kate?'

'She hasn't come back yet.'

Incredulously I saw the clock fingers pointing to a quarter to five.

'Why didn't you wake me?' I jumped up. 'Whatever will Colonel Darlington think of me?'

'He hasn't come. John has been watching. I'm afraid he won't come now. You may as well stay and rest for a while.'

'Rest? I've rested more than enough.'

I paid no attention to her: felt indeed bitterly angry with her, a selfish, interfering woman. Indignation, remorse, a wide range of anxieties sent me flying home to find Steadman at the gate, Emma on the steps, my grandmother in the hall where tea was laid and the Colonel as conspicuously absent as ever.

Explanations, conjectures, complaints occupied the next few minutes. I had not entirely shaken off the curious mood of apprehension and my head ached. Composing myself, I sat down to pour out tea and had no sooner lifted the cream jug than Steadman came to ask if we would see John, Mrs. Masson's handyman.

John was obviously an enterprising lad with more initiative than the tedious task of standing at the roadside required. He had taken it upon himself to walk to the church and thence to the village, where he had learned an astonishing fact. A fall of stone on the line had delayed all trains to Spandleby by one hour. At about one thirty a gentleman had driven into Barmote, had alighted at the Duke's Head, calling for a blacksmith or a fresh horse or both, had hurried up the hill, directing the driver to follow him to the Hall; and then about two hours later had met the carriage at the foot of the hill, jumped in and was heard to order the driver to return to Spandleby as quickly as possible. He was on his way there now.

John withdrew, rewarded for his pains, and

leaving us to explain these prodigies as best we might.

'There's simply no accounting for the behaviour of people who have lived a long time in a hot climate,' grandmamma said. 'You remember I told you about the surgeon who wrote to me from Gravesend. The wretched man had had sunstroke. It had left him quite confused. Colonel Darlington may have some softening of the brain. One can always recognise them by the pallor of their skin. People who have lived in India, I mean.'

She took a second macaroon and munched it with a slow relish that irritated me. She was glad that the Colonel hadn't come. Her reference to the inn at Gravesend roused me as I sat brooding over my untouched teacup. The occasion when my life had begun for the second time was like a door beyond which I had never been able to penetrate. There was no seeing beyond it without the Colonel's help and he had gone, perhaps for good.

I sprang up and rushed out to the stable yard.

'Simon. I want the mare at once. We're going to Spandleby.' I flew upstairs to change. It was a quarter past five when we rode off.

We had to go carefully down the steep hill to Barmote bridge. There was no sign of

155

Kate as we passed the church but I could do no more than glance. The mare was fresh and nervous on the loose surface. Beyond the bridge we climbed by woodland paths and bridle-ways until we came out on the moorland road. Here in open country one could see for miles in both directions. The Colonel's carriage was not in sight.

Our route had been shorter than his but even allowing for the slower progress of his hired horses, we could hardly have over-taken him. He must be ahead. After a canter on the smooth turf by the road-side, we branched off again, forded the river and followed the old packhorse way, cutting off a loop of more than a mile. It was a quarter to six when we saw below us Spandleby's two uneven rows of red pantiles and at the foot of its steep narrow street, the railway.

'There's the train, miss.'

A white curl of smoke drifted up from the trees. Simon was riding ahead. I heard him swear as an infuriating procession of cows came straggling out of a field and ambled home for milking. It wanted only five minutes to the hour when at last we could look down on the top of the waiting train.

In the station yard stood a pair of horses and an empty carriage. The driver was light-ing his pipe. The ticket-collector protested as I pushed past him and ran along the platform, up the steps and down on the other side.

'Hurry up, miss.'

The porter held open a door. The guard had his whistle to his lips.

'Was there a gentleman?'

I ran along the train, peering up from window to window.

'There was only one gentleman.'

The porter pointed to the last compartment of the first carriage. I never doubted that it was the Colonel: a yellow-complexioned, elderly man with a stiff grey moustache. He was leaning back, eyes closed, brows puckered, as if he had just sunk wearily into his corner seat.

'Colonel Darlington.'

His eyes opened.

'I'm Tessa.' I suppose I smiled. 'Tessa Jasmyn.'

What I expected, I hardly knew: a start of pleased recognition: an answering smile: he would jump up and come out on to the platform or at the very least let down the window.

None of these things happened. Nothing, I thought afterwards, happened at all, except that the engine gave a snort, drowning my voice, and raised between us an impenetrable white wall of steam and smoke. There was just time to see his frown without even leaning forward.

'Stand back, miss, if you're not travelling.'

The guard blew his whistle; the train moved. My last glimpse of the Colonel was of a cold indifferent face looking through me or past me as if I were one of the countless beggars of the Orient; as if I were no more than a pale wisp of the vapour that shrouded me from head to foot; as if I didn't exist.

I watched the train disappear into the wooded gorge; watched the track point into the shadow under the trees. Long after the porter had gone, I must have stood there, overwhelmed by a feeling of rejection, a depression so heavy that it was an effort to drag myself away – and above all by an intuitive fear of the strangeness of it all.

Alone on the silent platform I seemed to hear my own voice, wailing again and again, 'I'm Tessa, Tessa Jasmyn' with all the eerie melancholy of a lost soul.

I rode home slowly with a deepening sense of disappointment and loss. So far as I was concerned the correspondence was ended. How could I write to the Colonel again or he to me? If he had just smiled as the train carried him away, then I could have believed that his journey had simply been dogged by misfortune: a train delayed; a horse gone lame; he had realised within a quarter of a mile of the Hall that there would be no time to go further without missing his connection.

But there had been ample time when he left the carriage for even an elderly man to walk as far as the Hall; and when he saw me in my habit calling his name, even if he had not quite heard, he must have guessed who I was. We had been expecting him. The countryside was not likely to produce many young ladies anxious to speak to him and after all it was *he* who had been anxious to speak to *me*. That was why he had come. I had not read and re-read his letters without thoroughly knowing their contents, particularly the reference to 'a certain obligation' my mother had laid upon him. There had been more than one hint of apology as though he had failed in a duty.

I was sufficiently disheartened to feel that the duty must have been an unpleasant one; so much so that at the last minute he had felt unable to face me. But I was saved from brooding morbidly on these things by another incident unexpected enough to make me forget the Colonel. It had grown cooler as we wound our way over the packhorse bridge and through the woods. We came out into the open road directly in the way of a carriage going towards Spandleby. Two carriages in one day! I recognised this as the four-wheeler from the Duke's Head and drew in to let it pass: so that the two passengers were clearly visible: an elderly maid-servant and Kate in travelling dress.

It was humiliating to feel the now familiar sense of rejection. She too had intended to pass me by; but this time it brought me to life.

'Kate! Stop! Where are you going?'

She spoke to the driver, put down the window and leaned out. I saw that she had not passed me from indifference. She looked troubled and seemed for once unable to speak; but seeing no doubt a similar concern in me, she made an effort.

'Tessa dear. I'm glad we met. I didn't want to leave without saying goodbye.'

'But why? Why should you? Where are you going?'

She hesitated, quite without her usual frankness yet clearly unwilling to fob me off with anything less than the truth.

'I've telegraphed to Margaret Sutherland at Maresbarrow. She's been expecting me, you know.'

She had made up her mind suddenly; had packed one bag and a hat-box for the time being.

'Then you're coming back?'

'I don't think so. No, I shan't be coming back.'

Impulsive though I knew her to be, so very sudden a decision took my breath away.

'Then you did mean to go without saying goodbye. What's wrong with me? Why does everyone treat me so strangely?'

'Everyone?'

'Colonel Darlington...'

'You met him then after all?'

'Not really.' I explained briefly. 'I don't understand it...'

She stretched out her hand and took mine.

'I should forget him. There's nothing wrong with you. Far from it. It was because I hated to leave you that I didn't wait to see you in case I changed my mind.'

The mare was uneasy. I called to Simon to take her.

'I'll get down,' Kate said when I had dismounted, 'and have one more heavenly breath of it.'

The air was full of the scent of honey. Above the purple shoulder of Gib Rake rose the green brow of Long How. The whole landscape lay bare-faced and open under the sky. And yet as I watched, a cloud shadow lifted and a wall seemed to advance. A single grey stone in the heather moved and became a sheep. Another sheep lay still and might have been a stone. One couldn't be sure of anything – even of Kate. The same unpredictable forces had been at work in her too. In her manner, in spite of her seriousness, I felt a suppressed exultation. She looked – I reached the conclusion almost with awe – like a person who had seen a vision and been both uplifted and exhausted by it. Clairvoyant, that was it. She had undergone some change of spirit since I had seen her last.

'Something has happened to you, Kate,' I said timidly, wondering if she had suddenly fallen in love and if so, with whom.

Her eyes were brilliant as she turned to me.

'A change of direction. That's what has happened to me. I have found out...'

She stopped, drew another deep breath and seemed to forget me. The withdrawal reminded me of the last time I had seen her, staring with concentration at the harebells. By some enviable feat of mental discipline she must have made a discovery about her past. It was evidently a private matter. She offered no confidence. It seemed indelicate to ask; but presently sheer curiosity drove me to prompt her.

'You have found out...?'

'About life,' she said quickly. 'I've found out how sad and beautiful it is.'

I was disappointed, having hoped for some more concrete revelation.

'But that couldn't be the reason for your going away.'

'It has helped me to decide. My life is idle and useless. I've always wanted to do some splendid action. I used to think it would be a spectacular thing like saving the Queen's life.'

'You've found out what it's to be?' I

162

waited, eager to know.

'Yes. I have friends who work with the Cordingley Trust in the East End of London. I shall join them there and do something worthwhile with my life.'

Could she possibly have undergone conversion as Dissenters claimed to do?

'Yes, in a way,' she said when I ventured the suggestion. 'Conversion is as good a word as any.'

'But you liked living at the Lodge.'

'It has been an episode, a wonderful one, and now I must go on. I shall spend a few days with Margaret and then go to London.'

'Oh, I shall miss you, Kate. Please don't go. Don't leave me alone.'

'Alone? What can you mean? You have your cousin. You'll marry and be a perfect wife. You'll give the people at Betony a water supply and build a school. You must throw away that moth-eaten tiger-skin and live happily ever after.'

'Your mother won't want you to go.'

'Mother?' Her face was bright with tenderness. 'My poor mother. Nothing is to be as she wanted it. Only one thing, and she will never know it.'

Her rapt, exalted look estranged me from her. The feeling of some special bond between us had been an illusion. Unused to friendship, dazzled by her charm, I had imagined it.

163

Our two shadows had come to rest side by side on the heather. It was mine that moved away, Kate's that lingered.

'You will have a wonderful future, Tessa. You have your marriage to look forward to and until then... It will be a happy ending, I promise you.'

Her tone was comforting as if she were encouraging me to face some test of endurance; but I sensed in her manner, and remembered it afterwards, something else: a note of envy? or regret?

I motioned to Simon to help me to mount and rode off without glancing back. Presently I heard the carriage draw away and felt the distance grow empty between us as we went in our opposite directions.

12

I missed Kate even more than I missed
Reuben, who from long, unconscious familiarity remained as much a part of my life as
the places I could visit every day. As often as
I saw the well, the church or the cairn, I saw
him.

But Kate had changed Barmote itself or
had shown it to me in a different light. The
loss of her bright influence brought a sudden darkness, a crushing monotony whose
end I could not long for since it would
impose a new bondage that would last for
the rest of my life.

For a time grandmamma and I were quite
alone.

'Have we offended her, do you suppose?'
she asked when after a few days Mrs. Masson had not called.

'How could we have offended her? Don't
you remember, she wasn't well?'

A week later she called and gradually
resumed her regular visits. I could not think
she enjoyed them. She listened patiently to
my grandmother's rambling complaints
(when did I first think of grandmamma's
conversation in these terms?) and paid her

the little attentions she had grown used to; but there was a difference. Several times after she had sat silent, her eyes fixed on my grandmother with a new, sombre attentiveness, I felt sure she would not come again. But she always did. It was as though she could not stay away.

At first I tried to talk about Kate.

'She has gone her own way,' Mrs. Masson said. 'There's no help for it. I've lost her.'

The words were so simple that at the time their full implication escaped me. Remembering Kate's expression when she spoke of her mother, I did not believe that they had quarrelled. I felt rebuffed and resolved not to mention Kate again.

But that sombre expression on Mrs. Masson's face caught my attention. It helped to aggravate a nervous anxiety I had begun to develop. At first no more than a fancy, it grew, as such unwholesome habits may, into a constant preoccupation with the idea of deception. I had myself deceived my grandmother in corresponding with Colonel Darlington: nor had she any idea that I had seen him – however briefly – but thought that his train had left before I reached the station. Duplicity, like virtue, brought its own dubious reward: the conviction that I too was being deceived. There could be no rational explanation of Colonel Darlington's behaviour. I lacked invention to supply irrational ones, and so a cloud of suspicion settled on the incident, vague enough to amount to no more than the feeling: 'There was something...' With a similar uneasiness I recalled that Kate too had been less open than usual when we said goodbye.

Once imagined – and long before it took shape – the notion of deception hung in the air like a louring cloud; and if it threatened me, then of course it threatened grand-mamma. Mentally I sprang to her defence. Nothing must be allowed to excite or upset her. Nothing must bring on another attack and endanger her life.

Mrs. Masson's unsmiling gaze did nothing to dispel my fantasy. It reminded me of Ash-ton – and there was nothing fantastic about him. 'There is concealment,' he had said, 'I'm sure of it.' Mrs. Masson, I resolved, must be watched; and resolving, felt my brows lower and my eyes become more deep-set; more like grandmamma's. Yet always my longing for freedom overcame the caution Mrs. Masson aroused in me. It was understood that I would slip away for half an hour whenever she called.

One afternoon a sudden shower sent me home earlier than usual. Mrs. Masson's umbrella was still in the hall but I found my grandmother alone and asleep.

'She'll be about somewhere,' Emma said when I rang.

'Do you mean that Mrs. Masson doesn't always stay in the sitting room?'

'She comes and goes.'

'Where does she go?'

'There's plenty to do without following her up and down three flights of stairs, miss.'

'Does my grandmother know?'

'The mistress is inclined to drop off, miss, as you can see.'

She was sleeping more heavily than usual and did not stir. Some instinct made me move my chair back to its old position. I was sitting at her side when Mrs. Masson came in with a bottle of cologne in her hand.

'There!' She smiled. 'Mrs. Jasmyn asked me to fetch this and now she's fallen asleep. Were you caught in the rain?'

Again – and with resentment – I felt the exaggerated warmth of her manner. It seemed to me affected, like the quickly suppressed sigh with which she put down the bottle and took up her gloves. I rose. Together we looked down at my grandmother. In repose her face was without concealment but the strong mouth, puffed outward with every heavy breath, the slightly bulbous nose, (I had only just noticed the coarsening at the tip) did not tell the whole story; for naturally her eyes were closed; and it was in her eyes, I realised, that my grandmother's essence was revealed: an insistent force curiously at variance with her piety: a wilful fire, burning at times beyond reason and not entirely quenched even by age and illness.

'Poor grandmamma!'

Why, of all possible remarks I should have made that one, it is impossible to say. Even at the time I felt how limited a view of her it expressed. Mrs. Masson felt it too.

'In what sense' – she was not smiling – 'can she be thought of as poor?'

She was standing close to the chair, I a little further away on her left when grand-mamma awoke. It so happened that as her eyelids moved, Mrs. Masson put her finger warningly to her lips and laid her other hand on mine so that we stood hand in hand.

'Tessa.'

Grandmamma's voice was thick but its tone touched me. I was always her first thought. Had she not always loved me? Only – she was still half asleep – it was on Mrs. Masson that her eyes first rested.

'I'm here, grandmamma.'

It must have been disconcerting to find, instead of the one expected shape, two shapes hovering between her and the light: two hats, two feathers, two mantles not unlike in cut: more than disconcerting; startling. She gave a great gasp and tried to struggle to her feet. Mrs. Masson moved away.

'We've upset you.' I was annoyed, fearing

another attack. This nervous excitement was the very thing we had tried to hard to protect her from; and she was for a minute quite violently distressed. I groped hastily in the table drawer for her drops. The phial was almost empty. By the time I had measured out the dose, Mrs. Masson had left.

'No, I don't need it.'

Grandmamma waved the dose aside. The effect of her little fright was unexpected. She seemed, I noticed with surprise, galvanised into life. In fact she actually got to her feet without help. I had the impression, as she stood at the window leaning on her stick and looking towards the Lodge, that her mind was more alert than it had been for months. The mental activity, whatever it was, absorbed her so completely that when I suggested backgammon, she didn't even hear but gazed across the park with a look of brooding concentration, her dark eyes as round and resolute as they had ever been. The deep sleep, the sudden awakening, had evidently in some mysterious way cleared her head.

'It's possible.' Mrs. Masson looked thoughtful when I mentioned the change to her the next day. 'She's been well nursed. Her constitution is strong. She may make a recovery. On the other hand you mustn't build your hopes, my dear. The end could be sudden.'

All my fears revived. The end, the ultimate catastrophe, would come upon me when I was unprepared, thinking of something else. I must always be prepared, never think of anything else. By being constantly prepared, I could avert her death; and indeed though this could hardly have been the reason, grandmamma continued to improve in health. Though I sent for a new bottle of digitalin, it remained in the drawer unopened. Her rambling monologues gave way to a habit of absorbed silence. For long intervals she scarcely spoke, but sat staring into the fire and twisting her rings, not noticing whether I came or went. And yet, though I longed with all my heart for her to live and feared her death with a dread that kept me awake at night, her recovery did not make me happy. As the days shortened, my apprehension grew.

I remember how one evening I watched Steadman rehanging a picture in the hall after renewing its cord. When he had gone, I looked at it as I had never done before, carefully. The mythology was unknown to me then. It depicted Krishna's combat with the god Indra. Above a cluster of gilded domes, stretched a blue heaven full of contorted shapes of gods and birds. All at once I saw that the birds had unexpectedly vicious human faces, not only lustful but – it seemed to me as I stood in the lamplight –

positively evil. Averting my eyes, I looked into the gaping mouth of one of the terra-cotta figures. Its half closed eyes mocked my shrinking nausea.

The experience marked a new phase in my attitude to my home. The bronzes on the gallery table had been for me from child-hood an array of darkly definite but mean-ingless shapes. Now I really looked at them; dancing girls with fiercely pointing breasts, their incomprehensible poses both lewd and menacing. What were they doing, or about to do? One figure seemed to be a goddess with upturned palm; and I saw with a shock, having rested my candlestick at her side for a moment, that the shape curving like a handle above her head was in fact a cobra and the plinth she was stamping on, a crouching demon. It leered so hideously that I moved away, taking with me an impression of malevolence whose motives I did not understand.

Having revealed their character, these things assumed a silent watchfulness; a quality which naturally transferred itself to the people around me. Was it imagination that made me conscious of Mrs. Masson as now intently watching my grandmother? The sombreness I had noticed in her eyes had surely deepened. I suppose one must be aware of being closely watched and in defence become watchful too. It came to me gradually that my grandmother had taken to watching Mrs. Masson with all her old shrewdness.

There were times when their identical manner of watching each other so tried my nerves that I began to think of them as more similar than different and sometimes even to confuse one with the other. Once for instance, absorbed in a game of backgammon, I looked up triumphantly at my partner, for whatever else befell me, I remained phenomenally lucky in my throws, and remembered with a little shock of surprise that I was playing with Mrs. Masson. Grand-mamma had moved her chair nearer to the table and was watching our moves with unflagging interest. It occurred to me that she had moved without help from either of us and that she had more than once lately encouraged us to play together.

Inevitably there were lighter moments. Mrs. Masson and I once passed an enthusiastic half hour in the hall turning over old books of fashion plates and laughing at their quaint absurdities; until in a moment of silence I noticed that grand-mamma was standing quite still on the landing, listening. I had not heard her come though she usually moved heavily and was clumsy with her stick. Instead of speaking to her or going up to take her arm as I would normally have done, I casually turned a page; but I remember seeing in the simpering girl, dressed in a narrow gown with her waist under her arm-pits, a kind of innocent openness I myself had lost. It was with a feeling of quite sharp distaste that I presently became aware of grandmamma retreating along the gallery with surprising speed and no more than the rustle of her skirts to betray her. I felt Mrs. Masson's eyes upon me. Had she too heard?

'I thought grandmamma was coming down,' I said loudly and closed the book, my hand shaking.

'Alone? Mrs. Jasmyn is steadier on her feet than she was a little while ago. I had thought her quite confined to her chair.'

'It is delightful that her health is so much improved.'

'Delightful.' Mrs. Masson's face was grave. 'Let me help you to put away those heavy books.'

'They're draining my life away,' I remember saying to myself with a sensation of physical weakness. Sitting between them day after day in the stuffy room, I felt them mutually opposed yet united like the two extremes of a compass with myself as the pivot, except that my distance from each of them lessened as they drew me irresistibly into their watchful partnership. I became less and less detached and more and more nervous until at last a climax came; and even then I could not be sure whether the whole affair sprang from my own over-wrought imagination or whether there really was something. Oh, I know now, of course, that there was...

It was a cool day early in October with a keen-edged wind tearing away the leaves. I had been walking aimlessly in the garden. On such an afternoon the Hall was dis-couragingly bleak. We could expect no visitors; except – there she was in a purple mantle just by the laurels – Mrs. Masson. I kept out of sight. To sit indoors watching them watch each other was more than I could bear. Why, with all the world to choose from, did she choose to come here? What was there in the inhospitable country-side or in our own gaunt house – I looked at it with the critical observation that had grown on me of late – to attract a lady of means to winter here alone?

As the door closed on her, the apprehen-sion that had troubled me increasingly, sharpened into a mood of anxious question-ing. I had no personal fear of Mrs. Masson but an atmosphere of doubt surrounded her. She roused in me an uneasiness like the memory of an old distress. She was more than an acquaintance yet not a friend. Her continual calling had established an intim-acy in which she remained still a stranger.

Now that Kate had gone (if only she

would come back!), her mother's personality had grown more potent again as if she had moved out of the shadows though only into a partial light. The thought came to me when at last, having gone quietly indoors, I stood in the gallery under the portrait of Rodney Jasmyn where I had stood with Ashton, talking about the Indian gentleman. I looked down as I had done then, over the balustrade. As a child I had always expected to see a living shape materialise from the gloom below: the dusky face of Ali Baba rise from one of the porcelain vases. How startled I had been that day to see Mrs. Masson move into the firelight and tilt her head upward in its flower-laden hat!

'Who is she?' Ashton had asked. 'Who exactly is she?'

How did it come to me, the answer? With a thrill of fear, a quick new understanding, an inspiration as brilliant as the lightning on the flagpole and as devastating in its threat to the Hall. She had lived abroad; her skin had the ivory pallor of the Anglo-Indian; her speech was clipped. In that moment of illumination I thought of everything: her devouring interest in the family jewels and maps, even the tin-lined trunk.

'There is nothing one would not do for a daughter. No risk one would not take...'

She had come to spy out the land with some bogus claim to the estate: the very

176

thing grandmamma had always feared. Though I could not tell how, she must be connected with the Indian gentleman, a descendant. In my panic I tried in vain to think of dates. We had nurtured her as a guest while she awaited her opportunity. Not for nothing had she harped upon the subject of my grandmother's death. When that took place I would be alone at the Hall, a helpless ignorant girl, until my marriage at any rate. She wanted the property, it was as clear as daylight, for Kate; and Kate had discovered her intention, would have no part in it, had gone away without a word of betrayal. How noble and how loyal she had been! But Mrs. Masson had stayed, had persisted, would not give up. The sudden blaze of comprehension dazzled me. I clutched the balustrade, trembling, and with no thought of action beyond flight to my room. I could never face Mrs. Masson again.

The baize door to the library opened: quick light footsteps: she came right up to me, a bundle of letters in her hand, and stopped, taken aback. I had caught her red-handed among the family papers. Engulfed by the crisis, without time to prepare myself, I acted on impulse.

'Give those to me.'

She made no resistance as I snatched the letters without even looking at them and thrust them into my pocket. It was a moment beyond convention. All our polite exchanges of the past year might never have been.

'I've found you out. I know why you come here. I know why you came to the Lodge in the first place.'

She was equally unprepared. If I had felt any doubt, her fear would have dispelled it. She was terrified, shaking from head to foot. She leaned against the wall and closed her eyes, her face ashen.

'You came here with plans, didn't you?'

I had never in my life spoken so rudely. With my ancestors on the wall behind me I might have been facing a hostile army.

'Tessa, you...' She had to moisten her lips to speak.

'You have some sort of explanation no doubt. I suppose you claim to be some kind of descendant of my great-grandfather. We have experienced that sort of thing before.' The attitude was my grandmother's. I spoke with the tongue she had given me. After all I was her creature; and the Jasmyn property was at risk. 'You can't deny it, can you?'

Yet even in my excitement I was conscious of a meanness. I would not have wanted Kate, still less Reuben, to hear me.

To my amazement she recovered herself. The blood came back into her face. She even laughed shakily.

'Oh, how, you frightened me!' She made

no attempt to answer the charge, to explain or excuse. 'Here is the key to the writing-desk.' The unexpectedness of it deflated me. She walked past me and down the stairs. I followed, not wanting to let her out of my sight and caught her up in the hall. 'I'd better not say goodbye to Mrs. Jasmyn – in the circumstances,' she said. 'Are you going to tell her?'

'No,' I said with contempt. 'She mustn't on any account be upset. She thinks of you as a friend.'

I had no sooner said it than I knew it to be untrue and recognised, in contrast, the honesty of Mrs. Masson's bleak reply.

'Friend?' She might have been hearing the word for the first time.

'If she knew who you really are' – I caught myself positively striking an attitude. How extraordinary it was! I had the strangest feeling that it was I who was acting a part, not she – 'the shock would kill her.'

'Would that matter?' All restraint having been set aside, she spoke as freely as I had done; but much more calmly, cool as a statue in her heliotrope gown; and there was something judicial in her manner that both frightened and impressed me. 'She has lived long enough. You're keeping her alive by your devotion. She should have died long since. Why don't you let her go?'

I recognised not, after all, coolness but

179

cold dislike, deep-seated, long-accepted. It appalled me.

'You hate her?'

She ignored the question. A sudden weariness altered her face. For the first time I noticed its network of fine lines, her drawn, ravaged look.

'As for the estate, naturally you care for it. But hasn't it occurred to you that not everyone would want it? There's something about Barmote,' she glanced round the crowded hall as if it depressed her, 'that one would be glad to leave. At any rate it will soon be yours. When you are free, this should be a happier place. You'll become the girl that nature intended you to be, if it isn't too late. I must confess you are becoming more like Mrs. Jasmyn than I had realised.'

Her tone was sad. The sadness was unexpected. My anger had – disconcertingly – gone. I wavered, beginning to doubt.

'You've put off your marriage all this time for her sake. It was unpardonable to demand such a sacrifice.'

I felt all the irony of her mistake but could not bring myself to enlighten her. The touch of generosity made me feel again the smallness in my own behaviour. But her fear had been genuine. Ashton had been right. She had something to conceal.

'Then why...?' I looked doubtfully at her weary face, reminding myself that I mistrusted her. Afterwards I thought there had been a wistfulness in the way she answered.

'Why did I come here? Not, I assure you, with any wish to take from you what is yours.' She took her mantle from the settle and put it on. Normal values began to impose themselves. I thought with dismay of what I had said. 'Was there any harm in coming here to be at peace for a while – I thought – in this sheltered corner of the globe? When I first came and looked down on the fields at Betony, it was like a dream fulfilled. You are too young to know how a dream can keep one alive.'

'Mrs. Masson, I...'

She had let herself out, leaving the door open. From the top of the steps I watched her walking slowly away, her gown trailing over the sodden leaves. She had lost Kate. She had the look of a woman who had lost everything.

Naturally I was pleased to be rid of her. She was clever and dangerous but I had seen her for what she was and sent her packing. Through my resourcefulness Barmote was safe from the likes of her. I had more character than some people might suppose. But naturally too it had been upsetting: so upsetting that unaccountably my heart ached. The memory of my ranting language, the sheer vulgarity of it, sickened me.

And what nonsense it all was! Alone there

in the doorway with the keen wind ruffling my cuffs and hair and restoring me to sanity, I saw my suspicions of Mrs. Masson in all their cruel absurdity and writhed at the sight. There had been nothing in her behaviour or conversation that was not affable and even kind, save for her misjudgment of grandmamma and for that I must sadly acknowledge myself responsible, having given the impression that she had delayed my marriage against my will. No single shred of fact convicted Mrs. Masson of wanting the Jasmyn possessions. As for her presence here, some slight knowledge of Barmote village in her youth, perhaps, had blossomed into an impulse to come back when she heard from the Warmans that the Lodge was to let: a charming little place, just right for a widowed lady of means in search of rest and country air. And I had stood there, haranguing her in an attitude of righteous ownership, a small-scale reproduction of my grandmother, with the characteristics but not the weight of the original, like one of the stuffed parakeets in the glass case at my side.

There was no need to search my conscience to discover that I was becoming warped by mistrust of my own engendering. Had Reuben foreseen what would become of me? A pang of longing for his straightforward goodness made me look out over the grey meadow towards the cairn, before closing the door and turning back to face the dim clutter of objects in the hall. But at least I had dispelled the cloud of suspicion that had hung about the house. Mrs. Masson would not come back this time and who could blame her? Grandmamma must never know of the dreadful scene enacted between us. It would distress her...

Sounds from the sitting room startled me: a groping and shuffling; a rattle; the tinkle of glass; a familiar thud. Grandmamma had dropped her stick again. I found her sitting askew, her shawls in disarray as if she had sunk quickly back into her chair.

'I dropped my stick. Is Mrs. Masson there?' She was a little breathless but her voice had never been clearer. She positively rapped out the words. 'She went to fetch the Rev. Tobias Stacey's letters from the library. You know, we corresponded for a while. Their tone is so lofty and elevating. But I don't feel inclined to hear them now.' I retrieved the stick. 'We were going to drink a glass of claret.' The two glasses stood on the table. 'She is always so kind to me.'

In the circumstances the remark seemed inappropriate, the more so when, opening the table drawer to drop in the letters and the key, I saw the phial of digitalin lying on its side. I had opened it myself some weeks ago. There had been no occasion to use it.

But it was now empty.

In the sunless room the twin spheres of wine glowed red with a heartening effect of life. But were they after all identical? It was possible to imagine a fainter crimson in the right-hand glass and equally to fancy a faintly different odour as I bent over the glass on the left. So that I could not be sure of anything except that the digitalin was no longer in the phial.

'She should have died long ago...'

No one would have the effrontery to make such a remark having already... Besides, there was no reason, no reason at all.

'What are you doing, Tessa?'

I heard again the old note of authority and for a second felt every nerve tingle in response; but I could not take my eyes from the two glasses, so similar, yet for all I knew, so fatally different. Was it conceivable that the Rev. Tobias Stacey and I had between us saved grandmamma's life? I imagined Mrs. Masson handing the glass (which one?) and watching with gloomy satisfaction while grandmamma drank. The idea was so preposterous as to be gone in a second – and replaced by the even more preposterous question: assuming that there had been a hair's breadth escape, had the escape been grandmamma's?

Together in their still-life the glasses roused an equal suspicion. Had I not felt the same similarity in the two very different persons of Mrs. Masson and my grandmother? At any rate I felt it now. A strange new thoughtfulness made me take up the left-hand glass and say, 'Will you have your claret now, grandmamma?'

In the tiny pause before she answered, the foundations of my world trembled.

'No. It has stood too long. Besides, I'm not fond of it. It was Mrs. Masson's idea.'

'Perhaps I could drink it.'

My hand was steady as I raised the glass. It was as though a cool, impersonal newcomer had taken my place

'Certainly not. I don't wish it.'

Just for a moment I saw her face darkened again by a fierce petulance as with a sudden movement she heaved herself up, reached for the glass – and then the other – and threw their contents on the fire. A flame died.

'It's so strange, grandmamma, about your drops. I'm sure I opened a new bottle and you haven't had a single dose from it.'

'I have it here in my reticule.' She moved her hand. I could not see the phial but I saw the dry stain of claret on the lace edging of her sleeve. 'That must be the old one. You haven't outgrown your carelessness, Tessa dear.'

Of course. I remembered. There must have been two phials in the drawer. I had forgotten to throw away the empty one as I had intended. The relief, as I put it in the waste-paper basket, should have lightened my spirits but I felt only shame. The habit of mistrust had so taken possession of me that I would be suspecting grandmamma herself if I did not take myself in hand.

'How odd of Mrs. Masson to leave without saying goodbye!'

I sat down on the other side of the hearth in Mrs. Masson's chair. The hands of the clock crept round, marking the first minutes of a new stage in our relationship. We were alone again together. Steadman brought in the lamps. Presently I found – not having taken myself in hand with sufficient firmness – that Mrs. Masson had bequeathed to me not only her chair but her occupation, for it must have been then that I took to watching my grandmother and seeing her in quite a different light.

13

Two days later a servant brought over the keys of the Lodge. Mrs. Masson had already left. The following week we heard from Pawley that she would not be seeking a renewal of the lease at the end of the year.

My grandmother showed neither surprise nor regret. Her manner expressed more than anything else, patient suffering.

'Are you not sorry, grandmamma, that Mrs. Masson has gone?' I asked carefully.

'I'm sorry to have the Lodge empty again.'

'Her visits made a change for you. I thought you quite liked her.'

'She knew how to make herself agreeable. She will find new acquaintances wherever she goes. Mrs. Masson is a person who scrapes up connections where no connection exists. I shall tell Pawley not to look for another tenant, in spite of the loss of rent. The trouble of meeting new people is altogether too much at my age.'

For a few days she kept the alertness she had regained but gradually she lost the air of listening and watching. She sat turning her rings, her eyes uplifted to the window as though resuming communication with a higher power. It was harder than ever to escape on my own but when I did (and it was almost always to Betony), the feeling of release was like taking wing.

One afternoon, looking down from the narrow outlet between the stone walls, I saw Mrs. Bateman toiling up the hillside with her pitcher and bucket and went quickly across to join her at the spring. She was bending over the spout and did not even turn her head until with the pitcher half full she straightened up and put her hand to the small of her back with a groan.

'You're tired. Let me.'

I emptied the pitcher and filled it again. It seemed the most natural thing to carry the bucket down to the cottage. She made no protest. Her whole manner was apathetic. Inexpert as I was, I had slopped a deal of water over my person by the time we reached the door.

'You see. I'm always wet when I come to you, Mrs. Bateman. Do you remember...?'

She made no answer. The fire was low. She neither stirred it nor asked me to sit down. The room had lost its order and refinement. The bookshelf was empty.

'You miss him,' I said. 'Reuben.'

She made some sort of hopeless gesture and sat down at the hearth.

'Is there anything...? Are you quite well, Mrs. Bateman?'

'There's no need for such as you to bother about such as me.' The words came after a long pause and with such flat finality that I went to the door and stood unhappily looking down on the darkening valley.

'You can shut the door when you go. It does shut now. Reuben fixed it before he went.'

Accepting my dismissal, I went home. But I persevered and made up a parcel of plain sewing, determined to take it to Mrs. Bateman and pay for it myself. It took a little courage to knock at her door but this time she did ask me to sit down.

'You've given up the glove-making.'

The vice had been pushed aside on the windowsill.

'It was Reuben that used to fetch the skins for me from Maresbarrow.'

Her lack of enthusiasm for the sewing disappointed me. I was young and arrogant enough to have expected gratitude, but when I went again she had stitched the sheets and pillowcases and she thanked me for the money. If she had little appetite for the soup, butter and eggs I took her, at least she saw them as overtures of friendship.

One day, finding the bucket empty, I took it to the spring. Ferns had grown tall and turned brown again since the March day when I had been there with Reuben but the smooth folds of water were unchanged.

'When I'm married,' I thought, 'I shall come here sometimes. It will always be the same and–' I vowed in my ignorance – 'I won't change either.'

'You shouldn't have done that, Miss Jasmyn. Reuben made Tim Wagstaff promise to fetch water for me. He said I was to give him a penny now and then.'

But Tim was lax in his duty. I fell into the habit of occasionally doing it for him. It was a kind of expiation for the shortcomings of the Jasmyns as landlords.

More than once I had raised the question of a water supply with my grandmother.

'Those people are always pestering us for something or other. The more they have, the more they will want. Ashton agrees with me. Besides, as Ashton says, it isn't worth our while to make improvements at Betony if Packby is to start quarrying there. The people will have to move.'

'But not yet. They wouldn't want to go. And it was only piped water I was speaking of now that the well is dry.'

'I hope when I'm gone you won't pamper the tenants, Tessa. Remember the Lodge is empty again after all the outlay on drainage.'

When she grew excited I let the matter drop, basely sacrificing the interests of the Betony folk to my own desperate need to care for her health.

'I'll speak to Burnside,' she said once; but

190

since her illness the weekly interview with the bailiff had been discontinued. His next visit would not be until the end of the month. I made up my mind to speak to him myself; a momentous decision as it happened.

Meanwhile, as Mrs. Bateman and I grew easier together, she sometimes let me read Reuben's letters though grudgingly as if against her better judgment Together we sighed over the drudgery of his work at the hospital where he had found an opening as assistant to a surgeon. The long nights of study in the confinement of a cheap room would be harmful, we were sure, to his health. I went to visit her often, confident if not of a welcome, at least of not being repulsed until one afternoon when I had no sooner crossed the threshold than I felt a change in her manner. Afterwards, I understood it was from nervousness that she burst out at once:

'He's saving to come home next June.'

The news caught me off my guard. How could I hide the instant thrill of returning to life after being at least half dead? She must have heard the quiver of excitement in my voice.

'In June? That's wonderful news for you, isn't it, Mrs. Bateman?'

'I don't know.'

At the unexpected harshness of her tone I

looked up and saw at once that she knew our secret. Her eyes were cold. They taught me in a second, leaving no shred of doubt, the utter folly and hopelessness of the one dream that had brightened my life.

'It would be better for him to stay away, if you ask me.'

I took the preserves from my basket and laid them nervously on the table like votive offerings.

'Thank you, I'm sure,' she said, 'but I don't want them and I may as well say it – I don't want you.' I stared down at the table, trying with all my might not to show how much she had hurt me.

'You've turned his head, that's the long and short of it, and I want a stop put to it.'

'Has he said...?'

'He doesn't need to say. I knew before he went away and I can read it in every line he writes. He's wanted the chance to be a doctor since he was a little boy and now that he's got it he can't make the most of it because he's pining for what he can't have.'

The deal table swelled and wavered. It was no use. She could see that I was crying.

'He's miserable too,' she said bluntly. 'I don't want him eating his heart out for something that can never be.' She turned, ran her hand along the empty bookshelf and produced a duster from her pocket. 'You've brought bad luck to me since the day you came here in the thunder and lightning like a spirit in your white dress with your white face. I shouldn't have let you come back and I shouldn't have let you see his letters. But you've a way of worming your way into people's feelings.'

'What can I do?'

'You mustn't see him when he comes. If you do, he'll just go on hoping and looking forward to the next time until he's wished his life away.' She rubbed the duster over and over the shelf, into the corners and back over the surface, again and again. 'It's all right for you. You've always had an easy way of life with no troubles and always will. And you're engaged to be married, remember. It isn't decent.'

After a little hesitation, with the distracted feeling that everything I did was wrong and that even in this small act there was scope for some disastrous error, I put the food back in the basket, folded the napkin neatly into place and went to the door, stumbling over the uneven floor.

'I won't see Reuben again if I can help it; and I won't come here again, Mrs. Bateman.'

'I'm sorry, love.' To my surprise her own eyes were full of tears. She followed me to the door. 'I'm sorry,' she said as I went away across the grass.

The strangest feeling possessed me as I

walked home of moving over the ground without leaving any impression on it or making any sound, as though the substance had gone from my body; and in fact I came into grandmamma's room so quietly that she did not hear me; She was standing by her table where Emma had left a plate of the macaroons soaked in brandy that we sometimes gave her to tempt her appetite. There was only one left. She put out her hand to the plate, drew it back, hesitated, then seized the cake and crammed it into her mouth with an avidity that startled me. It was as though she could not be without it, so that I half expected to hear her say, 'I want it, want it,' as she had done once before, with her dark look beating me into submission. It revived the sickening impression of an obscene thing scuttling out of the darkness and back again. I stood quite still, waiting for it to abate. Seeing me she turned to the window, swallowing rapidly and I saw that though her head came level with the worn patch on the damask curtains as it had always done, she was not tall and slender as I had thought but rather squat and square.

It was remarkable how often and how clearly Mrs. Masson's remarks came to my mind. She had found in me a growing resemblance to my grandmother. Physically we were not alike. I glanced furtively in the chimney-glass only to be reminded of Ashton's unflattering comparison, which made it all the stranger when sometimes I felt my brows come down and my mouth droop; or surprised myself in an attitude of suffering with eyes uplifted, and knew I was looking like grandmamma as surely as I knew that the love and reverence which all the repressive harshness of my childhood had not dimmed, were now burning very low indeed.

But even in this time of painful disillusion it was possible to find a chink of light which unexpectedly brightened the coming winter. It came none too soon and by way of a revelation in other respects disheartening enough. I remember opening the front door for a quick look at the trees and grass before settling down to an interminable morning in the sitting room, one of the last golden days of autumn. It was Burnside's day for the accounts. As the first hour crawled by, I listened for the sound of his horse in the stable yard. A coal blazed, flaked and fell to ash. My back ached. I opened the book of sermons at random. It was almost time to read grandmamma to sleep. I had become expert at combining my own train of thought with that of the Rev. Tobias Stacey.

'Not that, Tessa. Not this morning. I have a fancy to hear his letters again. So very elevating. Now where are they?'

She groped, confused, among the books on the round table at her side.

'Don't you remember,' I said unwillingly, the subject being painful still, 'Mrs. Masson fetched them from the library. You gave her the key.'

I took out the letters from the drawer of the mahogany table and undid the frayed ribbon, wondering why she had bothered to keep them under lock and key. Who else would want to read them, dreary as they must certainly be?

The Rev. Tobias Stacey's handwriting was unexpectedly feminine, a youthful, formless hand. There were no more than four letters. The first was written from Simla and dated July, 1853.

It was at the Residency ball that Charles proposed ... so very brilliant an affair. The uniforms made it almost a royal occasion. I was quite overwhelmed...

I cannot describe how moving it was to step unawares into the lost world from which I had seemed for ever exiled; or how grateful I was to Mrs. Masson for having presumably picked up the wrong bundle of letters. The simple sentences brought a glimpse of moonlight and chandeliers, the scent of flowers, the last graceful days of a society already doomed.

I shall do my best to make him happy...

The innocent hope had outlived all that had been lost in sickness and war.

'Did you say you had the key to the writing-desk, Tessa?'

Her voice was sharp. I turned and saw with detachment the face between the cap-strings: the blotched skin; the self-willed thrust of the lips; the wide insensitive nostrils. She must have forgotten my mother's letters. She could not consciously have lied when she spoke of having destroyed them, she who above all else valued purity of conscience. Perhaps she had believed that the letters no longer existed because she wanted to believe it. Was that more – or less – of a moral lapse than to lie deliberately? A coldness settled upon my heart as I perceived that it was certainly more dangerous, threatening the very substance of reality. She was as convinced of my mother's duplicity as she was of her own selflessness. Neither was real. Feeling as if some venerable structure had crumbled to ruin, I saw her diminished, a victim of her own fantasies in a house of worn-out relics.

'Why don't you fetch Mr. Stacey's letters?'

'I thought they were here in the drawer,' I said, 'but they must still be in the library. The key is here. If you tell me where they are, I'll fetch them.'

'No.' Her eyes narrowed in sudden

thoughtfulness. 'It would take too long. You can read from the sermons instead.'

Stacey's folio volume was big enough to conceal the letters. I could glance at them as I paused impressively at the end of each of his monumental paragraphs. In a few minutes, grandmamma closed her eyes.

Captain Darlington has come and I have received the Jasmyn ruby at last. Such a very pretty thing. It goes charmingly with my green florentine but I intend to wear it always, awake or asleep, and if my baby is a girl she shall have it...

That had been written in December, 1855 when the Regiment had been stationed at Cawnpore, forty-eight miles from Lucknow. It seemed likely then that I had been born in the spring or early summer of the following year.

I have been lucky enough to find an English nurse. Her husband is a pay-sergeant in the Regiment. She and I are quite friends.

My nurse! Surely Colonel Darlington had mentioned her. I knew his letters almost by heart. He had said something about not having been able to give help and advice to my nurse: 'A faithful creature, Sarah – or Susan – I forget her name.' But she had managed well enough without him. She had weathered the four-day journey to Calcutta and the four-month-long voyage home without his help. Sarah? Or Susan? I sat up, suddenly alert, as a tiny petal of flame unfolded and fluttered in one of the black coals like a revival of life. She sprang into existence at first in a shape similar to that of the sad woman trudging to St. Agnes' with the sick baby in her arms. So many babies had died; but Sarah – or Susan – had brought me safely home. How close we must have been not only in the swaying dhoolie but from my very birth! To her I owed my life; and having delivered me into the hands of my grandmother, she had vanished, taking with her all that could be known of my early life. With a burst of childish chagrin I realised that she was the only person on earth who knew my birthday – or had been. For all I knew Sarah – or Susan (I inclined a little towards Susan), worn out by her melancholy adventures in India, might by this time be dead. She had been widowed, I remembered. Her husband must have died in the defence of Lucknow like my father.

Burning to know more, I found to my intense disappointment that the letter in my hand was the last. But I had not quite read to the end. There remained one or two sentences of extraordinary interest.

Is it not strange? She comes from Charles's part of the country. She was a Cade.

The sudden sense that she had come closer could scarcely have been more astonishing if I had found myself once again in her lap. Yet how little – I made the discovery with surprise – she had figured in that marvellous meeting at the inn at Gravesend. Without compunction I woke grand-mamma.

'Your nurse?' She seemed all at sea. Then her wits settled. 'You didn't have a nurse, darling. I did everything for you myself. I trusted no one to look after you. Did I ever tell you...'

'But my nurse in India. You saw her at Gravesend. What was she like?'

'Like? Hand me my shawl, dear. How can one say what such a person is like?' She took a little time to adjust the shawl to her satisfaction.

'You've never mentioned her.'

Of its own accord the statement turned into an accusation. I was roused almost to the point of confronting her with the letters but the habit of concealment had grown upon me as strongly as the determination never on any account to upset her.

'The woman made no sort of impression on me at all. I thought only of you, dear, as I've often told you. I wonder that you

200

should bring up the subject after all these years.'

Fifteen years, I calculated, and persisted.

'She must have been a good sort of person to have cared for me as she did.'

She sat up, looking dangerously flushed and seemed to force herself into composure before saying deliberately, 'A common soldier's wife – in India. You can have no idea of the degradation of their way of life. The woman was hardly fit to have charge of you. Such a person would be beyond the reach of any refining influence. I hope you are not going to sentimentalise over a servant, Tessa.' She thought for a moment. 'I gave her money, of course. So far as I recall, she was a stupid woman – or stupefied perhaps. She had been through a great deal...'

'Tell me about it. Was it morning or afternoon? Can't you remember anything she said?'

My questions irritated her. As I poured them out, she put her hand to her head as if distracted.

'You didn't hear anything from her about my mother?' I asked boldly.

'I didn't discuss the family with her. How could I? It was the surgeon who took me upstairs. But it's all so long ago. The wretched man had had sunstroke. Did I tell you? There had been such dreadful suffering. Could you move the screen a little, dear? And perhaps I should have my warm milk. My head swims.'

I rang for the milk and moved the screen by the exact fraction of an inch required, with the laborious care I gave to all her physical needs.

She had held me in her arms (Susan?) and comforted me so well that no disturbing memories lingered from the days in India: only a painless blank. The darkness and distress had come later, here at Barmote. I had not yet reached the stage of seeing my grandmother's arrival at Gravesend as a harmful intrusion like the swoop of a predator on innocent fields; but my view of the incident had altered. 'We are quite friends', my mother had written of this coarse, stupid woman beyond the reach of any refining influence; and she had actually been a Cade, connected however remotely with my beloved Betony. My grandmother had obviously forgotten this interesting fact. She knew nothing of the Cades, who had not been tenants and must all have left Betony soon after she came to Barmote. To my certain knowledge she had never so much as set foot in Betony; and that may partly have explained my affection for the place.

'Mr. Burnside's here,' Emma brought in the milk, 'if you're wanting him, ma'am.'

'No, no. He can leave the accounts.'

'I'll tell him, grandmamma.'

I found him in the stable yard, eager to be off.

'The well gone dry? You mean over at Betony?'

He listened to my hesitant questions about a water supply to the cottages.

'It's good to know you take an interest, Miss Jasmyn.' He gave me a sharp look as if recognising in me something more positive than the dreamy wraith he had been used to ignore. 'Things are slow here, especially since Mrs. Jasmyn's illness, but with your help we might make a few changes.'

'Only she mustn't be upset,' I put in quickly, 'about anything.'

'It's funny though about Cade's well. I wouldn't have expected it.'

'Cade's well?' The coincidence was positively startling. 'I didn't know it had a name.'

'It was the Cades that sunk it. They used to farm over at Betony Hay. It'll be above thirty years since they left. The old place is derelict now but the Cades go back a long way.'

'Where are they now?'

'It's difficult to say,' he spoke with un-expected humour, 'whether above or below. But what's left of them'll be in Barmote churchyard. So far as I know there's only Miss Abigail Cade still alive. She's living at Gib Cottage off the Spandleby road.'

So Chance set the globe spinning from east to west and pointed a finger, not at the gilded spires and minarets of Lucknow nor even at the inn at Gravesend, but at a cottage no more than half an hour's drive from home

14

She could not have heard me coming. Gib Cottage stood a little way down the slope with its back to the road. I had left the pony carriage at the lane end and walking along the soft green causeway, came unexpectedly level with Miss Cade's chimneys. Responding instinctively to the quiet of the place, I went softly down the garden steps and round to the front. The cat on the sunny door step watched, unmoved.

So that, as I said, she could not have heard me coming; in fact she was – I soon discovered – rather deaf. All the same she knew I was there.

'Come in,' she called. 'I was expecting you.'

'Oh, but I'm sorry.' I stepped from the flagged porch into the parlour. 'It must be somebody else you were expecting. I'm Tessa Jasmyn from Barmote Hall.'

She was sitting at a round table in the window: a plump woman in brown silk and a close-crimped cap, with the great sweep of Long How on her right; and on her left, covering every inch of the floor, an assortment of furniture so dense that I stood perforce inside the doorway, seeing no clear path by which to advance.

'I do hope you'll forgive my calling unannounced.' As she said nothing, I raised my voice. 'I wonder, are you Miss Cade?'

'Yes,' she said, not in reply but to reinforce her first statement. 'I was expecting you.'

'But how could that be?'

'It's all here,' a gesture of her mittened hand drew my attention to them, 'in the cards.'

I picked my way between two or three small tables and stood at her side. She must have been seventy at least but I did not think of her as old. The enthusiasm of her manner infected me at once with a sense of adventure.

'There and there.' She pointed to the Queen of Hearts. 'A fair lady: a stranger: very close to me; and I'll tell you why you've come.'

I looked at her in amazement; at the blue light dancing in her eyes.

'Yes, I'll chance it. I'll tell you. You've come for news. Am I right?'

'Yes. That's exactly why I came.'

'I knew it.' She beat her hand gleefully on the table. 'There's the Knave, you see.' If she could have got up I believe she would have made some more active demonstration but so far as I know she never moved without help. 'They're telling me more and more – the cards. I've tried them for years. At first I wasn't sure but now at last I know it. There's power in them. Sit down.'

I drew out the chair on her left, all agog to hear more; then recalled that soothsaying of any kind was ungodly. Besides, it was facts I wanted. I made an effort to guide the conversation into more conventional grooves and at the top of my voice. Her preoccupation with the cards, combined with her deafness, made communication with Miss Cade difficult.

'You must find it very quiet here.'

'What's that? Quiet? Not when there's so much happening.' She tapped the cards. 'All sorts of things are happening here all the time.' I felt that she was longing to try them again but instead she took up a brass handbell and rang it vigorously. 'You'll take something after your journey?'

The door to the kitchen remained unopened: but presently small sounds outside announced the approach of a very old maidservant with a basket of eggs. Without apparently noticing me, she crossed the room to the domestic quarters behind, where I heard her, to my joy for I was hungry, begin preparations for tea. Since these took almost an hour, I had ample time to explain why I had come.

My hostess was indeed Miss Abigail Cade, sister of Jonas Cade who had last farmed at Betony Hay. She had lived there with her brother and his wife. The parlour contained, I gathered, most of the household effects from their old home.

'Sarah? No. There was never a Sarah Cade.'

'Then – Susan?'

'No. There was Mary, Jonas's wife. She died young. Jonas was never the same after he lost her.'

'They had no children?' It was dispiriting when she shook her head again. 'When I was a baby in India, I had a nurse who was a Cade. I thought she might have been a relation of yours. But it must have been years since she left the district. Thirty years at least.'

I drew back as Molly thrust a lace-edged table-cloth past me and manoeuvred it into position. My journey had been fruitless but at least there was consolation to be found in the gradual appearance of scones, jam, tea-cake, sly cake and gingerbread. I removed my gaze politely to the everlastings in a pink vase with a blue Italian lake on its side; then to a pair of scornful swans on the fire-screen of painted glass.

'The Cades never strayed far from Betony,' Miss Cade observed as she poured out. 'The place was in their bones. I don't remember one that went to live elsewhere, unless–' She put down the pot. 'Well, if I hadn't forgotten her! But she wasn't altogether a Cade.'

'Who was that, Miss Cade?'

Cup suspended, I waited spellbound while she looked reflectively at the tea-strainer. A distinct cold shiver ran down my spine. The door had swung open in a breeze that ruffled the edge of the table-cloth.

'Susannah.'

She produced the name with pleased deliberation as if she had fished it up from impenetrable depths. I felt a faint premonitory thrill as though witnessing the creation of a new shape from formless dust; or was it the re-creation of an old one: the resurrection even, of a dead one?

'Did she die?'

It wasn't seemly to ask such a question at the top of my voice but I seemed to have found a pitch Miss Cade could hear.

'Very likely. I haven't heard tell of her from the day she left and that was many a year ago. Poor little Susannah! Did you say you knew her?'

'She may have been my nurse. I feel sure of it. Please tell me about her.'

'No Cade ever went so far afield,' she began doubtfully. But then Susannah was not entirely a Cade; only an orphaned relative of doubtful parentage whom Jonas and Mary had taken to live with them. Mary had died, leaving her to a Cinderella-like existence with Jonas and his sister.

'She wasn't your niece then?'

'No. Though I was Aunt Abbie to her. It was a hard life for all of us, especially a child. She was too much put upon. But Jonas wasn't a man you could appeal to; and I was put upon myself. She was a thin little thing, no better than a slavey. I've seen her toiling from that well with the wooden yoke bearing her down to the earth and her skirt hustled through her pocket-holes, so weary it's a wonder she didn't throw herself in and put an end to it all. Her life was a vale of tears. Toil from morning to night, that was Susannah's lot. Her one bit of happiness was watching the carriages full of gentle folk turning in at the gates of the Hall. You could say of Susannah that she was old before her time.'

'How dreadful!'

Whether it was due to Miss Cade's unexpected eloquence or whether there really was power in the cards, I felt my imagination excited to an unusual degree. A disturbing picture came to me of an aged child lifting the latch of the farmhouse door and stepping out into darkness and obscurity; for that was what, at the age of sixteen, she had done.

'Then she ran away?'

'She was driven to it, I thought afterwards. Jonas had used her cruelly but he wasn't a cruel man; when she was gone, it haunted him. "She'll come to harm, Abbie," he said.

"She'll be in that well," I said. He had himself lowered, just to make sure.'

She paused, remembering no doubt the hideous suspense, the relief.

'And she never wrote?'

'We never heard a word from her or of her from that day to this. And you say she was your nurse?'

She stared at me in disbelief; then wiped her fingers on her napkin and longingly took up the cards, clearly in search of more information. It was long past the time I had told Simon to bring the carriage to the lane end.

'Thank you, Miss Cade. I have so enjoyed my visit.'

'You're welcome, I'm sure. You'll let me know if you hear anything of Susannah?'

Having called her up, she seemed loath to let her go. She was old enough to slip easily into the past and see its characters more clearly than she saw me. Indeed, having recognised me at once as the Queen of Hearts, she had remained vague as to my actual identity.

'What did you say your name was?'

I had risen to take my leave.

'Jasmyn. Tessa Jasmyn.'

The flickering blue light in her eyes grew still. For the first time she looked at me with the steadiness of comprehension and disappointment.

'They didn't tell me that. They should have done.'

'Who?'

'The cards. I thought they would have told me that.' She took the pack in both hands, shaking her head reproachfully. 'They're not coming right, not yet.'

'She's mad,' I thought, liking her none the less.

'I'm hard of hearing, you know. I didn't catch your name the first time. I thought you might be the lady from the Lodge. Very finely dressed they say she is.'

'I'm sorry. She's left.'

'But the nurse you spoke about in India. That couldn't have been Susannah. She would never have worked for a Jasmyn. She was enough of a Cade for that.'

'But why not?'

'The Jasmyns should never have had that bit of pasture between the Hay and the river. Tod's Corner. That was Cade land.' Her plump face had lengthened. All its endearing whimsicality had gone. Her voice was implacable, hardened – by a long-dormant hatred I had unluckily revived.

She spread out the cards in a fan.

'Here. Take one.' I picked one out and showed it to her. 'That's more like it.' It was the Ace of Spades.

Before I had closed the door, she rang the bell.

'Clear the table, Molly, quickly.' She was already cutting the pack.

It was a little while before I shook off the feeling that all manner of strange things were happening on the table in the window overlooking Long How.

Susannah. The name imposed identity like a baptism. I thought of her – and I was to think of her often – as poised for ever on the brink of departure: scarcely visible, just short of vanishing-point. Time and again I was to feel her almost slip away; from the farmhouse into the night; from the inn at Gravesend into the rustic shade of Kent – or Hertfordshire – or Shropshire? from life even, into her grave.

But having once discovered her, I never quite lost her. Rather I caught and held her and gradually gave her shape. The ill-defined but ever-growing impression of falseness elsewhere in my life made me long to find in her, above all, sincerity. She had been lonely, unloved; but she had loved my mother and cared for me. She was faithful and good. She was coarse and stupid – or stupefied: a humble woman who had done her best and gone away unthanked.

From sheer necessity, out of loneliness, I made room for her in my mind, room to live and grow, though naturally with no notion of what she would grow into.

All this was before I had even set foot in Betony Hay.

15

It was an apple that tempted me: a late russet, if not the last that survived unpicked on a stripped branch overhanging the wall at Betony Hay. It lured me into the garden. The gate had lost its top bar and the windows a pane or two but the house had survived its years of neglect remarkably well. With the mild sunlight on its fading red creeper, it looked not only habitable but inviting.

The sweet tang of the apple amply repaid the damage to my skirt as I picked my way through nettles and damp grass to the front door. Above the lintel were carved the initials J.C. and the date: 1685. A slab of stone formed a single deep step.

From the flagged hall I went into a room facing south over a wedge-shaped acre of rough grass which I took to be Tod's Corner. Some of the cottage people had taken advantage of the empty rooms to store sacks of meal and potatoes but without too much disorder. The wainscoting was richly brown in the sunshine from the lattice and warm to the touch.

I spent a few minutes mentally furnishing the room with some of the contents of Miss

Cade's parlour: the pianoforte on the inner wall, the table by the window, the scornful swans in the hearth, and having constructed the setting, found the family creeping in: Mary who had died young, Abbie, aunt yet not an aunt, Jonas, haunted by his cruelty, for he was not a cruel man.

As for Susannah, her humble spirit was not to be found in the parlour. Still munching, I explored the catacomb of damp dairies at the back. Here, from a scullery window no bigger than a pastry board, she could just have seen the well as she hooked her buckets on to the wooden yoke and hustled her skirt through her pocket-holes. She could also have seen, when she had time and spirit to look up through the bracken, the track leading to the road where the carriages of gentle folk turned in at the Lodge gates. The rowans, barely rooted when Susannah was a girl, had since grown into strong slim trees.

And in the house where she had put down her roots, Susannah also grew, for me at least. All through the winter, though not more than a dozen times in all, at every opportunity to slip away, I went to Betony Hay. Except in the coldest weather the house was snug, sheltered from north winds by the tree-clad hill. Wrapped in a warm cloak, hands in muff, I used to settle on the window-seat and look down over Ted's Corner to a valley still undevastated by Ashton's quarry; or poke about in the warren of rooms hoping to find some trace of Susannah.

I came to know the house well; learned to negotiate the treacherous step down just inside the front door and to dodge the low-slung beams. Above all I loved its emptiness, the entire absence, as I thought at first, of things.

From a cell of a bedroom looking straight into the hillside, an intriguing back stair led down into a cupboard off the kitchen. It was in the cupboard that I made a discovery one day in spring when I had come down through the rowans and found the crab tree by the front gate, faintly pink, the house still as a picture; all Betony lovely as a dream of Arcadia.

I roamed happily about the ancient rooms, enjoying the smell of dust and wood and onions. A finger of sunlight reached even into the dusty cupboard under the stair and pointed straight to a serpentine shape: the letter S, scratched and scored into the wood as if to establish a territorial right. At my touch the panel proved to be a door opening on a spidery recess. Gingerly groping, I found two or three pieces of wood wrapped in rags and took them to the slightly less dim kitchen for a better look.

Clothes-peg dolls! Three of them, dressed in colourless gingham. I stood them up against the window frame. They were not absolutely identical. She had wound different widths of cotton quite skilfully round their waists and necks to give them shape. Which had she liked best? I thought of names for them: Susannah, Kate, Tessa ... and put Tessa in the middle.

It must have been then as I faced the inscrutable dolls, that my picture of Susannah changed. The down-trodden waif faded away to be replaced by an altogether different character. From the cupboard, the stairs, and three clothes pegs she had fashioned, I fancied, a world. The low cracket in the corner had been her seat. Unseen, safe for an hour or two, she would hear the grown-ups talking in the kitchen. But this place had been hers; and in its seclusion as the years went by, she had come at last to her great decision: to leave.

Roused by some small sound – was it the quiet drop of the latch? – I went almost in quest of her to the front door. On the roof starlings pursed and whistled their long notes. On such a day as this it would be hard to leave Betony, especially for a Cade – of sorts – with Betony in her bones. In her defenceless state, to go had been an act of pure courage; a refusal to tolerate any longer an intolerable servitude.

An intolerable servitude. In a moment of desperate honesty I felt the impossibility of ever going back to the particular form of it I knew. From the doorway I watched a group of ragged children splashing in the stream and saw with equal clarity scenes from a harsher childhood: not Susannah's but my own. 'You don't need a candle if your conscience is clear...' I caught again the last glimpse of my grandmother's face, warm in the lamp and firelight as I turned mute with terror to face the black passages at bedtime. I saw myself, feet still, shoulders straight, shivering in flimsy muslin, well back from the fire, while my grandmother, wrapped in layers of shawls dozed over her devotions. I felt again the pressure of her hand on mine as she tricked me into a promise that my whole life could not alter. Her gloomy doctrine of original sin had quenched my lightness of heart: it had turned my instinct to please into deceit. It had all been done in the name of love, and in the name of love, she had been as ruthless as if she had whipped me. She had been as cruel as Jonas Cade but, unlike him, she had not been haunted by her cruelty: not yet. And I knew that the small acts of repression formed no more than the surface of a deeper falseness, a dishonesty as unwholesome as a taint thickening the air. It seemed to me then a miasma as loathsome as any the seventeenth-century Jasmyns had feared when they built their house with its back to the sun.

218

The children in the stream had been joined by a playful yapping dog. It plunged about in its silly way, drenching their clothes, sure of their love.

'You were right, Susannah,' I whispered, turning to close the door as she had done, when she stepped out into the freedom of a friendless world. 'You were right to go.'

Then with my hand on the latch I waited, knowing that I was not alone in the garden.

He came round the corner of the house and stopped short, startled, delighted.

'I didn't expect to see you here. I was coming over to the Hall.'

'But I thought it was to be in June...'

'So it would have been if I hadn't had a real stroke of luck. There's a livery stable near my lodgings. I help the ostler there in my spare time, not that there's much of it, but the money helps. He told me about a gentleman wanting a horse fetched from Maresbarrow. I'm taking it up tomorrow by railway. I've just walked over from Maresbarrow and came to fetch some wood mother has stored in the barn here.'

His joy in seeing me, his pride in the lucky enterprise, kept him talking happily. There was time to see how city life had altered him; how months of working and waiting had sharpened his features, giving them a new delicacy. His eyes were heavier, he had developed a tendency to stoop and looked less confident, far more defenceless. There was time to remember how much I had harmed him: to see myself as a bringer of ill-luck and to remember my promise to his mother. This meeting had been unavoidable but I must see to it that there would not be another.

He had stopped. I saw in his eyes how much more intimate than any embrace a look of longing can be.

'I've counted the hours since I heard about Mr. Speckyard wanting his horse.' He waited, puzzled, when I said nothing. 'Then I thought, "Suppose you'd gone away"...' The sentence trailed off uncomfortably. He fidgeted with his collar and glanced away with a half-suppressed smile. 'It's looking its best, the old place.'

'I hope you enjoy the change, Reuben. It will do you good. Now I really must go.'

It had been easy to win his love: I had done nothing to deserve it; and it was easy to break his heart – by simply speaking coolly and moving past him towards the gate. There was no need really to say anything else; certainly no need for any harshness.

He came past me, put his hand on the wooden bolt and held the gate fast.

'I can't believe it,' he said, 'that you're so changed. You never spoke to me like that even before we ... when I was your groom.

You're like a different person. It isn't fair when I've waited and planned to come home with only you in mind. It isn't fair to treat me like this.'

A sudden scented breeze brought down a shower of blossom from the crab tree. A petal or two caught in the rough frieze of his coat. Involuntarily, caressingly, I raised my hand to brush them off.

'Don't touch me. Don't patronise me. It's the old woman, isn't it? She's warned you to keep away from me?'

Having his mother so much in mind, I misunderstood him and not wanting to betray her, lost what presence of mind I had so far kept.

'She ... she only...'

He misinterpreted my confusion. The resentment he had never shown before made him look at me with something like contempt.

'She's done it at last. Made you over in her own image. "Once a servant over-reaches himself, he will do it again."' The mimicry was ludicrous but cutting enough to show how the words had rankled. 'She said the same thing about your dog. Do you remember? "Once a dog takes to worrying sheep, there's no cure for it." Only to get rid of him for good.'

The parallel startled me.

'You were too fond of him. She had to

221

have you all to herself. It was the same with your French governess...'

I felt my face stiffen and turn pale.

'What are you trying to tell me?'

He hesitated.

'What's the use? You'll have to spend the rest of your days with her. The chances are she'll outlive you – and me. She'll live for ever. If you haven't found her out by this time, you'd better go on as you are.'

'What are you trying to tell me about Lance?' I demanded, but he had said enough already to prompt me to make certain swift connections I should have made long ago. 'Are you saying that she got rid of him on purpose? How could that be? She saw him go after the sheep, didn't she? Didn't she?'

From his silence I knew the truth. I understood his anger as he slammed the stones on the cairn.

'How did he get out? You saw him. You were watching.'

'There's no point in talking about it.'

He slowly drew the bolt and opened the gate.

'That's what she did,' I said. She had sent Steadman away and opened the loose-box door. I remembered the unaccountable pause before the carriage drove away. 'You saw her let him out.'

'Yes.' He was leaning wearily against the gatepost. 'She had to have him out quickly before Steadman came back. I saw her take the old broom handle and beat Lance out of the yard until he ran off with his tail between his legs, yelping. Into the wood. Then she fastened the lower door and left the top half open.'

I believed him as implicitly as if it were happening before my eyes but in imagination it grew into something even more repugnant: a black figure larger than life towering over Lance as he crouched, abject and beseeching; and raining blows on his pale coat with a wildness of cruelty I could not understand. What distortion of the mind had made her do it? Was it madness? And afterwards. She had pretended to see him in the field above Betony...

'Steadman didn't see him going after the sheep?'

'Steadman didn't see him at all.'

It had never happened. But she had been cunning enough to ask, 'Where's your dog Tessa?' just in case he had come back. The nightmare shape contracted into the familiar figure in the jet-beaded cape: the grandmother I had loved and trusted.

'Lance was killed for nothing.'

I remembered his thin tongue licking my hand, the way he yawned as he did when be was agitated or sorry. The sad waste of his beautiful fidelity affected me more at first than the cruelty. Together they brought a vision of destruction like the beat of black wings, a sudden swoop, the feel of claws, an aftermath of disaster and grief so intense that the whole experience might have been familiar, as if long ago it had happened to me before: as if at some unremembered distant time I had felt the collapse of love and security before the onslaught of their opposites.

'I can't bear it, Reuben. I can't bear it. Help me.'

'How can I help? I can't change what you are and who you are. There is no help for it.'

He went on speaking but I could not hear, deafened and blinded as I was by the first passion of my life. It was not love. When Reuben left me, saying something about never coming back, his going seemed a distant event without significance. I did not feel the parting though later I blamed myself bitterly for letting him go in such a way. It was a rage of hatred that seized me and made me grow and swell until the crab tree vanished, the hills shrank, the sky drew away and there was nothing in the whole valley but my fearful anger.

She had lied about Lance and murdered him, then taken me on her knee and stroked my hair. All my years of innocent trust, of longing to please her, had been lavished upon a lying hypocrite. There was no sincerity in her love, nor humility in her religion. Time and again I had searched my conscience and found in every dim mental hiding-place only herself, black-skirted, prayer-book in hand, relentlessly loving and forgiving. A fury of longing to cast her out and occupy in freedom the recesses of my own spirit drove me at last up the hill, along the muddy way between the walls, across the park.

I found her alone, sitting among her shawls. For once I stood over her, looking down.

'I hate you,' I said, speaking from a throat swollen with misery and anger, 'for the way you've deceived me. Are you not ashamed to have such a thing on your conscience? You thought no one knew...'

I never doubted that she would understand me. So monstrous a crime – as I judged it – could have no parallel in her experience. She could never for a moment have forgotten it Only afterwards did I begin to wonder whether the death of a dog could have justified the agony of suppressed guilt that declared itself in her sudden horrified stare.

'Who... Who...?'

'Reuben told me, the groom. He saw it all And you lied to me about my mother's letters. You didn't burn them. I've read them. You gave me a wrong impression of her. You disliked her just because my father gave her the ruby. What else have you lied to me about?'

I said much more, long since forgotten, paying no heed to her feeble attempts to raise herself, her relapse into helpless shuddering.

'You must let me go away. I can't marry Ashton. Give him the estate if you like. No one could be worse at managing it than we have been: more selfish and neglectful. Here.' I snatched up the bible and held it out, beside myself with grief and anger. 'There must be a way of undoing my promise.' I had in mind some ritual that would ease my conscience. 'You must know a way of setting me free.'

I broke off, defeated. My rebellion had come too late. Her dominion over me had lasted too long. She never relinquished it: she kept it, by simply dying there before my eyes. I saw it as a positive move, conclusive and triumphant. A violent shudder, an agonised breath and she was dead, her eyes fixed, naturally enough, on me. I was to feel their unwavering glare for years. I have never ceased to feel it.

The bible fell with a thud, leaving a torn page in my hand. A second thunderbolt rending the house from attic to cellar could not have convinced me more thoroughly of my wicked blasphemy. I stood shivering with superstitious dread, remembering the other time I had wished to be free, at the well. I should have learned from that first feeble spread of wings that there was to be no escape.

In a last desperate bid to bring her back to life and save us both, I felt in the drawer for the digitalin, then recalled that I had thrown the empty phial away long ago. I emptied out her reticule on to the floor and found another. It too was empty. In any case it made no difference now. I put it back, aware that its emptiness had some significance, some message, which in a more normal frame of mind I might have understood.

'Grandmamma.' I knelt beside her. One of her feet had slipped from the footstool and hung helplessly above the ground. Her cap had come off and lay crumpled between her straggling hair and the crimson velvet of the chair-back. 'It's Tessa.' Fearfully, I met the glaring accusation in her eyes. 'I'm sorry. Forgive me, please. Forgive me. I didn't want you to die.'

The door behind me opened.

'I've killed her,' I said, taking up the burden of my guilt. 'I gave her a terrible shock. It was my fault.'

'There now,' Emma said when she had got her breath. 'It had to be, I dare say. You were all she wanted and you were with her to the last.'

Everything she had done, I told myself, had been for love of me: the cruelty, the lies. I had made her as she was. She had made me as I was. For the life of me I could not have told which of us, in the long years we had spent together, had harmed the other more.

In the flurry that followed I took no part. Having acted with such devastating effect, I did no more; except for one thing. Before they carried her away, someone had taken the gold chatelaine from her dress and dropped it on the floor. When they had gone, I clipped it to my waistband and looked apprehensively at my reflection in the long glass.

16

Putting convention aside, I sent for Burnside before the funeral, even before Ashton arrived. Indeed I was determined to act before Ashton could intervene. Without waiting for the will to be read, without any legal entitlement to do so, I ordered Burnside to overhaul the cottages at Betony and put in piped water.

'Never mind about the cost,' I told him, having made up my mind to use the money set aside for my trousseau or to sell, surreptitiously if need be, some of the Indian treasures. 'I will want this work put in hand before I am married. Do you understand?'

'I do that, Miss Jasmyn.' He spoke respectfully. Since he had no plan with him, we went to the library and looked at an old map.

'There's the spring.'

I pointed it out with the gold pencil but the portent passed me by. I had just noticed the thick black line marking the boundary of our land. It passed south of Tod's Corner a few hundred yards on the far side of the river.

'You'll find it different on later maps,'

Burnside said. 'The farmhouse and the land to the east of it still belong to the Cades; to Miss Abbie, that is. But all the rest is Jasmyn land.'

'When did we buy that bit of pasture between the farmhouse and the river?'

'Well before my time. Mr. Pawley might be able to tell you. He'll have the deeds. But I'll see the surveyor of the Maresbarrow Water Company this very day and find out if we can get enough head of water from the spring.'

When he had gone I went back to the house with a shrinking courage. It was always quiet but now even the sound of the wind had sunk to a subdued whisper. Once again – it was becoming a habit – I caught myself listening, expecting her to call. It was a relief when Steadman came to see me about the servants' wages. Even without the symbolic act of putting on the chatelaine, I could not have escaped my duty; nor did any alternative occur to me. There was mourning to be got for myself and the servants; there were letters to be written. Tenants called to express their condolences.

Ashton arrived on the third day after my grandmother's death. This time he came in a new rôle. His very manner of taking off his Ulster and straddling the hearth-rug in the hall proclaimed him master of Barmote. It would have been no surprise to see him rubbing his hands as he approved the deep crepe swathing the trophies on the wall, and the design of the funeral cards.

'A draped urn. Dignified and appropriate. Yes, her life was an example.'

He was forbearing enough not to mention the wedding until after the funeral and almost too solicitous in protecting me from anxiety and distress.

'Leave it to me, Tessa,' he said half a dozen times when there were decisions to make.

Mercifully he spent a good deal of time on his own, going systematically through the rooms.

'Mr. Jasmyn has asked for the key to the cellar, miss,' Steadman informed me impassively on the day he arrived and added the illogical hint, 'The late mistress would very likely have taken him down herself.'

Rather to Ashton's annoyance Steadman came too and we made quite an expedition of it.

'Mr. Steadman was wondering if Mr. Jasmyn would like his things taken down to the Duke's Head now, miss,' Emma said as the afternoon advanced.

'I suppose I can have dinner here.' Ashton sounded irritable. 'You've surely enough stewed mutton and rice pudding for both of us.'

His unwilling departure to the inn left me to a long solitary evening with drawn curtains shutting out the spring twilight. Debarred from needlework or music, I made a hopeless effort to read some of the devotional books on grandmamma's table. By nine o'clock, silence, solitude and troubled thoughts had reduced me to such nervousness that it took all my courage to face the shadows of the hall and to pass my grandmother's room on my way to bed.

'She was an example.' The words haunted me with every possible inflection. It was not until Ashton handed me into the funeral carriage that the troublesome question, 'An example of what?' began to occupy my mind. Gazing above the tossing plumes of the black caparisoned horses, I considered it in some confusion. And to whom had the example been set? That question was easier to answer. The excessive deference of the undertaker's men like ill-omened birds with their crepe-swathed staves and black gloves, made it perfectly clear that the mantle had descended, however unsuitably, upon me. The property was not entailed. My grandmother had left it all to me, to be held in trust until my marriage, with Ashton and my grandmother's brother Thomas as trustees. When the will was read and it was no longer possible to postpone the discussion of our future, I summoned up spirit to take the initiative.

'I've promised to marry you, Ashton.'

'Good heavens, Tessa, you don't need to tell me that. We've been engaged for a year and a half.'

'Do you understand' – on this subject I was determined to be straightforward and in the relief of speaking openly, I spoke without finesse – 'that I promised because it was grandmamma's wish and not because I wanted to?'

He looked down at me indulgently.

'You were a child – little more – and you're still very young. Girls are sometimes afraid of marriage. There's no need. I'm not such a bad fellow, you know. You'll have a pleasanter time after we're married, I promise you. You can have more friends. We'll entertain the neighbours and go up to London sometimes.'

'She made me promise on the bible.'

He put his arms round me quite tenderly.

'No wonder it frightened you. One always felt this place reeking with the wrath of God. Marriage is a serious business, I admit; but your life here has made you altogether too solemn, my dear. Come now, you're still upset and shaken. I won't urge you, but shall we say the middle of July? Would that suit you?'

It would be for every reason a quiet affair. My unusual lack of relatives, Ashton thought an advantage. One of his Stydding connections, whom I had met briefly years before, would be my bridesmaid. Great-Uncle Thomas would give me away.

'Is there anyone else you would like to have with you?'

I thought of dear Mam'selle, now in an establishment for young ladies in Canterbury, but it was too far for her to come. Perhaps later...

'I know you don't care for her, Ashton, but I should so very much have liked to invite Kate Masson.'

'I'd forgotten the Massons. What became of them?'

'Kate made up her mind quite suddenly to go to London. She's living with friends and helping with the Cordingley Trust. I don't hear from her. And Mrs. Masson...'

How long it seemed since she had walked away, desolate, her gown sweeping the autumn leaves! The memory brought a similar desolation to my own heart. In that last dreadful interview she had in some strange way risen above the situation and put me to shame. She had spoken of my grandmother with authority but without passion; yet every word had been heartfelt. At that moment at least she had been absolutely genuine; and if her dislike had been genuine, what of the warmth, the wistful sympathy I had so often resented. Might they not have been genuine too?

'I don't understand,' I said, suddenly

bursting into tears, 'why I ever disliked her.'

Ashton drew me close.

'I've been thinking,' he said, 'you can't possibly stay here alone until the wedding. Emma has already thrown out all manner of hints. You must have some older lady to look after you. I'll write to Pawley. He can make enquiries in suitable circles. As for the Massons, you must try to forget them. Now,' he looked at his watch, 'what about our ride? I'll give you ten minutes.'

We turned left at the bridge and took the woodland path to the east side of the valley. Ashton pointed out where a road would be cut through Tod's Corner to connect the quarry with the bridge. Betony, I thought, looking out over the shining acres of my inheritance, would vanish with the last of my girlhood.

We crossed the stream by Miss Cade's cottage. Without Ashton I might have been tempted to call; but Miss Cade had spoken rather rudely about the Jasmyns. Turning to look back as we rode upstream, I caught a glimpse of something white in the doorway as if someone were waving a cloth or towel, but I heard nothing and rode on. If it had been a distress signal, there were labourers in the fields beyond. Almost at once we came in sight of Betony. Miss Cade had not after all moved so very far from her old home. By the river the distance could be no more than a quarter of an hour's walk; but a wooded hill cut us off from the hamlet until we were almost there, when all at once the ramshackle cottages rose above us on their natural terraces; and beyond, through tall grasses already in flower, we saw Betony Hay with the sun on its windows and its dairy roof white with fallen blossom.

'Look out, Tessa. You're dreaming.' I had almost caught my head on a low branch. 'What's Burnside doing up there, I'd like to know.'

He was standing by the spring with another man and a boy with a bag on his back.

'By Jove, they're taking measurements for something or other.'

'They must be starting on the improvements to the cottages,' I said as casually as I could.

'I didn't know Mrs. Jasmyn was planning anything of the sort. What in heaven's name is the point of making improvements when the whole place is going to be opened up for quarrying?'

We drew up and I looked round as if looking for the last time; hoping to imprint upon my mind for ever the willow-hung stream, the clover-scented meadows, the cottages sill-deep in flowers, the blue, distant hills. Betony had never been dearer to me, whether because its perfection could be followed only by decline; or because the well

– the spring – the farmhouse gate – aroused in me the aching sadness that comes from a glimpse of the unattainable. For whatever reason, in the hamlet's vulnerable beauty there seemed a sacrificial quality. So far – I found consolation in reminding myself – the Jasmyns had destroyed Betony's enterprises but not its people. Yet, from that moment, for no good reason, there stole upon me a foreshadowing of disaster as if, before the long history of Betony reached its end, there must be human sacrifice.

'I'd better have a word with Burnside.'

'Not now, please, dear Ashton. The work is already contracted for. Just a few things that should have been done long ago. Besides, it's your last day and I shall be quite alone when you've gone.'

Indeed I dreaded the solitude. Ashton was kind. I had grown used to his company. Since there was no changing it, I must accept my lot without complaint; without, if I could contrive it, too much regret. The one thing I had learned to do well was to submit. I would shoulder my responsibility and try to manage the estate as well as Ashton would allow. There must be no more foreclosures or cruel acts of distraint, no more neglect.

Long after the house was still, I sat brushing my hair by my bedroom fire. The very evening of my grandmother's death, I had come to my room and found for the first time in my life a fire burning. With the chatelaine it marked my change of status; and now, for the spring evenings were cold, it was as comforting as a companion. Again, as always, in spite of my resolutions, my mind slid away from the inescapable reality of my marriage as I spun for myself a fairy-tale with a happy ending. In it, for all my limitations, I did a splendid thing, worthy of Kate herself.

'Take it,' I imagined myself saying superbly to some unseen recipient: Ashton: the Indian gentleman (now grown exceedingly old): almost anyone would do: 'Take the house, the farms, the money. I don't want them, no, really...'

Then I would slip away to Betony, a Betony unchanged, to live happily ever after among the blossoming trees, above the river, between the sheltering hills. It was a dream soon to fuse, as I fell into a restless sleep, with other dreams of partings and loss, wanderings and vanishings: a dream to save me from despair.

17

We were fortunate in finding Mrs. Arrow, a clergyman's widow in reduced circumstances, who was so very happy to accept the post of temporary companion-housekeeper that it was a pleasure to have her at the Hall. After years of respectable poverty she found in a private sitting room and her own tea-tray all that she could wish for. We had luncheon and dinner together, sat together in the evenings and sometimes she came with me on my afternoon drive; for Ashton had left firm instructions that I was to ride or drive every day.

In the middle of May Mme. Ballard arrived with a trunk of samples and fashion books and two assistants who were to stay on at Barmote to work on my trousseau. The wedding-dress, Mme. Ballard said, would be a triumph: a creation of gauze and faille, a skirt slotted with ribbon and bunches of flowers and sixty yards of trimming.

'The dress,' Mme. Ballard said as I revolved listlessly while she took measurements, 'will help you. When other things are not quite as they should be–' she eyed me shrewdly – 'a beautiful dress raises the spirits.'

'Have you known other girls, Mme. Ballard, who would rather not...?'

'Others? Most of them. They overcome it, the reluctance, and make a life for themselves. The most important thing is that a match should be suitable. Only the things one cannot have are romantic. Now you can put on this dreadful black thing again. But after July you might slight your mourning. There are all the lavenders – and lilac – and white and grey. You will look' – Mme. Ballard became unexpectedly fanciful – 'like thistledown.'

'The girls will be nervous in this ghostly place,' she said as we stood in the hall waiting for the carriage to take her to the station. 'Perhaps you are fond of it.' She looked with distaste at the tiger-skin rug – and then more sympathetically at me. 'Is it permissible to ask how old you are, my dear Miss Jasmyn?'

'I don't know. I don't know my birthday or where I was born.' I explained reluctantly. It was like revealing a deformity, but she laughed.

'You are lucky. Most women would welcome a little latitude in calculating their age.'

'Emma,' I said when she had gone, 'would you please take away the tiger-skin rug?'

'Where to, miss?' She seemed divided between outrage and the necessity of humouring me.

'You can put it in one of the attics for the time being.'

'I've always thought myself it would be best hanging on the wall. It would show up better, especially the teeth.'

She lugged it away, leaving an enormous emptiness.

The more pressing problem remained. Once again I faced the ridiculous situation of not having been, officially at least, born, and foresaw further embarrassment. The clerk would write on my marriage lines: 'date of birth unknown', as grandmamma had done in the family bible; or worse still he might leave a blank, as though – the eerie thought come to me – Ashton would be standing at the altar alone. Had he been approachable, Colonel Darlington might have known the approximate date of my birth. The one person who had almost certainly known it was Susannah. Her husband had been a pay-sergeant in the Regiment. On an impulse I got out my writing-desk and wrote to Mr. Pawley, asking him to make some enquiries. Because there was so much I wanted and could never have, I set my heart on knowing this one simple thing, the date of my birth.

This practical step towards tracing Susannah was no sooner taken than forgotten, eclipsed altogether by the more exciting method of divination. Mrs. Arrow was not with me when one afternoon Simon drove me to Spandleby and back. We had passed the lane leading to Gib Cottage when we heard, sudden and clamorous enough to startle the ponies, the clanging of Miss Cade's brass handbell.

'There's somebody waving, miss.' Simon sounded regretful at the delay. He was always hungry.

It was Molly who stood at the gate, swinging the bell with her right hand and beckoning with the left like a mariner hailing a passing vessel. I got down and sent Simon home, saying that I would walk back by the river path.

'She wants you, miss,' Molly said.

Indeed she did want me though there was no means of knowing whether it was my arrival that had brought the pink flush to her cheeks or whether she had existed in the same state of feverish excitement ever since I had left her. Could it be almost eight months ago? I felt the onward rush of time like a chilling breeze. Altogether I must have cut a despondent figure, standing in the doorway with nothing to say.

'Come in, come in. Molly saw the carriage from the upstairs window. We've been looking out for you. You passed by a few weeks ago. "There's Miss Jasmyn," Molly said. "And well I know it," I said for it was just a minute before that I had laid out your card.'

'What nonsense,' I thought. 'A few pieces of cardboard.'

But I went further in, sidling between footstools and tables. The room was unchanged. The everlastings had endured another winter of their endless existence in the pink china vase; the disdainful swans floated amid the motionless reeds on the fire-screen; on the table lay the three rows of cards.

'I've been wanting to see you to tell you–' she broke off – 'It's been puzzling with all these Queens. Time and again they turn up. But it's the eight of diamonds I don't like. Nothing but worry and deception...'

My mood this time was not sympathetic.

'You look tired. Sit down.'

'No, thank you. I must go. Why did you want to see me, Miss Cade?'

She drew in her breath and looked at me jubilantly, the blue light dancing in her eyes.

'Because she's here.'

'Who?'

'Who do you think? Susannah. Susannah Cade.'

'Here?' I glanced round, half expecting to see a seated figure, hitherto unnoticed, in one of the more distant chairs.

'No. Here.' She tapped the table. 'She's been here ever since you came the last time. In fact I'm not sure she wasn't there before, only I didn't notice her. There she is.' She slapped the three of diamonds. 'S. or C. In this case both. She's there every time. And look there—' She pointed to the four of hearts. 'A woman from over the water. Oh, they're coming right.'

Intrigued in spite of myself, I waited.

'You're out of spirits.' She looked at me keenly.

'A little.'

'It's all this deception. Take a card.'

Indifferently I drew one out and watched her rapidly set out her table again.

'What do they say?'

'You're to be married,' she said without hesitation. 'There's plenty of worry and talk here but you're to be married. Oh yes, indeed. And there she is again.'

'Susannah?'

'Susannah Cade. After all these years. It can't be long now.'

'You mean, before she actually comes?'

'Before she walks in at that door.' She nodded. 'For come she will.'

The inner door was half open. In the kitchen Molly had been ironing pillow-cases and was now slapping and pulling the muslin bedroom curtains. She had evidently also been washing the ewer and basin.

'You're expecting her then? Susannah?'

'We're getting things ready.'

There was something so weird in this combination of practical housewifery and wild surmise, so precise a balance between the possible and the improbably that I wavered, half convinced. A loud knock at the door set my heart thumping. It was the postman.

'Gib Cottage?' He seemed in need of confirmation. 'I don't recollect the last time I was here.'

He positively started as Miss Cade called out, 'Come in, postman. You bring news.'

'She must have been expecting it.' He looked dubiously at the letter. 'From London. They say she's a bit...' He tapped his forehead and stepped inside rather hesitantly.

According to Emma they called her Mad Abbie in the village; and no wonder. All the same I carried away the curious impression that between us Miss Cade and I had once again raised a spirit. It was absurd to imagine that after all these years Susannah Cade would even remember Betony, much less come back – if she were still alive; and yet she refused absolutely to be dismissed. Miss Cade was actually expecting her. Nothing was impossible; nothing easier to imagine than her knocking at the door of Gib Cottage, slipping quietly inside (she would be a quiet woman) and sitting down at the table opposite her Aunt Abbie. Then in a little while she would pin on her hat again and take the river path to Betony to look at her old home...

It was not that day, so far as I recall, but a week or two later that I went there myself for the first time since my grandmother's death and almost turned back at the gate, so strongly did the place evoke painful memories of Reuben. Events had banished him as irretrievably into the past as if he were dead; and as if he were dead I mourned for him, no less deeply than if my black dress had been put on for his sake.

Was there – I paused at the parlour door – a tiny difference? The full sunlight of early summer falling on a patch of scattered meal in the far corner revealed a blunt triangle like the imprint of a narrow boot. I went slowly up the shallow stairs with my dress lifted to my ankles and imagined on either side of each tread a curve, as if a longer skirt had gone ahead of me, sweeping aside the dust. In the tiny bedroom I stopped short, startled by a square of bright green in the wall. The bracken had grown thick and filled the view. The door of the back stair had swung ajar. That was the way she would go down to the kitchen. I followed – to find with a shock of real disappointment that they had gone; Kate, Tessa and Susannah had vanished from the windowsill where I had left them standing in a solemn row. One of the Betony children must have taken them.

I dolefully traced the curves of the letter S on the little cupboard door, looked inside in the hope of finding other treasures and to my delight found them all there, lying on their backs in the darkness. But I was certain beyond any shadow of doubt that I had left them in the kitchen. Could the intruding child, whoever she was, have found Susannah's hiding-place? When closed, the door was indistinguishable from the flat panels on either side. It would take a sharp eye to detect it.

In a sudden panic I rushed out of door to find scarlet and brown hens strutting on the grass, a pair of grazing goats, the uneven garden walls hardly containing a spring-tide of currant and gooseberry bushes. By this time I knew the Betony folk. Mrs. Wagstaff nodded to me from her door. I stopped to pass the time of day.

'They're all little boys in Betony, except Mrs. Cotton's new twins,' I observed.

'There's Becky Porter. You won't likely have seen her, miss. She's that bad with the rickets that she doesn't play outside, poor little thing.'

She was a poor little thing indeed, crouched on a stool by her mother's wash-tub. Mrs. Porter seemed overwhelmed when I suggested that she should bring Becky to the bridge next day for a ride in the pony carriage. She must have sat up half the night patching and contriving to produce a spotless and utterly silent Becky. My impulse to help proved a trial to both of them. But Becky with her poor legs bent into a hoop could have had nothing to do with the mysterious adventures of the clothes-peg dolls. Then one of the boys perhaps ... and if not one of the boys, then...

Was it possible that other feet than mine had recently walked the stone floors? Could other hands have *returned* the dolls to their proper place? And were they hands and feet of flesh and blood? It was not surprising that I should have come to prefer fantasy to reality. Wavering more wildly than ever between the possible and the improbable, between the natural and supernatural, I settled at last in favour of a spirit. Betony Hay was haunted and by a spirit familiar with its nooks and crannies, a wandering spirit come home at last. Instead of calling on Miss Cade to establish the facts, I experimentally scattered a few handfuls of meal in front of the hearth, knowing very well that to find actual human footprints would be disappointing.

Some day perhaps they would call me Mad Tessa. I thought of myself, grey-haired and witless, searching for a ghost, and in spite of the experiment with the meal, resolved to stay away from Betony. And after all Mr. Pawley proved a more reliable source of information than Miss Cade. Shortly afterwards, he wrote that there had been a pay-sergeant in the 32nd named Edward Drew, whose widow, Susannah, had come back to England in August, 1858, bringing with her an infant, a girl. Since then nothing had been heard of her. Her movements could not be traced. All records of births and marriages within the Regiment between 1853 and 1857 had been lost and never recovered.

Not only must my birthday remain unknown: the whole Indian episode was as impenetrable as pre-existence. Regretfully I closed the chapter. It was as though my life had begun when my grandmother descended upon the inn at Gravesend and carried me away.

18

It came to me gradually, the conviction that I must go away. There was nothing dramatic about it; no glamour of flight or escape: there was nothing reasonable in it either: no moment of cool decision. It was simply that day by day with growing frequency I thought of myself as quietly going away until the idea clarified into a distinct picture. Beyond the instant of departure I saw nothing, any more than I made plans. Some shadowy scheme of going to London and finding Kate, or putting myself in the care of Mme. Ballard, or seeking out Mlle. Quéva, who had written to tell me of her marriage to a schoolmaster in Canterbury and urged me to visit them, was the utmost I could conceive. Travelling on the railway was not the desperate enterprise I had once imagined. I would take a few things and go away. A kind of spiritual exhaustion robbed me of any sense of responsibility as if I could wipe out the consequences of my action by absenting myself from them.

It was a summer of thunderstorms and heavy rain alternating with spells of sultry heat. With each passing day my lassitude increased until almost any activity became a burdensome duty. Yet the idea that I would go away persisted. Whether it was saving me from a melancholy sickness or driving me into it would be hard to say.

Our banns were read for the first time on the last Sunday in June. After morning service I spent a few minutes by grandmamma's grave and came to the lych-gate to find myself face to face with Reuben. For a second he seemed a shabby stranger. He was thin and serious. The hollows in his temples and under his eyes shocked me in spite of the delight and relief that he had come home after all. It would have done no harm surely to speak kindly to him; but the shame of having brought ill-luck to his house reminded me of my duty. I felt a despair so intense that I must have gasped with the pain of it, before walking on without a smile or a word.

'That young man,' Mrs. Arrow had looked round discreetly on the pretext of adjusting her cape, 'seemed to want to speak to you. He looked quite ill. Do you think we should…?'

A glance at my face silenced her. We walked on without exchanging another word; but at the gate into the park I turned and ran all the way back to the church. Reuben had gone.

Some feeling of obligation to Mrs. Arrow helped me to endure the ordeal of our midday dinner.

'You're not eating a bite, my dear. Is it the heat? Or the excitement,' she added. 'It's very natural, I'm sure.'

The moment she went to her room, I went to mine. In those days we had postal deliveries on Sundays. Emma had laid a small parcel on my bed. It would be another wedding present, no doubt. I dropped it unopened into the depths of the wardrobe and dreamily took out a hat and a summer cape and collected a few necessary articles – a hairbrush, a pair of slippers – laying each object slowly and uncertainly in a carpet bag with a feeling of unfamiliarity as if they belonged to someone else.

No one, so far as I know, saw me cross the park, but in the carriage road the positive necessity of going somewhere revived me; and all at once it came to me quite naturally that I would go to St Agnes'. The sisters would help me as they had helped the woman with the baby. They would usher me into some little cool windowless room where no one could find me. The decision brought me to a more rational state of mind. I would go by way of Betony and Reuben must not see me. Like a shadow I slipped between the screening thornbushes. There was no one about: not a soul. They might all have gone away, so deep was the summer quiet.

252

The afternoon was hot; the clouds were heavy and low. Not a breeze stirred the leaves of the crab tree in the garden of Betony Hay. There could be no harm in taking a last look from the parlour window. A mouse scuttled to safety behind the sheltering sacks. There must be a colony of them big enough to have made short work of the meal I had scattered on the hearth; or tidy enough – in my trance-like state the idea was not acceptable – to have brushed it aside. An uneven line of it lay at the right side of the hearth like flotsam washed there by a wave. An ancient birch broom lolled in the corner behind the door. It was possible to note its presence there for the first time without surprise, all my thoughts being given to leave-taking.

By the well the elder was in bloom again. I lingered there, leaning my arms on the cool coping, and hung my head above the empty darkness, until the blotches of black and grey cleared to show bright green patches of moss and between them the faint glimmer of slime. From the depths there rose again the breath of the earth itself, bringing a message older than memory; but now there mingled with the odours of stone and damp a more sickly smell as if the tainted air the early Jasmyns had feared had settled and festered there at the very heart of the hamlet, where the most ancient bond between Betony and its people had been broken: the primal need for water.

The perception came to me dimly, no more than half understood, to stir a grief far deeper than my own personal sorrow. I pulled down a creamy spray of elder. Flies rose with a hostile buzz from the rich pannicles of bloom, hovered about my hat, then settled one by one to crawl on the stones lining the well. In the sweetness of the blossom as in all the hamlet's Arcadian beauty, I sensed a warning of decay.

I knelt there, thinking that I must go. There are depths of unhappiness in which it is impossible even to form a wish. In such cases a wish may form itself as once, long before, a wish had come unbidden to define a secret longing. Perhaps now, in spite of all reason, a lingering hope survived that the implacable powers of earth and sky would hear my appeal.

'Save me, save me. Help me, please.'

This time there was no lightning fork, no thunderclap, not a sound, not a breath. The people in the cottages might have sunk into the earth, leaving no trace, not even a thread of smoke from a chimney. The hills floated in a vaporous haze. Framed in the motionless elder flowers, the valley hung like a picture.

Then in the right-hand corner of the picture something moved: a stirring: a change of light by the river at the base of the wooded hill. I stared so hard in the warm stillness that the whole hill moved towards me, receded and settled again as a form came out of the shade of the trees and advanced along the path: a brown shape: a human figure: a woman.

Stiff as the stones of the well, I watched: and in spite of the distance between us I felt the strength and energy of her movements. She walked steadily but quickly, was over the stile in a single stride. Would she cross the stream by the bridge? Instead she turned left into the wilderness of Tod's Corner and disappeared among its ox-eye daisies and cow parsley, then came out from the mist of flowers into the path that curved up to Betony Hay.

She was wearing a chip hat and a plain brown dress and even coming uphill she walked with the tireless plod of a strong country woman. She did not see me crouching by the well but I saw her face clearly. As soon as she pushed open the farmhouse gate and vanished behind the apple trees, I ran down to the lower wall in time to see her unlatch the door and step down confidently, negotiating the steep step inside as if she had known it all her life.

What, having conjured up a spirit, does one do next? Astonishment and disbelief kept me motionless just outside the door. But she was no mere spirit. So far as I could judge she was chopping sticks at the back of the house. Bewildered, pleased, ashamed, doubtful of everything on earth, I knew that in one respect at least my instinct had not misled me. She had never, no matter what she wore, walked like a lady but always like a countrywoman born and bred.

She came suddenly back into the passage, ducking her head expertly to avoid the low beam.

'Tessa.' Her voice was tender.

'Mrs. Masson, I don't know what to say. It's so strange to see you here.'

'Is it so very strange to come home?' she said. 'I lived here when I was a girl. The strange thing is that I ever went away.'

19

She had changed, as though in putting on country clothes she had laid aside a disguise. Her eyes – they were blue – were tranquil. The intently watchful look had gone. All the same – I saw it at once – a settled sadness remained.

'So you came back.'

'I couldn't stay away.'

We sat down together on the window-seat. At first I could feel only the miraculous strangeness of having witnessed the fusing of two people, the known and the imagined, into one. Yet there was nothing supernatural in her presence there. She had simply found an intolerable emptiness in her life and come home at last three weeks ago to Aunt Abbie and the country life nature had designed for her.

'I wrote, asking her to take me in for a while. It has been so peaceful and natural. We sit at the table, talking about old times.'

'She was expecting you.'

Susannah laughed. As Mrs. Masson she had scarcely ever laughed.

'Dear Aunt Abbie. Her faith in the cards is now unshakeable. She doesn't know how many times I walked along Gib Lane when I was living at the Lodge, wanting to call...'

I looked away, sharing to the full her embarrassment in speaking of the episode at the Lodge.

'It's been,' she went on, 'not so much a coming as a going back to my very roots. Growing older, one feels the need.' She leaned her head against the panel of the shutter and looked out over Tod's Corner to the hills. 'I actually found my old clothes-peg dolls, the very first time I came. It was like finding the little Susannah I once was.'

'What shall I call you?' After the first bewildering minutes I could talk to her more naturally than to anyone else I had known, except Reuben. There was restfulness in being with her. 'Mrs. Masson sounds too distant. Besides, I should like to start again.'

She hesitated.

'You used to call me mamma, imitating Kate.'

'After mother died?'

She nodded.

'What was she like? You loved her?'

'Alice Jasmyn was the light of my life when everything else was dark.'

'Colonel Darlington wrote that she died very suddenly.'

'It was cholera. She was taken ill at noon. Before midnight I wiped the death dews from her brow.'

Even now the distress of it altered her face. She closed her eyes with a deep shuddering sigh.

'May I call you Susannah?'

'I'd like that.'

'When I thought of you at the inn at Gravesend, it didn't occur to me that you would have a little girl of your own. I thought only of myself. But you had two of us to care for – and Kate was so delicate.'

Our talk as we sat there in the dusty parlour was fitful. There were no long explanations. She would bring out a fragment of information and I would placidly fit it to those I already had, like a piece of patchwork.

'When you heard that the Lodge was to let...'

I laid the subject before her and she took it up.

'Can you imagine? It was like a door opening. To be mistress there for a while...'

I thought of the little Susannah peeping through the rowans at the carriage folk. How delightful a change of fortune – and how strange!

'And naturally I wanted to see how you had grown up. What you were like.'

What sort of figure had I cut; self-centred, suspicious, grasping, like all the Jasmyns?

'Was I different,' I asked, hoping that she would show me a more flattering picture of myself, 'from what you expected?'

'I loved to watch you on the brink of life, so much in love ... and I feared for you too. You were oddly lonely in spite of your engagement.'

'Could you not,' I interrupted quickly, coming at last to the heart of the matter, 'have told me?'

She got up and was a little time in replying.

'It was wrong not to tell you. It made me ill, the deception. But there was Kate.'

'She didn't know – that you had been my nurse.'

We had then, in our infancy, been almost sisters, Kate and I. The sense of closeness, the pain of separation from her, had been founded not in imagination but in memory. A closeness had existed, a parting had taken place before, long ago.

'Kate knows nothing?'

'She knows that I am staying with an elderly relative at Gib Cottage.'

I saw the dilemma. Kate's upbringing had been that of a lady, far superior to my own.

'Why did Kate go away?'

'The time had come, I suppose. Her stay at the Lodge was a breathing space. It changed her. She was more thoughtful than I had ever known her; then suddenly she made up her mind – and left.'

There was no estrangement; only a parting; they had taken different paths.

'After all,' I said to comfort her, 'Kate only did what you did,' and as she looked startled, 'You went away. I've often thought of you lifting the latch and going out into the darkness. Was it night?'

At first she seemed at a loss.

'Yes. I had almost forgotten.' With the faintest suggestion of a shiver, she remembered.

'It was a brave thing to do. Kate has inherited your courage.'

'In my case it was an act of madness.'

But she seemed to consider the proposition as if it were new to her and it occurred to me that there could be other things Susannah had not thought of.

'It isn't likely that I shall see Kate again,' I said, 'but if it's a secret still, you can be sure that I shall never tell.'

I turned the conversation to the safer and more enthralling subject of our life in India and gradually came to understand the ordeal she had survived and only just survived. The deaths of her husband, their first child, my parents and many others had left her almost friendless. Months of privation, heat, sickness and the agony of seeing Kate decline, had reduced her by the time we reached England to skin and bone.

'I had no spirit left, no judgment. I had nothing – but money.'

There had been plenty of that. Edward Drew had been with the 32nd at the sack of Multan in 1849 and unlike his fellows, had made good use of his share of the booty, a small fortune in jewels.

'Most of the men sold what they had taken for a few rupees to buy drink but Ned was a careful, prudent man. Yes, I had money, and Kate.'

They had lived quietly with Ned's mother until she died, by which time Susannah had recovered. The spirit that had rescued her from Jonas and worse afflictions revived and strengthened. Her second marriage to Richard Masson had been prosperous, though short. Kate had been so young that she had never known Richard was her step-father. India was best forgotten. The attitude did not surprise me: I was used to it.

'Money can do almost anything,' Susannah said.

That too I understood, recalling what it had done for the Jasmyns. Money had been the means of elevating not only Kate but Susannah. As Kate learned, she learned, shedding her country ways with memories of Alice Jasmyn as her model. She had learned to speak like a lady though with the too careful precision Ashton had noticed. The one thing she had never lost was her country-woman's walk. She could not have known or she would have altered that too.

Her resources of character, I was beginning to realise, were formidable.

But the elegant clothes had helped to create a new Susannah. To discard them had been a deliberate act, symbolising another phase in her adventurous life. It was characteristic of her to slough off the old skin with an energetic twist and enter on a new existence. It had been, I believe, a relief; but the motive had been a sad one.

'I had lost Kate – and you too.' Then seeing my embarrassment she said, 'The fault was mine. Concealment is always wrong. But it seemed wiser not to offer information where to offer it might have made things worse.'

If some hovering idea came to me that she had done a little more than withhold information; if some recollection stirred of her terror when confronted with my charge (absurd and wholly at sea as it had been), 'I know why you came here,' they were forgotten; she had been thinking only of Kate. Scarcely a shadow fell upon that first hour we spent together. I remember it as an interlude of quiet happiness, all the more memorable in its contrast to the period that was to follow.

One subject we left almost untouched.

'If Mrs. Jasmyn had recognised me,' Susannah spoke after a pause and with deliberation, 'I should have explained the position and appealed to her discretion.'

How reasonable it sounded! How unremarkable, after all, the whole incident had been! How nearly Ashton had diagnosed it: a woman of means rising above her station. How pardonable, entirely justifiable when Susannah's early life was taken into account! Detecting in myself a touch of superiority, I recalled the transformation of Barmote Farm into Barmote Hall, of pasture into park. And how delightfully Susannah's worldliness and social ambition had been balanced – or rather outweighed – by the sentimental longing to see Betony again, and me!

All the same, reasonable as it was, the remark carried an inflection which combined with an additional stillness in her manner to suggest uncertainty. Was she absolutely sure of having escaped recognition? The question served as dramatically as any spell to fill the room with the watchful presence of my grandmother. If in her wide black skirts and flowing sleeves she had suddenly appeared between the meal sacks and the broom, I could not have experienced a more painful confusion of loyalties; but in fact she was not there to testify as to whether or not she had recognised in her elegant visitor the downtrodden nurse of fifteen years ago: or why, in such a case, she should have refrained from saying so.

With a discipline of mind that grandmamma herself would have approved of, I banished her with the safe observation, 'You had changed so much.'

'It was years ago... We met for only a few minutes. She scarcely looked at me.' Susannah's face had hardened. 'She took you away without a thought for my feelings and gave me to understand that no further connection was possible. One shouldn't speak ill of the dead.'

Leaving me to wonder whether the announcement of grandmamma's death had hastened her return, she went on to speak instead of my wedding. That too had been announced in the *Morning Post*. One attitude from the old life had survived to flourish in the new: her whole-hearted approval of my marriage. It was generous of her, especially as she had no fondness for Ashton, and in view of her failure to contrive a successful marriage for Kate. I described my dress and the half dozen of every kind of petticoat in my trousseau, from embroidered lawn by way of quilted silk to winter flannel; and told her how I longed for a cuirasse bodice. In a discussion of berthas and net fichus our magic hour ceased to soar and brought us safely back to earth.

'Your birthday? 25th August, 1856,' she said promptly, and instantly my feverish interest in the subject evaporated. What did it matter when I was born? Or that I would be not quite eighteen when I was married?

'You'll stay with Miss Cade,' I said when by mutual consent we prepared to go.

'For a while. But I shall settle here, Tessa, at the Hay. Aunt Abbie has already altered her will, leaving it to me. You must help me to plan the improvements. Can you imagine how beautiful it will be? I shall sit here when I'm old, looking down the valley.'

The dreadful thought that she would be looking at the Jasmyn and Packby stone quarry made me lead the way out into the warm afternoon rather more quickly than was my inclination. Tod's Corner shimmered in a hot haze of flowering weeds: a tangled wilderness as useless as an acre of land could be; except – I suddenly perceived – that it could have effectively barred the outlet of stone wagons from the valley had it still belonged to the Cades.

At once my attention was distracted by the sight of Tim Wagstaff who had appeared on the bank of the stream with a bucket. By the time he had waded in, filled it and returned to pour the water into a pitcher, I had run down and caught him by the collar of his tattered shirt.

'What are you doing, you wicked boy? You know you're not to take water from the stream. Why didn't you go to the spring?'

I threw away the slimy bucket and gripped the frail shirt more tightly, tempted to give him a good shaking. Overwhelmed by the descent of a whirlwind – as it must have seemed – the poor child burst into tears.

'Have you ever taken water from here before?'

He nodded, quite broken down; and I saw remorsefully that he was not well. He was shivering and yet his hand was hot.

'I'm sorry, Tim. You're poorly. I'll take you home.'

'Mother's poorly too.' He snivelled and shivered.

With foreboding, I felt again the silence of the place and looking anxiously round, formed a swift impression of shuttered windows and closed doors.

'Tim isn't well.'

Susannah had joined me. She felt his hand and forehead.

'He has a fever.'

We took him home. I remember my shame at the sight of the crumbled step, the warped window-frames, the earth path puddled by heavy rains. From some rotting mess by the door a swarm of flies rose with a glitter of blue-black wings. The fetid darkness and sickly stench of the room turned me faint. Mrs. Wagstaff was lying on the mat by the empty fireplace, coughing and muttering, her knees drawn up in pain.

'Wait here.'

Susannah pushed past me and bent over

her, then went quickly up the winding stairs to the room above.

'The husband is ill too,' she said when she came down. 'They must have been ill for days. They have the rash, the soreness in the body, the fever.'

'What can we do?'

We went outside into the purer air, talking in whispers.

'The trouble is,' she glanced at Tim crouching miserably on the step, 'there will be others.'

The Porters' cottage stood close by but on higher ground. I saw the door move. At first there was no one to be seen; then at floor level Becky appeared on her hands and knees, looking out. Something in her wordless beseeching look as she caught sight of us warned me of what I would find when I picked her up and went inside. It was too late to help Mrs. Porter. She had died without help or consolation, close to the wash-tub from which she had never long been parted.

'Put the little girl down, Tessa,' Susannah said when we had stood for a minute or two wretchedly wondering what to do first.

'Do you think I'm afraid of infection?' I hugged the filthy child and held her close.

'This comes from infected water.' Susannah hesitated. 'It is enteric fever.'

On the hill above the houses, brown

glazed pipes lay abandoned. Heavy rains had interrupted the work of installing tanks and conduits. The water supply would come to Betony too late. The mournful sequence of neglect had come inevitably to death, fulfilling my premonition. But no foreboding could have prepared me for the awful reproach of Mrs. Porter's silence.

'You must go, Tessa, and send Burnside. We shall need a doctor. Young Dr. Staple from Spandleby would be the best.'

But I could not leave without finding a temporary home for Becky. In all but two of the eight cottages we found at least one member of the family suffering from symptoms of the fever: pain, coughing, headache and rash. The old couple in the end cottage seemed in normal health and they willingly took Becky.

Susannah and I met again at the well.

'What is this, I wonder?'

'It's mine.'

I took the carpet-bag and hurried homeward. But as I emerged from the tangle of fruit trees and flowers that overgrew the cottages by the stream, a woman came running round the nearest garden wall: a thin, agitated woman: Mrs. Bateman.

'Can you come?' She clutched my hand. 'I've done all I can. I can't go on by myself.'

I left her panting behind me as I ran to her door and up the stairs. Reuben was lying in a low bed under the sloping roof. The room was as hot as an oven. I took his hand. But this time it was he who stared without recognition. He was too far gone to know me.

20

I stood in the twilight at the Batemans' door and watched a little procession of our own servants and people from the cottages wheeling handcarts and carrying baskets and bundles down to Betony Hay: murky figures seen through the smoke of the bonfire to which Burnside had consigned every scrap of perishable food to be found in the hamlet, and most of the bedding.

Mrs. Bateman had put out a chair for me but I was not tired – or hungry – or even, so far as I knew, sad, being totally possessed by the single determination that there must be no more deaths. The sight of Reuben on the point of becoming such a pitiful thing as Mrs. Porter had already become, had shaken me free of every sentiment but the passionately felt necessity of saving him. No effort would be too much. No money should be spared if I had to sell or pawn every article the Jasmyns had accumulated throughout four generations of greed and neglect. The stringency of my mood made me immune – not only to the disease, as it happened – but to the implications of Dr. Staple's grave face when presently he came down from Reuben's room. All I suffered from was the delusion that by giving everything, one could settle even with death.

Dr. Staple made me a perfunctory bow. His curtness to me as the representative of the Jasmyns would have been hurtful if I had any longer been capable of being hurt.

'He hasn't much chance, poor fellow. A pity! His mother tells me he's been wandering about with fever and headache for some days. It was only at noon today that he gave in and took to his bed. He seems exhausted and underfed. I understand he's been working at the Royal Free Hospital.'

'Reuben wants to be a doctor and practise here some day.'

'He'll find plenty of work in these parts if he pulls through.'

Dr. Staple spoke grimly. He was a slight, wiry young man. Burnside had brought him from a farm on the other side of the valley where a labourer had been seriously injured by the fall of a tree. He had been up all night and looked tired to death. It was evident he saw no charm in Betony. Dusk had robbed it of its changing colours, its enchanting steeps and hollows. The cottages, appearing fitfully through the acrid smoke and lit from time to time by a burst of flame, might have been habitants of the damned in an infernal region.

'The fact is, Miss Jasmyn, you've let the

place fester to death. It's a plague spot. Those heavy rains have washed effluent into the stream. The hillside reeks. It's a breeding place for flies in this sultry heat. Over the years a settlement like this is bound to pollute its own water. Still, there's one thing to be thankful for in a sorry business. We have Mrs. Masson. We're in a state of siege here and she has been used to sieges.' He went off to attend his other patients.

Of the tiny population of Betony ten people had contracted the disease, most of them young: it was the older ones who escaped. At that time the controversy as to the cause of both cholera and the enteric fevers still raged. But those who still believed like the earlier Jasmyns that fevers were spread by the air itself, had already lost ground to the followers of Dr. Snow, who reasoned that they were fly- and water-borne. Old Molly Buckle at Wheel Cottage blamed the wind, or lack of it.

'When it blows down from the Gib again with a nip in it, that'll take the pest away,' she said and in my heart I believed her, thinking of the purifying wind as a sign from heaven to watch and wait for.

But fortunately Dr. Staple and Susannah belonged to the other school of thought. It was by boiling all the water and milk that we limited the spread of the epidemic. Even so, nothing like it had been known in our part of the world since the cholera outbreak at Spandleby in 1842.

It was Susannah who knew how to construct makeshift filters from leaking buckets and charcoal until the newly patented ones could be got from Harrods. She knew how to save distilled water from under the kettle lid to give to Mrs. Cotton's twins. Somehow she contrived to bring order and cleanliness to the dreary homes where there were invalids, working tirelessly from dawn to dusk and sitting up with the worst cases night after night. She became my example. All that she did, I learned to do. Between us, with two of the sisters from St Agnes', we changed and burned foul linen, made cooling drinks and applied every device then known to ease the terrible headaches and coughing. At each door we hung a curtain soaked in carbolic to keep out flies and we stretched butter-muslin nets over the narrow windows, which had to be left open in the continuing heat. In a few days, even in hours, I had learned to emulate Susannah's quiet ministrations. The exacting rhythm of nursing came easily to me.

We had adopted a similar costume of a thin cotton gown and a huge enveloping holland overall with big pockets. With linen bands round our heads we looked almost as much alike as the sisters in their habits.

'You are early, Mrs. Masson,' Sister

Monica said as I went to relieve her at Tim Wagstaff's bedside one morning; then seeing her mistake, 'You are relatives, perhaps.'

'She was my nurse.'

'She has taught you her ways.'

We slept at the Hay on truckle beds brought over from the unused servants' rooms at the Hall. At first Susannah tried to insist on my going home and staying there.

'You must think of your situation, my dear, and of Mr. Jasmyn.'

'I shall stay here,' I said, 'until things are better or until I die.'

She smiled and shook her head; but for me there was no melodrama in it. The suspension of normal life was complete. Everything that had happened before seemed as trivial as a game of backgammon. Nothing that had seemed to matter, mattered at all. If only the sick could get well; if, above all, Reuben lived, there would never again be anything to wish for. Even in my happiest fantasies I had never dreamed that Reuben and I would marry: that was impossible. But our lives, I had thought, were bound together in a way that did not depend on circumstances. We could move about the earth in our separate spheres, each feeling the love and sympathy of the other, however distant, for as long as we lived.

Meanwhile as I fetched and carried for his mother and took turn and turn about with her in sitting by his bed, the belief never left me that if I expended every ounce of my strength on his behalf; if to the limit of my powers I atoned for any harm done to him by my family or myself, then he would be saved; until, as time carried us inexorably into the second week in July, the illusion that the old life had altogether ceased, itself faded. Dr. Staple spoke of complications. My obstinate confidence began to waver.

Susannah was taking one of her brief spells of rest in the farmhouse parlour. A couch, a rug and crockery made it already, for all its rough simplicity, a home. As a final touch, I had brought my fairing and set it on the mantelpiece. She watched me as I polished it with my handkerchief and moved it this way and that.

'You think me a perfect baby, don't you?'

'Yes.' She smiled. 'But it was as a baby, remember, that I knew you best and as a baby you *were* perfect.'

Sunlight gave a heightened gloss to the gentleman's black curls. Apart from his colouring he really was remarkably like the pictures of the late Prince Consort. With a pang of fear I remembered what His Royal Highness had died of.

'Have you ever known anyone who got better – of a fever like this?' I asked desperately.

'Yes,' she said. 'I did.'

I turned to her in astonishment and relief. 'Then there really is hope. And that explains something that puzzled me. Grand-mamma thought it was my mother who had been ill for weeks with a fever. She mis-understood what Mr. Hoggatt the surgeon told her, or perhaps his sunstroke had confused him.'

'She never did pay attention to other people.' For all her compassion, Susannah's dislike of my grandmother had not abated. 'And I never heard that Mr. Hoggatt had had sunstroke.' Then as if regretting her sharpness, she went on quickly, 'I was lucky enough to escape cholera and smallpox at Lucknow. It was while we were waiting to embark at Calcutta that I was struck down with a fever very like this. Mercifully I was over the worst by the time the *Indian Queen* docked. Otherwise the captain would not have taken me on board. But I was ill for most of the voyage. Mr. Hoggatt was a true friend. In the end it's constitution that counts. What else could have saved me?' Then she seemed to dismiss the episode. It was unusual for her to speak of herself. 'Wherever did you find that thing? I've never seen it at the Hall.'

'Reuben gave it to me.'

'He was your groom, wasn't he? I remem-ber the day he brought you home after the thunderstorm.'

'He wouldn't have been a groom if his family had not failed in their manufactory. He's very clever, you know.'

It was possible, in this time of extremity, to indulge in the rare pleasure of talking about him. I went to the window. In the presence of the quiet hills, the love and grief I felt for him were not eased, but purged of disquiet as though they passed into the structure of the place itself to become a living part of it.

'How strange!' I said. 'In spite of all the suffering, I have felt alive in a new way during these past weeks.'

Like a prisoner turning from daylight, I faced the dreariness of life without Reuben; and how short the daylight had been! On every meeting had lain the shadow of parting. Minute by minute the next parting was drawing nearer. A sudden clear understanding that this would be a parting of a different kind made me heedless of everything but the simple truth.

'If Reuben dies, I don't think I shall want to go on living.'

'Tessa!' Susannah had sat up and was looking at me with alarm. 'Are you telling me that you love Reuben Bateman? Do you mean to say... Are you not happy about your marriage?'

'Happy?'

I must have spoken wildly. She looked – more than startled, deeply dismayed.

'You don't love your cousin? Then why did you accept him? You could have refused. A woman is always free to refuse.'

'I suppose so.' For a moment I could not recall why a refusal had been impossible. 'But it's too late now. Ashton would never release me. It's all to do with the estate, the hateful property, and the name. If only I hadn't been born a Jasmyn! Why didn't you hide me from her, Susannah? Why didn't you keep me with you? You should have let me die in the Mutiny. I would rather have died.'

Her feeling for me must have been much deeper than I had ever imagined. She had got up from the couch and stood close by me while we talked, but gradually she drew back and sank down on a chair, her lips pallid. If a mortal blow had crushed her, she could not have bowed her head more hopelessly, lower and lower until it rested on the table. I actually thought she was dying and rushed to fetch a restorative from the medicine chest in the hall.

'You've been working much too hard, Susannah,' I said, reproaching myself for my hysterical outburst. 'Do please stay here tonight and rest.' She raised her head and drank the draught. I put a shawl round her shoulders but she refused further help. I was on the point of leaving when the scullery maid from the Hall appeared. She had been sent by Emma to remind me that Mr. Jasmyn would be arriving the next day and to ask for orders. I must go home.

Instinctively I went by way of the Batemans' and from the higher ground saw Dr. Staple leave one of the cottages and untether his cob as if ready to leave. To my surprise Susannah came running from the door of the Hay to intercept him. He produced a paper, pen and pocket ink-well and resting them on the garden wall, Susannah wrote quickly and handed him the folded paper and some coins. Tired as she was, she would spare no effort to help the poor souls she had befriended.

Mrs. Bateman was dozing in her chair by the window. For the hundredth time I crept upstairs to look through the door and persuade myself that the contortions of pain were less agonised, his colour more normal. He was lying still but his eyes were open. Many a time I had rehearsed what I would say if ever he looked at me again with understanding but now I could only say:

'Reuben. I'm here. Reuben.'

I fancied he recognised me, and felt an exquisite lightening of spirit that remained, when after a moment or two he closed his eyes.

'Mrs. Bateman. I believe – he looks better.'

I waited while she went upstairs and sensed, as she came slowly down again, that she was afraid to speak; that the fear came from new hope. We stood on the doorstep as we had done on the summer day when I first found shelter there; when we had seen Reuben in all his strength and vigour coming up the hill. He had lifted me as easily as if I were a child – as indeed I was: an ignorant, light-hearted child, unawakened until that day to any understanding of other people's needs. If he could live, there was nothing just then that I wanted for myself. It was the nearest I ever came to unselfishness.

Molly Buckle had brought a chair to her door. She had been sitting there in mob-cap and shawl since the outbreak of the epidemic. I had seen her late at night and early in the morning. For all I knew, she had taken root there, her dim eyes under the frill of her cap fixed ferociously on Gib Rake.

'Do you think it will be long, Mrs. Buckle?'

'We always have a nippy wind from the Gib between hay and harvest,' she said, without removing her gaze from the hill where the first patches of heather were coming into bloom. 'It'll mebbe come with the change of the moon.'

I lingered for a few minutes under her spell; but the distance was still blurred, the air heavy and thick.

'You'll be staying at home now, miss-ma'am.' Emma corrected her form of address but did not change the tone of firm persuasion she had used since I was a child. 'To have a rest and see to your hair and hands?' Somehow she converted the question into a command. 'Mr. Jasmyn won't want to see you looking like that. There's no need to remind you, I'm sure, what happens next Wednesday.'

Yet in a sense the reminder was necessary. To forget beleaguered Betony for a while and give my attention to my wedding and future husband required an effort of will almost beyond me. The conflicting demands of my two worlds were brought into sharp confrontation at that very moment by a loud knock at the front door and the simultaneous appearance of Steadman from the back of the house.

'A message from Mrs. Masson, miss, to say that Reuben Bateman has taken a slight turn for the better.'

In my relief and gratitude, in the revival of pure happiness, I was unaware of what Emma and the cab-driver were doing as they lugged a great box into the hall; until Emma said with a smirk of pleasure:

'It's your wedding-dress, miss. It's come. There now, I haven't seen you looking so happy for weeks.'

21

By the time Ashton arrived my appearance
must have changed.

'You're like a ghost, Tessa.' He kissed me
uneasily. 'You haven't been going into any of
the houses over there, have you?' Avoiding a
direct answer I made some remark about
the suffering. 'Yes, indeed. A thoroughly bad
business. I called to see Packby on the way
here and we agreed that it must be kept out
of the newspapers. There's a fellow on the
Maresbarrow Gazette, a thorough Radical.
When he gets hold of the story, he'll make a
scandal of it. The annoying thing is that by
next summer those cottages would have
been cleared. The legal side is going to be
slow but Packby is willing to go forward
with the quarrying on the security of some
of the property until we can lay hands on
the capital. I thought of Roper Farm. What
do you think?'

We faced each other that evening at dinner
with the length of the table between us and
Mrs. Arrow halfway down to nod sympathetically while he enlarged on the future
of Betony. Some day I must exert myself.
Somehow, if I could not manage the estate

myself, I must learn to manage Ashton: but in my heart, listening with a dreary sense of the distance that separated us, I knew that he was too strong for me. I had escaped one form of tyranny only to face another; and how much longer it would be!

'We must do something for Becky Porter,' I said abruptly, 'and I'm afraid Tim Wagstaff may be homeless too. You don't know yet: his father died yesterday.'

'Poor fellow! But you mustn't involve yourself personally with these people's problems.'

'I feel so much involved,' I said, rising, 'that Betony will haunt me to my dying day.'

'You're exaggerating, my dear.' He looked uncomfortable. 'Epidemics of this sort are not unusual in the kind of weather we've been having. You might say they're a feature of country life; a regrettable one. We'll find good homes for your orphans,' he spoke as if they were kittens, 'and you can send soup and jellies and so on. But keep away from the place. I should have a good night if I were you. You look fagged out. By the way, this is a rum thing, Mrs. Masson turning up again. But she's making herself useful. Steadman has been telling me…'

'How fortunate it is,' Mrs. Arrow observed when Ashton had gone off for a stroll round the out-buildings, 'that Mr. Jasmyn takes such a practical interest in the estate. I really don't know what you would have done without him. He will be master of Barmote in the true sense of the word.'

I left her to her tranquil crocheting and with the intention of taking Ashton's advice, went to my room. The fire was laid. I put a match to it and watched the flames rise. It was still daylight – we had dined early – but despite the warm windless weather, the house was cool. I went to close the window, and caught the scent of Ashton's cigar from the terrace below. Peeping out, I saw the top of his fair head, then his whole figure as he sauntered up the steep path as far as the gate opening on the park: the master of Barmote at home, at ease. He had waited a long time and now the waiting was almost over. In spite of his narrowness, he was a good man; and good or bad, soon we would be man and wife, one flesh for the rest of our mortal days.

And as I watched him, the course of my life changed. Its current ceased, or was checked for a terrifying moment as if seeking another direction in which to flow; seeking and finding it, with the rush of pent-up water freed. For I could not do it. I could not marry him. Nothing in heaven or on earth could make me. No matter how sacred the promises I had made, how binding the legal contract, how just my moral obligation to Ashton, I could not, would not do it. If it was blasphemy to break a promise made in the sight of God, then God must be mocked. But I understood at last that the promise had nothing to do with God.

Twice before I had gathered all my spiritual strength in a longing to escape: once I had brought down a thunderbolt; once I had killed my grandmother; experiences which had taught me not to tempt Providence again for fear of a third disaster infinitely worse. But no threat of disaster could stop me now. Whatever happened, I must free myself before it was too late.

With the new confidence came a marvellous exhilaration like an intake of new life. It demanded movement. I pulled the pins from my hair and shook it out, stood on tiptoe and stretched my arms so that they almost touched the bed-canopy, flung open the wardrobe, and saw my wedding-dress, alone in its separate compartment: and that was a mistake.

White, still perfect, it had so strong an identity, so assured an existence, that my mood changed. I came down to earth. I knew what I would not do; but what, instead, remained to be done? I must tell him. Just to anticipate the agonising embarrassment of it made me hot, feverish, ill. I would be very ill. I would have the fever. Perhaps I had it already. My marriage would be postponed. I would die. A vision of death like the inner darkness of the well brought a brief comfort, soon to pass. The subterfuges were contemptible. As if from above, I observed my shallow manoeuvres, knowing that they would not do. I must tell him.

I pushed open the window again. What better time than now – at once? Ashton was still there but he had gone through the gate. He seemed to be looking with some intentness towards the nearest tree. Its heavy foliage cast a deep shadow. The sun was low. I thought Ashton spoke, then could not be certain whether he moved first into the shadow or whether someone came towards him: but there was someone; a woman. I could see no more than the shape of her dress. They melted away between shadow and light. For the time being, my opportunity was gone. In my excited state I felt no curiosity as to who the woman was, but some inner prompting brought Susannah to my mind. She was taking the air, no doubt, before going to bed.

I went to close the wardrobe and found the dress caught in the door. In disentangling the floating gauze, I found the unopened parcel, a miserable reminder of the awkwardness to come; and dropped it like a hot coal on the ottoman by the fire. It would have to be acknowledged and returned with the other gifts. There must be yet another announcement in the *Morning Post*. But these were the least of my problems.

The enforced delay in speaking to Ashton had shaken my purpose. Would it not be wiser and kinder to wait until morning? A few hours could scarcely matter when a man's entire life was to be so cruelly altered. Yet fear that I would weaken made me long to tell him and have done with it. I wavered and was inspired. Since the arguments in favour of delay exactly balanced those in favour of instant action, I would refer the decision to Chance.

I went softly down to the sitting room and took from the chiffonier the dice we had used for backgammon. Odds, I would tell him now, at once. Evens, I would wait till the morning. Shakily I threw a double six and almost gasped with relief, having scarcely gathered up the dice when Ashton came into the room.

'Tessa, I wanted to see you.' He spoke absently. His face was flushed, not with brandy as I first thought, but with agitation. 'Tessa, my dear.' He took my hand, then dropped it as if he had been mistaken as to what it was. Certain facial movements suggested that he was bracing himself to impart some unpleasantness. With admirable resolution he imparted it at once. 'I have sometimes felt that the thought of our marriage was – shall I say – distasteful to you. You have never been enthusiastic about it.'

Seized by an extraordinary prescience, I waited.

'There is a good deal of difference in our ages. It occurs to me – it has often occurred to me – that I may not be the man to make you happy. Oh, I know this is not the time. It must seem to you base and unforgiving to say it now. You have your dress. There are the wedding gifts. But – in short – it is better now than later...'

I liked him too well not to pity him. Who better placed than I to appreciate his acute embarrassment in the very dilemma from which he had so unexpectedly rescued me?

'You're a good child, Tessa. It makes me unhappy to see you standing there so submissively. You have been too much put upon, I believe. But taking everything into account, I ask you to respect my judgment. It would be better, I'm sure, to break off our engagement now than to marry and regret it.'

Having crossed this first most difficult hurdle, he moistened his lips and looked away over my head with the pardonable relief of a man who has not been found lacking in courage. From my hopeless astonishment and confusion one unmistakable fact emerged.

'You do understand, Ashton, of course, that grandmamma left everything to me.' For a second, and unaccountably, since

Ashton was behaving for once entirely without self-interest, I was struck as never before by his resemblance to Rodney Jasmyn. 'I thought you … looked forward to sharing the property.'

'I did. To be candid, I have looked forward to it for years.' His discomfort could have been no greater if he had been drowning: a situation in which subterfuge would be impossible; and yet the word 'candid' struck a false note: or rather, it drew my attention to all that Ashton was leaving undisclosed. Waiting for Barmote Hall had been the chief, the only motive of his existence. He was now not far from middle life. What unimaginable circumstance could have produced in him this sudden change of heart?

My silence alarmed and distressed him.

'Believe me, Tessa, were it not that I believe this to be the best – the only course – I would be bitterly ashamed of causing you so much humiliation – especially…' Here some invisible barrier halted him. He left the sentence unfinished. 'I shall always acknowledge – be keenly aware of my obligation – or at least my desire – to look after you in whatever way is suitable. You are very young to learn how uncertain life can be; how strangely unpredictable. Even I…' His generalisation brought him again to the invisible barrier and he lapsed more agreeably into genuine warmth of feeling. 'My poor child. Dear little Tessa. I don't know what will become of you. I shall always...'

At this point I rescued him. Thanks to the brief but concentrated rehearsal in my room, I was able to behave perfectly. It was simply a question of reversing the roles. Ashton had taken my part. I assumed his, bringing to it all the tact and understanding I had scarcely hoped to find in him.

'I'm sorry for your distress, Ashton. You mustn't feel anxious about me.' Appreciation of that part of him that had been truly kind brought, most appropriately, tears to my eyes, and he looked more wretched than ever. I slipped the ring from my finger.

'I – I absolve you from your promise – and I wish you very well, Ashton dear.'

'No, no.' He put the ring aside. 'You must keep it, please, as a token of our long...' He seemed to have difficulty in supplying a word for our curious relationship. 'Besides, you may ... your future...'

The barriers raised themselves thick and fast. No thought that occurred to him seemed capable of full expression except the one that had set me, unbelievably, free of him.

He got himself away at last. Bereft of all hope of becoming lord of the manor, did he look in some way diminished? Or having acted with scrupulous honour, did he bear upon his brow some new touch of nobility? In one way or another and in the short space of an hour he had either changed his nature or – I had learned the Jasmyn trick of calculation – his plans. The change puzzled and worried me as when so often I had seen in the continual interplay of light and shade some feature of the landscape alter: a rock move, a hill become a cloud.

It was too soon to be happy. The sudden reversal of fortune left me perversely despondent and lonely. It was not long before I discovered the cause of Ashton's heroic renunciation: my own unsuitability as a wife. It outweighed all my material advantages. Even the simile of the white mouse was nothing to this humiliation, and for all my dignified behaviour, I had conducted the most important interview of my life with my hair (the discovery made me cringe) hanging down my back, like a child.

From the exhausting emotions of the day I found relief in tears and recovering a little, congratulated myself on at least not having broken my solemn promise. I had always been extraordinarily lucky with the dice.

The servants had gone to bed. I took a candle from the hall table and lit it. As the flame flickered and steadied, I hesitated, reluctant to go upstairs, until I became aware that on the brink of my tiny pool of light they had gathered again to watch me as they had watched me from the days of my infancy, the enigmatic faces in the porcelain vases, the cold-eyed parakeets, the motionless girls in the yellow garden. The house was theirs. How could my grandmother have imagined that it would ever belong to me? Night after night, year after year, they would be there to watch me take my candle and go to bed alone. They would see, as the slow days passed how, moment by moment, a girl could fade and gutter out: how one black-skirted woman with a chatelaine at her waist could be replaced by another, exactly the same.

As I retreated up the staircase, the antlers on the wall reached forward in the passing candlelight; on the half-landing the lustre of the jade pieces warmed to yellow and paled again. My grandmother's door stood open. With an effort of will I glanced into the silent darkness of her room and reached my own in safety. I mended the fire and watched the light burnish the looking-glass, the satinwood box, the panels of the wardrobe. Now that I would never wear it, I felt a kind of compassion for my wedding-dress and passed my hand not so much regretfully as pityingly over its soft folds, its myriad puffs and ribbon knots and bows. And all the while I was conscious of filling in time, of waiting, as though the crisis of my life lay, not behind me, but ahead: as though the parting from Ashton, overwhelming as it had been, were no more than the first movement of a straw in the path of a hurricane: as though, close at hand, here in the firelit room perhaps, there loomed some huge catastrophe.

As I drew the ottoman to the fire, my hand touched the unopened parcel. For the first time I felt some curiosity as to its sender. Our presents had come from family connections and from Ashton's friends, some few from tenants. I took scissors from my workbox and cut the string, to find inside a letter, and a strongly made box containing an oval object wrapped in soft paper. It was no inkling of what it could be that roused my uneasiness but the sight of Colonel Darlington's handwriting, reminding me of all the unpleasantness surrounding his visit.

Dear Tessa,
You must have wondered at my long silence. I am still recovering from a bout of illness which has laid me up for almost a year. The announcement of your wedding in the Morning Post *has roused me to a sense of neglect. I was shocked to see the reference to the late Mrs. Jasmyn...* [He went on to express condolences.] *The gift will not come as a surprise to you: nor must you thank me as I am not the giver, only the instrument...*

The Colonel's assumption that I would not be surprised was at a piece with the rest of his inexplicable behaviour. I unwrapped the gift and looked at it without in the least comprehending why he had sent it. So profound a sense of mystery did it rouse in me that it seemed more than a material object: a token or fetish from some altogether different world. I had long felt that there lay, touching the frontiers of my own narrow existence, a darker region of unexplained circumstances as obscure to me as the deepening night outside. From that region the Colonel's gift had come.

I read the letter again, right through to the end; and I was terribly afraid, as lost and lonely as a spirit might be, having left the body and found no other resting place.

I leaned forward, staring into the fire: but it was not the caverns and palaces in its glowing heart that I saw. A door, long closed, had swung open with a crash, to reveal a room at an inn at Gravesend and I gazed in, appalled, and with almost unbearable pain, at the evil thing enacted there.

22

The scene in that dingy upstairs room on the afternoon of a day in August in 1858 had been presented to me at first as a magical event, its details as simple and significant as those of a fairy tale: the journey by post-chaise from Barmote: the narrow stair: the child alone in the room 'like a flower' among the cushions: the instant miraculous sense of recognition. Even when the colours and pictures began to change, to become blurred and contradictory, they had never faded into the drab light of reality. For years it had seemed a rapturous experience involving only the two of us, grandmamma and me.

To introduce Susannah into the scene had been difficult: impossible. In so far as I had imagined her there at all, she had appeared erratically, undergoing constant changes: a spiritless drudge, a homely nurse, Mrs. Masson in an amber or heliotrope gown, sombrely watching my grandmother.

Now, my wits sharpened by desperation, I tried to see the incident more clearly. It was Hoggatt the surgeon who had taken my grandmother upstairs. That could not have taken long: yet in the short space of a few minutes she had found him to be confused by sunstroke, whereas Susannah, who had known him well for months, claimed to know nothing of his affliction.

The room was empty except for myself. 'You held out your arms...' It must have been touching, a mystic sign of kinship. But was it true? Or was this one of the many things my grandmother had made herself believe because she wanted to believe it? The answer could never be known. Susannah had not been there. She had taken Kate into the bedroom; not the Kate I knew but a sickly emaciated infant struggling to breathe: a child given up for dead more than once. My grandmother had never mentioned the nurse's child.

I knew no more, except that she had snatched me away, giving no time for a tender leavetaking. That – even allowing for Susannah's prejudice and for the terrible doubts now troubling my thoughts of her – I could believe: not only because my grandmother had admitted to having ignored the nurse but because her dark, swooping figure had imprinted itself upon my mind long before I identified it; and because she wanted me so much, 'the little fair creature' in whom the lifeblood of the Barmote Jasmyns had been against all likelihood preserved.

Poor grandmamma! As she rose in

memory before me, my attempts at sober thinking floundered. I could only feel a trembling bewilderment as if I had come again from the warmth of the womb into the cold tumult of an unwelcoming world. Even then I would have cast the Colonel's gift away and closed my mind to all its implications, had it not been for the extraordinary change in Ashton. It convinced me that the truth I was just beginning to grasp was already known to him. Susannah herself must have told him, just before he had come to extricate himself from so unexpected a difficulty.

Firelight fell on the Colonel's letter and on the gift. It was a likeness in water-colour in a gilded frame.

'It is Alice to the life,' he wrote. *'A speaking likeness.'*

She wore a low cut green gown – the florentine, no doubt – and at her throat a pendant of some sort: a red stone. With a pang of sadness I looked at the lost ruby. And how lovely a face it was in its symmetry and softness, with its delicate dark brows and fine features! It was indeed a speaking likeness. Except that she wore her dark hair looped over her cheeks: except that she looked older as if her expression, in the flesh so full of vivacity, had been caught and fixed in an unchanging stillness, it was a speaking likeness – of Kate.

You are so like your mother [the Colonel wrote] *that when I saw you at your easel on the occasion of our happy meeting in Barmote churchyard, I might have been seeing Alice herself: her eyes, her mouth: only you were quieter. Thinking it over, I regretted having talked so much. Forgive a sentimental old man. You were kind enough to ask me to keep the likeness since I treasured it so much; but now you must have it and your mother's wish will be fulfilled at last...*

The gift was Kate's, not mine. Sick and shivering, I reached for the shawl on the nearest chair: Kate's shawl, her chair, her room, her house, her inheritance. Kate was not only cleverer than I, clever enough to see at once the significance of her meeting with the Colonel: she was nobler too. She had gone away in silence, leaving it all to me, an impostor. I saw myself reduced to a homeless figure in white, pale-faced as a spirit, wailing and protesting, 'I'm Tessa, Tessa Jasmyn,' the syllables as sad and hollow as fading cuckoo notes. Instinct and reason told me that if Kate was Alice Jasmyn's daughter, then I was Susannah's: but I could feel no certainty or comfort; only a shrinking dread of my new identity. I longed to be reassured that I was at least still Tessa: that it was in both senses my first name: my own if nothing else was mine.

It may have been a similar longing for reassurance, or the sheer inability to be active in any other way that drew me from my room into the corridor, then to the drawing room, and so to every other unused room in the house except my grandmother's. Quietly opening doors and holding up my candle, I looked with a curious painstaking anxiety at all the assembled host of possessions, one by one. The careful tread learned in childhood took me soundlessly between chairs and tables, glass cases and cabinets, past the still surprisingly motionless hooves of the gilded chair from the palace of Ranjit Singh, over the elephants perched absurdly on their coronets in the sitting room carpet and brought me at last to the hall.

It was there that the change struck me: not a change in the vases, gongs, pictures, swords, but in my way of seeing them. I was aware of a fellow-feeling. They too were there against their will, exiles, as out of place in the house as I was. The sad faces on the vases, the weary girls in the yellow garden, seemed infinitely pathetic. Nerving myself, I went and looked at the bronze figures and found them writhing without hope like the damned. There would be no release for them. Kate would let in a fresh gust of wind and sweep them up to imprisonment in the attics. But for me…?

The clock in Rodney Jasmyn's tower stuck midnight. At each thin stroke the air trembled; with fear or hope? It was the hour of transformations. Was it possible then to become another person? To break the mould and be free?

Day was breaking over Long How when I came down to Betony. The casements of the stricken cottages still glowed with candle and firelight. Through the Wagstaffs' kitchen window I watched Susannah leaning over the bed by the wall. She saw me and came out.

We sat down on the bench under the window. She pulled the linen band from her head. Her hair fell lank and matted over her brow. She was hollow-cheeked, heavy-eyed as she must have been when she came home from India, widowed and wasted with fever.

'You've seen him, Mr. Jasmyn?'

Her level tone conveyed a hopeless weariness such as she must have known then. I nodded.

'He wanted to end our engagement.'

'I felt sure that he would release you when he heard what I had to tell him. I've telegraphed for Kate to come.' I saw that she was desperately nervous. 'When she comes, I shall have something to tell you both. Both of you.'

'There's no need. I know. You were my mother, weren't you?' In the painful necessity of actually putting the truth into words, I had no thought for her feelings. The choice of tense expressed my view of our relationship exactly. I handed her the letter and the likeness. 'Kate has known for a long time.'

Had I been older and wiser, I would surely have spoken more gently. As it was her look of sudden illness frightened me. With what must have been an enormous effort of will she conquered it and read the letter; but as she looked at the likeness, tears rolled down her cheeks.

'Alice Jasmyn,' she whispered. 'Forgive me.' Then to me, 'I dread telling Kate. She'll never understand. She'll forgive me but she won't understand how it happened. Perhaps you...'

She paused, discouraged by my silence.

'You see the path up there through the rowans?'

It was not yet light enough to see but I knew the way from Betony Hay to the carriage road.

'I used to go up there and watch them, the gentlefolk in their carriages turning in at the Lodge gates, and especially her when she came there as a bride. It wasn't envy I felt. Their settled easy way of life was too far beyond me. It was more like a vision, or a play to watch and have no part in. Then years later when she drove up to the inn at Gravesend, it was the same. I watched the flurry and fuss from the upstairs window and saw her get down. It was like watching the play again. She looked confident, strong, rich; and then I did envy her.'

Envy had burned in her, the first feeling she had known for months.

'I was like a dead thing. A woman had died on the voyage. Oh, there was more than one: but she left a baby alone in the world. Nothing seemed more likely than that I would die; except that Kate would die and you would be left. We'd come from a world of death.'

In the growing light the trees and bracken were green again. Under the willows the poisoned stream was treacherously bright. She was so tired that her voice only just served her. It was cracked and dry.

'Well, I took Kate into the bedroom next door to sponge her face and try to revive her a little. I left you in the armchair. Mr. Hoggatt brought her upstairs. It wasn't until the sitting room door opened that it dawned on me what would happen. She was expecting to see her grandchild. She would see you first. You were,' she put out her hand to touch mine then drew it back, 'irresistible. "This is little Tessa", he said.'

'"A lovely child," he said. "Wonderful when you consider that her mother was ill

303

for weeks of a fever." Then he lowered his voice but I heard him say, "Nurse is attending to the other little girl. She is dying, I'm afraid, Mrs. Jasmyn. There's no hope. I'm sorry." He went away. "My love," I heard her say, "my beautiful child." "It's happened," I thought, "exactly as if Fate had planned it, not I, as if I were helpless." In a second (I was hardly in my right mind) I saw all the misery of my childhood made up for by your happiness. I felt an insane pride that my child was so much more winning than any Jasmyn could be. You know, I had lost a baby out there, a boy. That makes a woman feel guilty. More than anything else I wanted you to be safe. The whole future came before me in a clear bright light. Kate would die. I would die. You would live, safe, rich, loved.'

'Yes. That part came true. She loved me.'

'Her first words when I went into the room were, "She knows me already. I thank God for the miraculous gift of this child." You reached up and tugged at her bonnet strings. She cried. She wasn't then as she was later. I had no doubt that she would love you; but I didn't dream ... I should have known.'

'Poor grandmamma!' It was difficult to speak. A stubborn reticence had kept me until then almost silent. But an unexpectedly consoling thought made me burst into speech. 'I have worried so much since she died. You know, it was I … I upset her and it caused her death. But now I see – and it's such a relief – that it was better for her to die than to know that all her hopes were based on a – mistake. In an way I saved her from knowing.'

The relief was such that I felt the blood rush to my face. Susannah was looking at me so attentively that she scarcely seemed to breathe. Her stillness was absolute, as if all her faculties were concentrated in listening and watching.

'It makes you feel happier – to think of it like that?' she said at last.

'Oh, yes, yes. Just think, if she had known…'

So close had been our interdependence, so overpowering her influence, that I actually lowered my voice, seized with the irrational dread that she would hear and learn that her love had been lavished on a servant's child.

'Dear grandmamma!'

Was it surprising that I forgot the circumstances which had made her, at the end, so much less than dear: that I clung to the memory of the secure old days at the Hall?

Susannah looked at me steadily.

'She was not your grandmother.'

So deep, so far beyond reason had been my closeness to her that it was quite impossible for me to grasp just then, or indeed ever after, that we had been in no way connected: that she was Kate's grand-mother, not mine.

'No, of course not,' I said doubtfully. 'You were telling me...'

She seemed unwilling to go on and when she did speak, it was with a resentment she had not yet shown.

'She was so unfeeling. "I shall be leaving at once," she said, and when I said something about having packed, "No," she said, "I want nothing, only the child." She pushed money into my hand. Fifty pounds. I put it into the poor-box of the nearest church. She didn't even let me hold you or kiss you goodbye. It was like tearing the heart out of my body to let you go.'

'And no one knew?'

'Mr. Hoggatt knew. He came upstairs after she had gone. He was aghast. "It isn't too late to put things right," he said. "I'll go after her myself." He was a good man, so used to suffering that he didn't judge me. "She'll be far better with her," I said. "It was a mistake that was ordained. A thing that's heaven-sent can't be a sin." And later when I heard of your engagement, I thought it justified what I had done. In the sight of Heaven you would actually become a Jasmyn. "And what about this one?" Mr. Hoggatt said. I still had Kate in my arms. "I'll care for her as if she was my own," I said. But gradually, as she began to thrive, I

306

realised how I had betrayed her dear mother and robbed Kate herself. She was Alice Kate but I took to calling her Kate after that so that I wouldn't be reminded.'

'Kate might not have lived if she had come here instead of me.' Warming at last to her need for comfort, I searched for consolation. 'No one would have nursed her as you did.'

And no one knew better than I how easily a frail child might have succumbed to the hardships I had survived.

'That's true. What strength I had was spent on her – and later, things were easier. But you'll always feel I wronged you; that I gave you away. You'll never think of me as your mother.'

I could not deny it.

'Would you ever have told if it had not been to save me from marrying Ashton?'

'Never. I thought I had drunk my cup to the dregs until yesterday when you said, "If only I hadn't been born a Jasmyn". That was my punishment for letting you go; to know that nothing had been gained, everything lost.'

She smoothed the linen band in her lap and put back her uncombed hair with an instinctive gesture that recalled to me – faint and distant – the elegant person of Mrs. Masson in one of her impeccable gowns and exquisite hats, her carefully modulated voice taking on only rarely a deeper tone as when she said, 'Yes, I have a beautiful daughter... There is nothing one would not do for a daughter. No risk one would not take, no hardship one would not endure...' with the tenderness she could not conceal. The pride and pain had been for me, not Kate; and how she must have suffered in coming to the Hall, from her first visit to her last!

The cruel daylight did not spare her sallowness, her greying hair; it showed every crease in her anxious brow. I took her hand. We watched the sky turn blue and the hills take shape as she must have done long ago when she came to the well with her wooden yoke, before ever she set out on the adventurous road which had brought her back at last to her starting-point. The sympathy I had felt for the small Susannah would grow perhaps as she herself had grown into the strong, self-contained, deeply loving woman at my side.

In one of the gardens a cock crowed. The morning air was cold. A sharp breeze brought down the scent of heather from Gib Rake and set the trees in motion: and more than the trees. In the porch of Wheel Cottage a still figure stirred and came to life. Molly Buckle got up from her chair, went in and closed the door, her long vigil ended. The cleansing wind blew down from the hills and changed the sky.

23

When I came out of Gib Cottage, Reuben was waiting. He took my basket and offered his arm. We walked through the rustling leaves, spinning out the distance and the time.

'She must miss you now that you've moved into the Hay,' Reuben observed.

'Aunt Abbie? She pretends to miss us, but now that she's alone again, she has more time for the cards. The Queens don't trouble her any longer but I'm afraid there's no doubt that you're going back to London tomorrow, Reuben. Aunt Abbie has turned up a departure three times. I saw it myself.'

'Then I've no choice.'

His face was tanned again after long days of leisure in the open air but the look of delicacy had not left him.

'Dear Reuben, are you sure you're well enough...?'

'Quite sure. Just this last week I've felt a difference as if my feet were firm on the ground again. Only it's today I'm going, Tessa, by the evening train from Spandleby. I've wasted so much time.'

We drew closer, walking very slowly

between the autumn hedgerows until we came to the lych-gate.

'But it won't be for so long this time,' I said. 'We shall be coming up to London for a visit and you'll come home every summer to see your mother.' We went through the gate and sat down on the bench by the wall. 'But I had hoped for just another day.'

'It's in the cards,' Reuben said, 'I'm bound to go. Only,' he paused, 'Miss Cade isn't always right. Didn't she say that you were to be married?'

'Perhaps I shall be some day.'

With sudden exhilaration I discovered the joy of looking forward, even though time, which had seemed always to be rushing me on to a future I dreaded, would now begin to drag. But I looked down with suitable decorum at the toes of my leather boots.

'In a few years' time I shall be thinking of marrying,' Reuben said, 'if I can find a suitable wife.'

'Suitable!' I exclaimed in alarm.

'As a doctor I shall want a wife worthy of my station in life. It won't be easy to find one in these parts.'

'My father was no common soldier,' I said. 'He was a pay-sergeant in Her Majesty's Indian Army as well you know, Reuben Bateman.'

'But your mother was in service, Tessa Drew.' He looked down at me, smiling. 'Still,

310

it was good service. It isn't everyone who is lucky enough to work for the Jasmyns.'

He grew serious and spoke of my mother's generosity. She had persuaded him to accept a small loan to pay for his board and books; and she had found him lodgings with a former servant who had married a pastry-cook in Holborn. The couple were famous for their mutton pies and would feed him well. As Reuben said, men had advanced in the world by even more dubious means.

'When I've saved enough to set up on my own, I shall settle here at Betony. Will you wait for me, Tessa? I've loved you for seven years and more. Will you wait?'

'I love you, Reuben, and I don't know how I shall live without you. There's nowhere else in the world I want to live. After all I'm a Cade of sorts and Betony is in my bones as well as in yours.'

'But?' He sensed the reservation almost before I was aware of it.

'I never want to promise again – and I don't want to be loved too much.'

'You think it was pining for love that brought me to death's door?'

'No, of course not; and it wasn't love that kept me watching by your bed day and night either. But people can love too much. They impose their love on others.'

'That isn't love,' Reuben said. 'Whether I'm here or in London, every stone, every blade of grass, everything I see is bound up with my thoughts of you. You're with me wherever I go. But if I loved you too much, I wouldn't be going away.'

We had talked so much of the past that there was nothing left to say. We talked for a while of the future, and for a while not at all. The sun was warm on our faces and on the resting places of the other Batemans and Cades. Beyond the two un-named and greening mounds where Tim's parents lay, the eye was irresistibly drawn to another memorial: a draped urn of dark polished marble and fine proportions: tribute to an exemplary life. Having rested upon it for a moment, the gaze, I found, turned with relief to other things: jackdaws on the tower: the crimson hips and purple bramble leaves sprawling on the low, weathered wall. But the dark shape prevailed. I took Reuben by the hand and drew him to his feet.

'Some day we'll go to Barmote Fair,' he said. Then we sauntered along the lane like real country people until we came to the narrow way between the stone walls and so to the gap above Betony. There we kissed and said goodbye and in the sudden anguish of parting I forgot my dislike of promises and promised with all my heart to wait for him for ever if need be. I watched him out of sight, then dried my eyes and went over the hill to call on Kate.

It was some time since I had seen her. The alterations to Betony Hay and our removal there had occupied much of my time since the summer: the rest had been spent with Reuben. Moreover Kate was not regularly or officially in residence at the Hall. The legal complexities of her unusual situation dragged on. 'A detestable business,' Mr. Pawley called it. He was looking, according to Burnside, greatly aged by the affair. Not that there was any rival claimant to the Jasmyn property. Colonel Darlington's testimony had been corroborated by that of old Mr. Hoggatt, now a ship's chandler at Gravesend. Together, with the evidence of the likeness, they had supported Susannah's story. Since I had never succeeded to the possession of the property, no transfer of ownership was necessary. But there was much talk of affidavits and the wording of the will proved a stumbling block. Nevertheless Kate contrived to spend a good deal of time at the Hall. It was, as she said, hers.

More than once I had spoken of her marvellous unselfishness in going away without claiming her inheritance. Her face would cloud a little.

'Yes, it was marvellous,' she said once. 'I felt uplifted and almost saintly. But I could never do it again. It was only because I didn't know what I was giving up. In those circumstances it seemed right to go. But

313

now that circumstances have changed, it seems right to take what is mine. And yet surely, Tessa, whether a thing is right or wrong shouldn't depend on circumstances?'

My own confusion at the time as to what was right or wrong, true or false, prevented me from offering any guidance.

She received me warmly. I had expected to see changes but not the particular change that confronted me the instant I stepped into the hall.

'You've put it back!' I exclaimed as the tiger and I resumed our old antagonism.

Kate looked embarrassed.

'I found it in the attic. It seemed rather a shame. Don't you think after all it looks – right?' and before I could reply, 'I do wish, Tessa, you would take your dresses away. They positively haunt me.'

'I've told you, Kate dear, that I can't take anything.'

It was possible to be high-minded in the matter because the clothes I was wearing were so becoming. Life at the Hay, we had decided, was to be gracious but unpretentious. My skirt, looped up over a blue and brown striped petticoat of finest merino seemed to me to strike exactly the note of unassuming gentility our situation required.

'There is no need,' mother was fond of saying, 'for simple clothes to be inelegant. Boots must be well-fitting, of course.'

She had found an excellent bootmaker in Maresbarrow. Our feet were exactly of a size. In retrospect, I am not sure that our shared interest in dress did not bring us more rapidly into harmony and enable me more sincerely to forgive her than all my earnest prayers.

My trousseau had been happily disposed of to a client of Mme. Ballard, a young lady going out to India to be married and anxious to sail as soon as possible.

Knowing that Kate had plans for opening up the drawing room, I moved towards the stairs.

'No, not there. I've been using the sitting room. It's more comfortable. For some reason there's always a wind blowing upstairs. Did you ever notice that? I rather like this room.'

She motioned me to my old place and sat down in the crimson velvet chair by the round table.

'I've been looking through papers. There seem to be so many bills.' She had been puzzling over an account from the Maresbarrow Water Company. Her appearance was subdued. She had anxiously considered whether or not to wear mourning and in the end had decided against it; but her dress had in general a toned-down air. She looked – and I was sorry for it – a trifle harassed. 'Cousin Ashton thinks these water charges unnecessarily high.'

'Ashton? Has he been here?'

'We met in London entirely by chance. He was exceedingly kind and offered to help me in any way possible. We have corresponded.'

Her involuntary glance towards the mantelpiece drew my attention to an envelope propped against the clock. 'I have seen quite a different side to his nature; and he is so practical. As a matter of fact he has helped me to find new tenants for the Lodge. It isn't easy as you know and I didn't want it standing empty for another winter.'

Ashton had behaved impeccably. After one furious outburst when my mother had first placed the facts before him, he had exercised an extraordinary restraint, accepting them without recrimination.

'Some people,' I remember saying confidentially to Reuben, 'might have threatened to take legal action. After all, it was a serious crime, I believe.'

'He may have seen another way of going about things,' Reuben said, 'and as for the crime, as you call it, there could be two ways of looking at that,' and he would be drawn no further.

'As Cousin Ashton pointed out, being a trustee, he has an intimate knowledge of family affairs,' Kate said. 'He has offered to come down to Barmote.'

'That was kind.'

It was perhaps more than kind. Despite her recent experience, Kate was too candid and open to suspect that people were not always what they seemed. Whatever my upbringing had failed to do, it had taught me guile; and if, a short time after, I too took advantage of her innocence, there was good reason for it; for I saw at once the danger of Ashton's coming to Barmote and calling, as he certainly would, on his friend Packby. The threat to Betony loomed nearer.

Presently Kate brought out the jewel cases.

'I want you to take something, Tessa dear. You must have a favourite piece.'

She laid them on the tablecloth, handling them already, I thought, with the pride of ownership: the seed pearls: the jade comb: the gold half-moon set with jargoons...

'This was my favourite.'

'Oh, yes. Do have it,' she said with a little too much promptness and enthusiasm. Her expression was guarded. I laid the necklace down.

'Isn't it a pity,' she said, and with just a trifle more peevishness the words would have had a familiar ring, 'that the ruby should have disappeared?'

If it had remained at Barmote, how different my history might have been! It had been sent out to Alice Jasmyn in a spirit of bitterness that never abated. I can see that

317

now; but then I was less enlightened: my picture of the incident at Gravesend still lacked one significant brush-stroke.

At any rate there the ruby was in the likeness, which Kate had set up on the mantelpiece. We would neither of us ever have a nearer view of it. It lay on Alice Jasmyn's bosom like a drop of blood, symbolising some rare and precious quality which, in the sad tangle of our lives, both Kate and I had lost. Yet I found in Alice Jasmyn's face a gentle but unwavering tenacity. Against all odds, she had had her way. The great wave that broke over Lucknow, carrying so much away, had spared the fragile thing of watercolour and gilt for her daughter to see; and Barmote was hers and hers alone; at least for a time.

The resemblance between the face in the frame and the face at the other side of the table seemed to me now less striking. The tranquillity on Alice's brow was not to be seen on Kate's.

I put the jargoons back in their case and pursued my own purposes.'

'Believe me, Kate, I would rather not have any of the jewellery or anything of value. As it is, I feel – surely you must understand – that I have occupied your place unjustly all these years and used your things all my life. It would be painful to me to take away any reminder of it.'

'It wasn't your fault.' She spoke with all her old warmth; but she closed the jewel cases and if I was mistaken in detecting relief in her manner, there was certainly no regret. 'But for you to have nothing – that is unjust too.'

'If you would really like to give me a present, I should prefer it to be some quite commonplace thing suitable to my changed way of life; of no value in itself. Something you would never care about or have any feeling for.'

'You have only to ask, Tessa dear.'

She was so good and conscientious, so noble, that I hesitated, tempted to be open with her. But she was a Jasmyn; and Betony was very dear to me.

'There's a scrubby little bit of land between Betony Hay and the river; no more than an acre. It's all overgrown with weeds and only good for grazing a few goats. It's Jasmyn land but it did once belong to the Cades. In all the world, Tod's Corner is the only thing I want.'

'Why, of course.' There was no doubting her readiness this time. 'I can't imagine why you want it but perhaps you'll be extending your garden some day. I'd love you to have it. It won't be possible until all this legal business is settled but...'

'And you may change your mind.'

'Never. It's a promise, and I'm glad we've

settled on something you really want.'

She was relieved, I remorseful; but the thought that Gib Rake could not be opened up for quarrying without my permission was wonderfully consoling.

In spite of these skirmishes, Kate and I were happy together as we must have been – we were both confident of it – when we were nurslings at the same breast. Kate abandoned the high-backed chair and we sat on the hearth-rug talking. She was convinced that even without the dramatic encounter with Colonel Darlington, she would somehow have discovered the truth. Barmote had affected her strangely so that she had been, if not prepared, at least in a frame of mind disposed to accept some revelation. Nevertheless the appearance of Colonel Darlington as she sat sketching in the churchyard, had been as awe-inspiring as the mythical descent of a god bearing a gift. She had guessed at once who he was, the pale military gentleman who came wearily through the lych-gate and sat down on the bench. Catching sight of her, he had come nearer, presumably to ask the way to the Hall – then stopped dead.

'Alice Jasmyn,' he said. Then, 'I mustn't frighten you, my dear. I know of course that you must be Tessa but you are so like your mother...' There were tears in his eyes and it was the tears that restrained Kate from making the obvious immediate denial. 'It might be Alice sitting there as I've seen her a score of times at her easel. Look.'

Fumbling in his pocket he had produced the likeness.

'It was terrifying, Tessa, to see myself. The one thing I was sure of was that I must not speak for fear of harming someone: her – or you. I realised that we were involved in some sort of tragic mistake...'

Fortunately she had been as if struck dumb; faint; sick with fear. He had been alarmed. She had begged him to let her sit and rest while he talked...

We thrashed it all out again as we were to do at intervals for years to come, until it was time for me to leave; and after all, I did not leave empty-handed. I ran upstairs to speak to Mrs. Arrow, who had sedately, and without pause in her crocheting, become Kate's companion-housekeeper instead of mine; and then went to my old room to collect a few small personal things. There Emma found me. Her mood was affable.

'I'm not one to scorn the downfallen,' she explained when we had exchanged more conventional remarks, 'and I'm sure it's hard that you should have nothing to remember *her* by. This was put aside with some old things. Nobody else will want it...'

Pleased with her own enterprise and generosity, she thrust it into my hand, grand-mamma's reticule, it's black moiré dull with

321

dust. I pushed it into my basket and escaped to the hall, where Kate was waiting between the porcelain vases.

'I wanted to ask you, Tessa,' her manner was confidential, even timid, 'did you ever hear a story about an Indian gentleman who had some claim to the estate?'

'It's utter nonsense,' I assured her. 'Don't think of it. There's no such person.'

I left her on the steps. She looked lonely, a pale figure in the dark doorway. The most suitable companion for her would be a husband, I thought sagely and, it must be confessed, smugly: nor could I restrain a certain jauntiness as I made my way between the turnip fields, with Tod's Corner, in a manner of speaking, in my pocket.

It was just as I reached the turning to Betony that a carriage breasted the hill. I stepped on to the grass to let it pass.

'Barmote Lodge?' the coachman asked.

As I directed him, the window was put down and a lady looked out.

'Is it far?'

'Only a few minutes round the bend in the road – at the Hall gates. You can see the Hall there on the left.'

A dip in the fields revealed a pair of gaunt chimneys and the dark shape of Rodney Jasmyn's tower.

'The Hall!' I detected in the lady's voice a note of dismay. 'Surely that can't be...'

She made some remark to her companion and drew up the window. The carriage rolled away, leaving me an uninterrupted view of what she had seen: a sombre farmhouse among ragged trees and something like a tall pepper-pot in stone.

24

I turned my back on the tawny sunset above Gib Rake and pressed the latch. My mother sat by the fire with her embroidery. Her movements, as she turned to greet me, stirred reflections in the copper lamp-stand, in the polished wainscoting and the rosewood panels of the pianoforte against the inner wall. I had pleaded for the swans but Aunt Abbie was not yet quite reconciled to parting with them. Otherwise the room was as we wanted it to be. Mother's taste and mine were completely in accord. Our means were modest for my mother had spent lavishly for years; but they would be sufficient to maintain a household with two servants and Tim, who was to be trained as a house-boy until he was of an age to know his own mind. Becky remained with the old couple in the end cottage.

The house fitted my mother like a glove. For the first time I sensed in her an air of permanence. She was settled at last.

'I've found them all,' she said, 'all the monthly parts of Mr. Hardy's latest novel in the *Cornhill*. They will last us until Christmas. You read so well, dear, and I shall be able to finish this while I listen.'

She was embroidering a fire-screen. Failing the swans, we had reached agreement on a hunting scene in tapestry work.

I laid my outdoor things on the sofa and caught sight of the reticule in my basket. Reluctantly I took it out, a dusty relic of a time already remote, but not so remote as to have lost its power to prick my confidence and make my hands shake as I turned out the contents on to the table in the window: a lace-edged handkerchief, a few macaroon crumbs, a vinaigrette, an empty phial that had once held digitalin.

They had the pathos of trivial things left behind by the dead; and their potency. As softly as the sigh of wind or the rustle of silk they summoned up like shadows the watchful women in the close room; yet as forcibly as the gun-shot that once split the air above the meadow, they propelled me into a new maturity of understanding. There had been two phials: the one I had thrown away; and this one. I had opened it but there had been no occasion to use its contents. I no more knew what had become of them than I knew whether one of the glasses had contained more than claret; or whether, as grandmamma had emptied the wine into the fire, her brows had been contracted in anger – or disappointment. But I knew that – for all that had been told – there remained in some corner of the web wherein Kate and I had been caught, a secret still undisclosed.

'Mother.'

She started at the change in my voice.

'Why should grandmamma have hated you, enough to want to kill you?'

Stark as the question was, it had been speculative. I was astonished to see that there was an answer and that she knew it. She showed no curiosity as to why I had asked, but deliberately ran her needle into the canvas, put the frame aside and braced herself as if to face an ordeal she had long expected. But she sat with her hands clenched, saying nothing.

'You said that grandmamma couldn't possibly have recognised you. Even if she did, she would just think of you as my nurse.' And she would soon have sent her packing, I thought, picturing grandmamma as she had been in her prime: authoritative, alert, and I remembered how for a few weeks the authority and alertness had come back: how she had sprung from her chair as we had bent over her, similar figures in our hats and mantles. 'Even,' I said, 'if she had seen some resemblance between us as Sister Monica did, it would mean nothing to her.' I looked at the tightly clenched hands. 'There is something you haven't told me.'

'Everything I told you was true,' she said, 'but I didn't tell you everything.'

'About grandmamma?'

'She was not your grandmother,' she cried out in sudden passion, *'and she knew it.'*

The change of perspective was so violent that I felt the whole world tilt sickeningly awry.

'When?' I whispered. 'When did she know?'

'From the beginning.'

With a cruel distortion of memory I saw my whole childhood take on a new and sinister colouring. Every word became a lie: every instant of that close companionship a deception.

'It was a bargain then between you?'

'No, not that.' She spoke harshly. 'Only – we understood each other,' and presently, as if there had been no interruption in the story she had told me as we watched the day break over Betony, she went on, 'I brought Kate to her...'

They faced each other, each holding a child, in that dreadful symmetry I had felt when long afterwards they had watched each other at Barmote, each having and withholding an equal power to make the other suffer.

'"This is Alice," I said and held her out, a little dark-looking, gasping thing. I saw the shock in her eyes before she turned away in disgust and laid her cheek against yours. Her whole heart was already fixed on you. "I want her, I want her," she said. But it wasn't a bargain, Tessa…'

There had been between them a look, an averting of the eyes, a similarity of interest, a confluence of wills.

'When I came to Barmote, she never dreamed… She had persuaded herself that you were her grandchild. Towards the end I wondered if she had recognised me, not from her memory of me as your nurse, but from some similarity between us. We aren't strikingly alike, dear, but a family likeness doesn't depend on features and colouring. One can see it without being able to explain it. But by that time I was too unhappy to care. She would never have told. And now,' my mother gave a long sigh, breathing into the very depths of it the satisfaction of a heart at last unburdened, 'you know everything.'

But how – I seemed to stand above a deep chasm and from its brink look across at her far away – how was it possible to believe her? The two had hated each other. Hatred could distort one nature as well as another. Between them they had destroyed the open-hearted trust I should still have been cap-able of.

And yet – I turned my back and watched a cloud lengthen and deepen until it spread its wide sleeves across the sunset – I saw how easily it could have happened. No words could have been more effective in reviving the antagonism against her daughter-in-law than the simple statement: 'This is Alice.' Spite and wilfulness could never have been more instantly welded than in the moment when she feared to lose me and longed to be rid of Alice Jasmyn's child.

And if it really was so, the tricks and lies I had tried to forgive because they seemed to come from excessive love for me, had been part of an insane but settled determination to turn me into the creature she had wanted me to be. To the hoard of unrightful possessions at the Hall she had deliberately added another; a child. I was to be tempered, beaten, given shape and finally in my marriage stamped with the hallmark Jasmyn. That she had tried to change me I had long known: that she had actually tried to change me into someone else seemed a piece of evil witchcraft to confound reason. No object in the crowded rooms, no wildly twisted shape, human or bird, had been the product of a more fantastic and diseased imagination than hers.

I contemplated the outrageous wickedness of what she had sought to do; and I recoiled from it, as if, having looked at her portrait, I put it away in an unlit corner or hung it with its face to the wall. The figure in the crimson chair has, in my memory, certain unchanging attributes: the cap, the sparkle of rings, the open book. But the features and expression are often undefined; and often I can even pretend to myself that the eyes are as soft, the lips as sweetly curved as I believed them to be when I looked up at them in innocent trust, longing to please her.

The painful sense of outrage possessed me entirely to the exclusion of any emotion so limited as anger. Its very intensity made it short-lived. Gradually there grew within me a slow, triumphant joy. She had failed. Without pity (the pity came later: much, much later) I saw that her guilty fear of discovery had been the death of her. I had survived. She had no doubt done me incalculable harm but I had escaped. She had no more conquered me than sword, knife, gun or fever had done in the days of my adventurous infancy. Moreover I had regained what was mine, my own spirit, as if it had come home to its own place.

My mother had reached the end of what must have been a long speech, not a word of which I had heard; but the note of finality reached me. When she came and put her arms round me, the action was significant, as though she had progressed yet again from one phase of existence to another.

'After all–' her voice was full of love – 'it cannot matter now. It's all over.' She gathered up the reticule, the handkerchief, the vinaigrette and the phial. 'I'm sorry to have upset you, dear, but it's better for you to know. And now that you have so much to look forward to, the past is best forgotten. We'll have a quiet evening. I'll fetch the first number of the *Cornhill*. It's in my room. You can't imagine how wonderful it will be to have you all to myself.'

She kissed me and went upstairs. The tender words lingered, waking a faint, uneasy memory.

I have sometimes wondered whether the Dardanian maidens thought fondly of the parents who sacrificed them to the sea monster. If one of them had escaped, would she have settled happily by the parental hearth, bearing no grudge and submitting to be loved to death in recompense?

The wide-sleeved cloud had merged with others into the grey of evening. An early star was reflected in the deep pool of shadow below the horizon by a faint light from one of the windows of St Agnes': a lamp to guide benighted wayfarers.

I turned back to the warm room. Mr. Hardy's novel would certainly be more entertaining than the works of the Rev. Tobias Stacey. The comparison combined with my mother's last remark to make me all at once, alert. Something familiar in the arrangement of the furniture – my mother's chair and footstool – my own armless chair – the hearth-rug – the fire – sounded an alarum note.

331

Of the two women who had so far dominated my life, I never doubted that one was as selfless and good as the other was treacherous and base. But in one respect they were alike. In their ability to stifle me with their affection, there was not a pin to choose between them.

It was this conclusion that dictated my movements during the next few minutes and brought me – I thank God for it – to the bravest act of my life.

I put on my hat and mantle. The few things in my basket must serve for a while. There was just time to find pen and paper and write the note. It would grieve her deeply but she would recover: she had grieved before. We had both of us already survived worse ordeals.

Dearest Mother,
   I shall come back to Betony as you did but not for a while.
   My love,
   Tessa.

Then just as she had done, I lifted the latch and stepped out into the freedom of the cool, unloving night.

This Large Print Book, for people
who cannot read normal print,
is published under the auspices of

THE ULVERSCROFT FOUNDATION